Club Wicked:
MY WICKED DEVIL

Ann Mayburn

LooSe Id®

ISBN 13: 978-1-62300-740-9
CLUB WICKED: MY WICKED DEVIL

Originally released in e-book format in May 2013

Cover Art by Fiona Jayde
Cover Layout and Design by Fiona Jayde

Printed in the U.S.A. by
Lightning Source, Inc.
1246 Heil Quaker Blvd
La Vergne TN 37086
www.lightningsource.com

DEDICATION

Dear Beloved Reader,

I've had people ask me if there is a lot of abuse in My Wicked Devil because it's a story about a Sadist and a masochist. No, there is absolutely zero abuse, because from my point of view abuse is an infliction of mental, emotional, or physical pain that is done to an unwilling person.

"But Ann, how can there be any S&M with no abuse?"

Because, my darlings, what Lord Bryan gives Kira is completely and 100 percent consensual, and he does it for her pleasure.

"What? Pleasure from pain? That's poppycock."

Yes, pleasure from pain. Some people are wired like that, and for those masochists who crave the mixture of the two, there are always Sadists who love providing what the masochist needs in order to feel complete. Now I'm not saying Lord Bryan takes a baseball bat to Kira or strings her up with barbed wire, but he does mix the pleasure with the pain enough to get her into the subspace she needs and give her absolutely mind-blowing orgasms.

"So if I try S&M, does that mean I'll have mind-blowing orgasms?"

Maybe? It all depends on how you, my beautiful little snowflake, react to things.

Personally I just can't get off on pain. I'm not wired like that. But I do have sadistic tendencies when I'm matched with a masochist. No blood, because it makes me pass out—not sexy—but watching my submissive endure discomfort, knowing that he/she is going deep into subspace, and witnessing the transformation from suffering to ecstasy is amazing.

So, I had a point somewhere in there... Oh yeah. Don't be scared away by the title of "Sadist." It doesn't equal dangerous psychopath. They're people just like everyone else. They have jobs, get married, have kids, pay taxes, and bitch about politics. They probably do such unsexy things as laundry and have the occasional bout of the stomach flu, which they piss and moan about like anyone else.

They're human beings, and just because their sexual tastes run to what is considered edgy doesn't mean they should be feared or shunned. And yes, while there are bad people out there who call themselves Sadists/Doms/Dommes/etc. and who cross the line between consensual and abuse, there are bad people everywhere. No cross section of our culture is going to be free of evil. You're going to find scary assholes everywhere, from an ice-cream man to the CEO of a major corporation who loves to abuse, degrade, and destroy people.

But in My Wicked Devil, *every ounce of pain given by my Sadist to my masochist is done out of love.*

Find that hard to understand or believe? Take a peek at My Wicked Nanny. *I begin to delve into a slightly masochistic sub's mind in that book, getting you ready for Lord Bryan and Kira's love story. All kinky fuckery aside, that's what all of my* Club Wicked *books are: love stories for people who like their vanilla ice cream covered with fudge, nuts, whipped (snork) cream, and cherries on top. Oh and sprinkles. Can't forget sprinkles.*

Now I want ice cream.

Ann

P.S.—Before you try any new sexual practice, please please please be careful and seek the help of an experienced practitioner. I'm really for real about this. Like for real for real. Safe, Sane, Consensual.

ACKNOWLEDGMENT

Beta readers, you suffer so much for me. Reading through prose that could have been written by someone who failed English... repeatedly. With great vehemence. I appreciate that you find the willpower to push beyond your disgust at my haphazard use of commas to find the story within. Your suffering makes me smile and warms my heart. ;)

Mistress Ann

CHAPTER ONE

Kira Harmony took a deep breath, the scents of perfume, cologne, and sex filling her nostrils. Before she'd heard of Club Wicked, she'd never known that people having lots and lots of sex in one building left a pheromone haze in the air, something that would make her almost instantly aroused. But now that she was here, surrounded by hedonism on a scale she'd never even imagined, set against the opulent splendor of the club, she took another deep breath and smiled as she looked around the massive entrance. A double staircase led down from the floor above, and a balcony stretched around it. Statues of women in long robes in states of partial undress flanked either side of the stairs, and Kira was pretty sure she'd seen similar statues at the Acropolis Museum in Greece.

An older man called out, "Ms. Harmony." She turned and found a smartly dressed and very big man offering his arm.

"Good evening. My name is Mr. Grant. Master Hawk is waiting for you at the bar. Since this is your first time here, he asked me to escort you and beat off any Doms that get in the way."

Laughing, she glanced down at her outfit. From the tour she'd been taken on after being granted membership at Wicked, she knew that inside the club people wore pretty much next to nothing. Her teal halter dress, a vintage piece from the fifties, would normally be risqué. With her size 16 body came a nice set of breasts that were all but spilling out of the top. With her long auburn hair up in a French twist, her freckled back was bare and exposed. Add a pair of nylons with the seam running up the back, and she felt sexy, in a Marilyn Monroe in *The Seven Year Itch* sort of way, but nothing any man would come running for.

A stunning woman with long, carefully curled blonde hair glided past them in a G-string. The other woman's perfect, wobble-free body made Kira suck her gut in.

No matter what sadist she ended up with, she would never, ever do a public scene.

Realizing the gentleman, Mr. Grant she believed was his name, waited for her to respond, she forced a smile. "Oh, I think I'll be safe, but I wouldn't mind the escort. Right now my knees are about to give out."

Mr. Grant laughed and placed her hand on his arm in a very old-world gesture of civility. He was older, probably late sixties, but he was also self-assured. "Darling, I may be a submissive, but let me tell you. You look amazing, and any Dom would be thrilled to have his collar on your lovely, swanlike neck."

Kira couldn't help her pleased smile. His sincerity warmed her from the inside out, giving her the courage to follow his lead as they made their way to the Hall of Mirrors bar. They started walking through the opulent foyer of Wicked, and Kira tried to keep from feeling overwhelmed. For fuck's sake, she'd done a free-fall jump from the top of the Eiffel Tower when she'd been an actress, with a split second between getting the shot and pulling the cord on her parachute. This should be a piece of cake. There was nothing in this massive space to suggest this was anything but a magnificent private club that catered to the extremely wealthy outside Washington, DC. It certainly didn't look like the premier BDSM club on the East Coast, but it was, and by some miracle, she'd gotten in.

They reached the massive polished-brass double doors that led to the public bar. Two big men in black tuxedos opened the doors in unison and let them in. Normally she would have giggled at such a choreographed display, but the space beyond took her breath away.

Gilt mirrors, crystal chandeliers, and beautiful, naked people.

Mr. Grant took them to the left, along a massive dark-wood bar that occupied one entire wall of the room. Behind the bar, ornately framed mirrors extended up to the two-story ceiling, and on the opposite side immense windows allowed you to observe a nighttime garden illuminated by tasteful lighting. Having been raised as the daughter of a very successful plastic surgeon, she was used to money, but this place had something money couldn't buy.

It had class.

She scanned the crowd and couldn't help the rush of excitement speeding her pulse. The public bar area was crowded, and every couch and chair was taken. There were even those who stood with submissives kneeling at their feet.

Another thing she didn't think she'd ever be able to do in public. Fuck, she was going to make one shitty-ass submissive, but she had no choice.

This had to work.

Soon the familiar sight of her old costar's long black hair and strong Native American profile came into view. Tonight his hair was held back by a silver clip, and he wore a tight black T-shirt and dark brown leather pants. Sexy, sinful, and oh so obviously in love with the pretty bartender smiling at him.

Sunny, the bartender, had a very gamine beauty about her. Tall, slender, with massive dark chocolate brown eyes and perfect skin. Her pixie cut made her already high cheekbones even sharper and her full, natural pout all the more sensual. The way the other woman looked at Hawk let Kira know Hawk's devotion wasn't one-sided.

Kira had met Sunny a few weeks ago at a party hosted by their mutual friend, Jesse Shaw, for a charity Kira was active in. While Sunny had been there as Hawk's friend, not girlfriend, Hawk had still treated her like his date. Kira found Sunny to be a blast to hang around, and she was grateful the other woman was here tonight.

Mr. Grant smiled at Sunny. "I have a delivery for Master Hawk."

Hawk turned and smiled. "Ah, Mr. Grant, you're looking handsome as always."

Mr. Grant chuckled. "Master Hawk, you could charm the pants off a monk." He turned to Kira and gave her hand a kiss. "I hope you have a wonderful evening. If you ever have any questions, please let me know. I enjoy helping people, so please don't hesitate."

Charmed by his good manners, she smiled, then gave him a light kiss on the cheek, making sure not to smear him with her lipstick. "Thank you so much, Mr. Grant. I hope you have a lovely evening as well."

She waved as Mr. Grant left and turned to find Hawk smiling at her. Goodness, he was a handsome man, but they'd never had anything even close to a spark between them. It was a case of the totally wrong chemistry for romance and the right one for friendship.

"Kira, so glad you made it. You look amazing." He stood and gave her a strong hug. "Welcome to Wicked."

Sunny reached across the bar and gave Kira's hand a squeeze. "Hey, sweets. What can I get you?"

"A glass of champagne would be nice."

"Got it."

Hawk sat and gestured to the empty stool. "Have a seat. Are you ready to go sadist hunting?"

She swallowed hard. When he said it out loud like that, her idea sounded not only stupid but dangerously stupid. "I guess." He raised one eyebrow, and she lifted her chin. "I mean, yes."

Sunny returned and set Kira's glass next to her. "I talked with Master Hawk, and he thought it might go better if I went with you. I know all the Doms here by either sight or reputation—us submissives do gossip—so I can tell you which sadist would probably be the most helpful for you."

While Kira took a healthy drink of her champagne, Hawk nodded. "Besides, I really don't want to go and talk about some guy's dick and how good he can fuck you. No offense."

Laughing, Kira set her glass down. "Good point. I'll be more than happy to talk all day with you about stunt work, but we'll skip the sex stuff. It would be like talking about it with my dumb-ass younger brother."

Sunny giggled and managed to choke it back at Hawk's glare. "A word to the wise, Kira, as a submissive, I'd really watch lipping off to any Dom. It could end badly."

A woman passed them with what looked like weighted clamps hanging from her labia. She had to walk with an odd, wide-legged stance to keep from dislodging the weights as she followed an older woman dressed in a conservative suit. Kira tried not to stare, but the woman's obvious humiliation was made all the worse by the fact that she was so aroused her honey had dripped down her thighs.

The sound of snapping fingers brought her attention back to Hawk and Sunny. "What? Sorry. I was distracted."

Hawk stood and reached over the bar, easily lifting Sunny from the other side. For a brief moment his hands lingered on the bartender's waist, and Kira almost got knocked on her ass by the blast of sexual heat coming from the two of them. Then Hawk took a step back and let Sunny go.

The other woman's nipples were hard as rocks, and the pulse in the side of her neck banged. Kira felt sorry for the young woman and slung an arm over her shoulder, helping to break the tension. "So, where does one go sadist shopping at?"

Kira stood at the end of an extremely long hallway with Sunny. Massive viewing windows on either side allowed people to look into the different theme rooms, and most people wandered from window to window. One couple appeared to have been so overcome by the scenes inside that the Master had his submissive giving him a blowjob right there.

With a giggle, Sunny tugged her forward. "Come on. There are a few Doms I want you to see."

"Are we window-shopping?"

"Yep." Sunny paused and leaned closer. "We'll find you your sadist, Kira. Don't worry."

Oh, Kira wasn't worried. She was terrified. When she was standing on the edge of the exit out of a plane, about to jump for some skydiving fun, she was also terrified, but in a way that made her want to scream with joy.

Now she just wanted to scream.

The thought of allowing a stranger to hurt her on purpose made Kira's stomach lurch. But that is exactly what she needed, maybe even wanted. If she did, she wasn't quite ready to admit it to herself yet. She'd always been fiercely independent, so the thought of totally surrendering her will to anyone made her leery. Yet, if she wanted to really get over her issues, she needed to be able to trust whomever she picked. Trust someone to hurt her enough to get her off, but not enough to really hurt her. How the hell was she going to be able to do that? A leap of faith of that magnitude was crazy, but that is what it was going to take. Everything she'd read about BDSM and talked with her friends Jesse, Hawk, and Isaac about, all stated trust as being the most important aspect of any successful BDSM relationship. So, she was going to have to trust a stranger enough to really let go and submit to whatever Master she picked. She needed to find a single man, one she had chemistry with, who also had a taste for making women hurt but wasn't a psychopath and could still inspire her respect.

Yeah, sure. No problem.

The first window they reached showed a burly man in gray leathers inserting small-gauge needles into a woman's nipple.

Kira recoiled. "Oh, hell to the fuck no."

"Got it. Next."

Sunny dragged her past a couple more windows. This one was decorated to look like the interior of a barn. A woman was tied upside down to a ladder while the Dom slapped her face. The way he hit her, the taunting and arrogant look on his face as he did it, annoyed the shit out of Kira and made her want to hit him back. No, that wasn't the kind of guy she could see helping her learn how to take pleasure from pain.

Three rooms later and Kira was now disgusted, angry, and scared. She was also ready to cry. This had been her last hope. So far none of the men Sunny had shown her had made her anything but apathetic, angry, or icked out. The last one had taken a piss on his submissive, and both Sunny and Kira had gagged and left.

Sunny put her hand on Kira's shoulder and gave it a squeeze. "It's okay. These are only a few of the single sadists we have here. We'll find him."

Turning her head to the left, avoiding Sunny's sympathetic look, Kira stopped in her tracks.

On the other side of the glass was a theme room designed to look like a medieval chamber. And sitting on the massive wood-and-gilt throne, with his leg slung arrogantly over one arm, was the most devilishly handsome man Kira had ever seen. Instant heat filled her body, and for the first time, the negative wad of feelings in her gut began to vanish.

He had pitch-black hair, dark eyes, and a goatee that framed an entirely too sensual mouth. With his shirt off, she got to enjoy the impressive muscles of his chest and abdomen, as well as the fat outline of his cock against his leather pants. His features were aristocratic, with a strong jaw and solid cheekbones. He held two floggers, one white and one black, probably in complement to the women sixty-nining in front of him. The woman on the bottom had skin as pale as Kira's, while the woman on top had lovely dark skin and long, beaded braids. Both were plump and beautiful, the kind of women Kira was attracted to.

Four years earlier Kira had been in a terrible motorcycle accident after a stunt went wrong in a movie she was starring in. It had fractured her pelvis and screwed her up so any penetration during sex gave her cramps similar to the contractions women experienced during labor. While her body slowly healed, she had found sexual release with women, but none of them had what she wanted in a relationship. Still, the sight of the women having what looked like really good oral sex with each other brought back pleasant memories.

The man stood and descended from the throne steps to the main floor below where the women continued to play with each other. Kira's breath caught in her chest as he had them stop, then turn over so they were both on all fours. The sight of their wet and swollen pussies, the involuntary twitches, and their tension only added to the eroticism of the scene before her.

She stepped closer, placing her fingers on the glass separating them. It must be one-way, because no one on the other side noticed her. The man strode around both women, his attention totally focused on them. Lean, muscular, graceful, he moved like a panther and had enough charisma to bring Kira to her knees. During her time in Hollywood, she'd been around many charismatic, extremely handsome men, but they didn't hold a candle to this guy. The hair on her arms stood up, and deep inside her soul a tiny flicker of hope began to brighten and burn.

She didn't know anything about him, and he could be a total douche bag, but oh my goodness, did she want to be the one on her knees before him. Intense sexual fantasies burst through her imagination like fireworks, and a powerful wave of heat made her pussy swell. Evidently her body was totally on board with anything she wanted to do with this mysterious man. Her attention on him deepened until it was almost like she was alone watching him on the other side of the glass rather than surrounded by a growing audience.

Her breath caught as he slapped the black flogger over both women, their buttocks jiggling from the strike. Stepping back, he said something, and the women put their faces to the floor, leaving their bottoms exposed and vulnerable. She couldn't help but think of what it would be like to be in that position, to have him being the one making her arch, making her moan. Thank goodness this viewing wall didn't have a door or she might have gone in, flipped her dress up, and assumed the same position next to the other women.

A few more glancing blows to their hips, shoulders, asses, and thighs before he stepped back, and his sensual lips moved as he spoke. Kira strained to make out the words, to catch some sound of his voice, but she might as well be on the outside of a dreamer's head looking in. Or in this case, more like watching an incubus torment and pleasure two helpless women. Fuck, there was no way a man could be that sensual without having sold his soul to the devil.

More people had joined her by the window, and they commented on his ability to create a scene, and other complimentary things. Behind the glass, the man rolled his shoulders and wrists, upping the tension, making the watching audience, herself included, hold their collective breath. Energy buzzed along Kira's body, setting her skin aflame and soaking her panties.

Then he really worked them.

Whirling the floggers like they were martial arts weapons, he began an intricate dance around the two women, hitting them simultaneously but at different positions and with different strengths if the extra effort he put into his swing hitting the blonde was any indication. The dark-skinned woman received a lighter treatment, though she was the first to begin crying. The blonde appeared to be moaning, but it was hard to tell because no sound came from the room. In fact, the only thing Kira could hear were her own pants and the thud of her heart as it sped in time to the man's movements.

What would it feel like to have him strike her ass like that? To leave bright red marks on her skin? He paused and held both floggers in one hand. With his free hand, he leaned over and played with the dark-haired woman's pussy. Kira couldn't see what he was doing, only that it seemed to be driving the other woman wild. She bucked and thrashed beneath his touch, her lips drawn back in an almost snarl Kira found incredibly sexy.

Sunny tapped her shoulder, then dragged her from the window. "Kira, did you hear me?"

Unable to look away, to even speak, Kira shook her head.

With a soft laugh, Sunny turned her so she could no longer see the erotic scene being played out. "I said that is Lord Bryan, and he may be more than you can handle."

Resisting the urge to shove Sunny out of the way so she could go back to drooling over the wickedly handsome man, she cleared her throat. "Why is that?"

"Bryan is what I like to call a Master's Master. Whatever it is that makes a Dom, he has in spades, but his tastes run dark."

Kira stole a quick glance and found Bryan was now fucking the blonde with the end of the flogger while she ate the other woman's pussy. "Holy shit."

"Come on. You need to listen to me."

Sunny dragged her down the hall until Kira felt like a puppy being pulled on a leash. As they left Lord Bryan behind, she could almost feel an intangible energy flowing from her body back to him, wanting to stay. Wanting him.

It had been so long since she'd had a man. Her last attempt at a relationship had gone up in flames when she'd been unable to hide the pain of penetration. She'd screamed into her pillow, but he'd heard her and freaked out, telling her he couldn't see her again.

Lord Bryan was the sadist she'd been looking for. No one had ever completely enthralled her like this. If she was one of those flaky chicks who believed in soul mates and all that stuff, she might think he was the person she'd been waiting her whole life to meet. Either that or all the sexual frustration had put her into a state akin to a cat going into heat.

Goodness knows she wanted to rub herself up against the wickedly handsome man just like a cat.

"Kira, to be honest, I don't know if you'd be the best match."

"Why?"

"Lord Bryan is pretty high-powered with his submissives. His scenes are intense and not for the faint of heart. Plus he expects total obedience...which I guess makes sense. With as much edge play as he does, he could really hurt a girl if she didn't follow his directions. I don't know how well you'd do with him. He's like driving a Ferrari when you haven't even learned how to roller skate yet."

"Do you think he would do it?"

Sunny rolled her eyes. "I can ask Master Hawk."

Feeling embarrassed and vulnerable but having to ask anyway, she looked away from Sunny. "Do you think he'd be, you know, attracted to me? I'm not a size 4 anymore."

"Of course he would. I'd kill for curves like yours." Sunny gave her an unexpected hug, and Kira could feel all the bones of Sunny's back. "You are exactly his physical type, so don't let any doubt enter your mind as far as that is concerned. I'm more worried about your tendency to be a smart-ass getting you in trouble."

Pulling back, Kira made a note to talk with Hawk to see if Sunny might be anorexic. Now that Kira was looking closely, not so focused on herself and her own fears, she could see that other than Sunny's naturally full cheeks, the rest of her was terribly thin. While Kira wasn't good enough of a friend to bring it up, she knew Hawk was.

Sunny gave her an odd look, and Kira forced herself to smile. "So, I've picked out my sadist. Now where can I get him gift wrapped?"

"See? You're going to get your ass beat so often you won't be able to sit down for months."

Looping her arm through Sunny's, Kira began to walk with the woman back toward the public bar area. "Lord Bryan, is he cruel?"

"He's a sadist."

"I mean, does he ever, like, hurt anyone when they don't want to be hurt?"

"No. That's not his style. All the submissives he's been with adore him."

"Has he been with a lot?"

Sunny shrugged. "I'm not sure. I usually don't come back here. I will say he's been with Wicked for the last three years, and he has to go through the same rigorous health checks that you did by the club's doctors. Oh, and he doesn't always have sex with his subs. Some of them he just beats."

"Why would he do that?"

"I guess because some women need it and they can go to him without worrying about him wanting sex."

"Doesn't he like sex?" The dry look Sunny gave her made Kira laugh. "You know what I mean."

"Yes. Considering he belongs to a BDSM sex club, I would say the chances he likes sex are pretty high. But just because something is available doesn't mean you have to take it. He's picky about who he takes."

That thought made Kira feel both better and worse. She didn't like the idea of a guy having banged every woman here, but at the same time she did want an experienced sadist. But shit, Bryan was the kind of guy who could walk into a room and a draft would be caused by all the women dropping their panties at once. The thought that such a sex god would want her with her fucked-up body and would want to help her get over her fucked-up fear of penetration seemed slim to none.

Sunny stumbled, and at first Kira thought it was because the other woman wore killer six-inch heels. Then Sunny leaned against Kira and whispered, "Migraine. Hawk."

Kira winced. She'd had a migraine once in reaction to some medication for allergies. Everything had hurt. Light, sound, a breath. Everything.

"Okay, Sunny. I understand. You have a migraine, and you need me to get Hawk. Will do. I need to get you someplace where you can sit down."

Moaning softly, Sunny muttered, "Lounge. Ahead and left."

A Dominatrix and her hunky boy toy paused as they passed them in the hallway. The tall brunette in a black leather catsuit looked closely at Sunny. "Woman, I swear to God if you didn't take the medication I prescribed you, I'm going to rip your spine out and beat you with it."

For a moment Sunny rallied, but tears were pouring down her face. "No drugs."

Kira hefted Sunny up as she sagged. "You know her?"

The Dominatrix nodded, her whole body vibrating with anger. "I'm her physician, Dr. Pershelle."

Kira nodded. "She asked me to get Hawk for her."

Dr. Pershelle nodded to her submissive. "Go run and get Hawk. Tell him we'll be in the warming room."

Without another word, the man took off, his extremely toned ass providing an instant of distraction as his loin cloth flew up with his movements.

"Girl, what's your name?"

"Kira, Ma'am."

"There is a warming room nearby. We'll take her there." Dr. Pershelle got under Sunny's other arm. "Let's go."

In what seemed like record time, they made it into a small, super cozy, and extremely relaxing room. The scent of vanilla and a hint of cinnamon filled the air. Against one wall there was a king-size daybed with mounds of pillows. Kira and Dr. Pershelle set Sunny down, and the woman immediately curled on her side.

Dr. Pershelle pulled a blanket over Sunny and jerked her head at Kira.

Leaving the other woman curled up in a ball, Dr. Pershelle leaned in close to Kira. Dr. Pershelle smelled like expensive perfume and sex. "Are you a friend of Sunny's?"

"Yes. I know her through Master Hawk."

"Good. Can you please tell him to make sure Sunny takes her pain medications? I know she hates them, but I detest seeing her like this when she doesn't have to suffer if she'd just take her damn meds. Someone needs to get through to her, and he's the only one she'll listen to."

Kira's breath hitched. "I…yes, of course. But why Hawk? Why not her family?"

Dr. Pershelle pressed her lips together and shook her head. "Can't say. What I can say is that Sunny views Hawk as her Master. I know they've never done anything sexual together, but she loves that man and will do things for him she wouldn't do for anyone else. Do you know what I mean?"

Before Kira could say anything, Hawk raced in. He didn't even look at them, just went to Sunny's side as quickly as he could. As soon as he reached her, he knelt next to the bed and extended his tanned hand across the silk sheet to Sunny. The other woman put her hand in Hawk's and drew a shuddering breath. Next to Hawk's vibrant Native American good looks, Sunny seemed as frail as spun glass.

"I'll talk to Hawk," Kira said.

"Good."

CHAPTER TWO

Lord Bryan Sutherfield reclined on one of the throne-like leather chairs, looking down into the pit at Club Wicked. The entire floor was transparent, so one could sit up here and watch the happenings below in a mellow, subdued atmosphere. The only lighting came from the room beneath his feet, so this space was dimly lit shadows and silence. Dominants often liked to come here to relax and rejuvenate. Watching the scenes at their feet, appreciating the beauty of the submissives, soothed a hole in their hearts.

Below, Bryan was observing a baby Dom letting one of the more experienced submissives top from the bottom. Normally he would have frowned on anyone letting a sub get away with that, but in this case, the submissive was helping the young Dom learn his craft. The guy was probably in his early twenties, and the submissive in her early forties, so it was fascinating to watch the dynamic between the two. The exchange of power and emotion.

That was what he was interested in.

The connection, that brief and elusive kiss of the divine that happened when a Dominant and a submissive truly connected. He'd had it once or twice, but for various reasons, those relationships hadn't worked out. It had been almost a year since his last relationship ended, and he was feeling irritable, needing that connection.

It kept him grounded and sane.

And right now he was so fucking bored. Nothing excited him like it used to. Everything was just kind of...blah. He'd tried different submissives, even considered a male sub, but everything he'd considered had left him feeling as empty as he did now. Last week he'd had two female subs, and while that had been fun to watch, it didn't totally engage him like it should have. Maybe he'd go on another long ride up to Canada before autumn hit and brought his motorcycling options north of the border to an end. He should go see the Rocky Mountains and let his soul rejuvenate.

Someone sat next to him. The moment a pair of worn cowboy boots kicked up onto the glass table in front of them, he knew who it was. When two beers clinked on the table, he reached forward and silently took one. He and Jesse Shaw had never been good friends, but over the past month, they'd formed an unusual bond. Dove, Jesse's submissive, was in Paris, and the man was missing her fiercely. Right now, Jesse was too pathetic to irritate Bryan.

Besides, he understood how the man felt.

Taking a sip of the rich English stout, Bryan sighed, then rubbed at his goatee with his free hand. His nickname at Wicked was "The Devil." He found it amusing. He guessed he could be seen as somewhat demonic. The submissives certainly enjoyed it. There was nothing like the tremble of a woman right before she felt the kiss of the belt or cane. The only thing better was her relaxation a minute later when she learned your intent was to pleasure her, not beat her.

Jesse cleared his throat. "So you're in between submissives?"

Arching a brow, he barely turned to look at the other man. "Yes."

"Huh."

The other man's leg twitched, his foot tapping a fast pace against the edge of the table. If Jesse didn't spit out whatever he was trying to work up the courage to say, Bryan was going to choke him. "For fuck's sake, man. Say whatever the fuck you came to say and then fuck off."

Jesse laughed and sat forward, slowly spinning his beer between his hands. "I have a favor to ask you."

Immediately suspicious but interested because Jesse clearly needed him for something, he waited for the big Texan to continue. They had similar taste in submissives, so there had been some competition between them. Dove had briefly interested Bryan, but he saw right away how those two were gaga over each other. From there on out, Bryan had only flirted with her to irritate Jesse. Dove knew, so she'd play along until Jesse would pick her up and take her somewhere for her "punishment."

Wondering if maybe Jesse wanted him for a threesome with his deliciously full-figured submissive, he cleared his throat. "*And?*"

"I have a friend who needs your help."

Taken off guard, Bryan leaned back in his chair, then looped his leg over the arm in an arrogant manner that never failed to irritate Jesse. It was so much fun fucking with that man's head. "If she wants financial advice, have her set up an appointment at my office. Oddly enough, I didn't bring my laptop with me tonight."

"Not that kind of help." Jesse actually had a flush to his cheeks, visible in the bright lights shining up through the floor. "She needs a sadist, a good one."

"Pardon? Was that a compliment?"

"Stop being an asshole for a second. This is serious." He looked over at Bryan; his gaze was straightforward but weary. "Hear me out before you say anything else."

Bryan pantomimed zipping his lips, but he was actually intrigued. While Jesse certainly liked to fuck his women rough, he didn't cross the line into darker things. Bryan lived in those murky shadows, dim places filled with sighs, moans, and crying. Not tears of pain but tears of release. The kind of orgasm that lifted a submissive to a different level of consciousness, a state not easily achieved but so worth the effort.

"I've known this woman for the past five years. She's a friend of Hawk's, is on a couple charity boards, and one of the smartest people I've ever met. And I know rocket scientists, so that's saying something."

"She's ugly, isn't she?"

"What?"

"Well, you're going on and on about her attributes, but you've failed to mention anything physical about her. So she must be hideous."

"Don't be such an asshole."

"But irritating you is so much fun. Fine, tell me more about this girl with a great personality."

Jesse took a long drink, looked at Bryan, then took another pull from his beer before setting it down.

Bryan made an impatient motion with his bottle. "So, back to the lovely damsel in distress that needs Lord Pierced Dick to save her."

"She is also compassionate, funny, and so sarcastic it makes my teeth hurt." He squinted his eyes at Bryan, then picked his beer back up. "She reminds me of you."

"Should I be flattered or appalled?"

Jesse took a sip of his beer and flipped Bryan off before continuing. "Keep that thought in mind. My friend used to live out in Hollywood. She left her home here in DC as soon as she graduated college and went in search of fame and fortune. She found both but at a great cost."

"Drugs?"

"Nope. I don't think she's ever done anything heavier than smoked weed. It was her adrenaline-junkie side which took her out. She had a motorcycle—"

"What kind?"

Bryan had nine motorcycles in the ten-bay garage at his home. Riding had been a passion for him since the moment he set foot in the States. Coming from England, he'd been stunned by the size of the country and had bought a top-of-the-line touring bike that day. For the next six months he rode across the US and into Canada, going wherever he wanted. A good deal of that time was spent camping at the national parks and being amazed anew at the world. It had certainly refreshed his soul, and when he decided to make Washington, DC, his home, he felt like for the first time he was someplace where he could be happy.

Now if only he had someone to share that happiness with. A nice, quiet, soft little submissive who would let him take care of her. The kind of woman that would be waiting for him at the end of his work day, naked and begging for his cock.

Jesse shifted, bringing Bryan's attention back to him. "Some kind of crotch rocket. I think it was pink."

"Pink?"

"Yep. Baby-doll pink."

"Sacrilege."

"Anyways, they were doing another take of one of the scenes for the movie, a chase scene. My friend is a rather well-known actress who did all of her own stunts, and while she was taking a turn at forty miles an hour on a winding California road, the stuntman chasing her lost control of his bike. It clipped her bike, hard enough that she got thrown into the handlebars before flipping over the front. Luckily she landed in a safety barrier or she would have gone down the side of the hill and probably died."

Bryan sucked in some air through his teeth. Anyone who rode a motorcycle knew the risks. What Jesse was describing must have resulted in some pretty bad injuries. "Is she okay?"

"Yeah. That happened four years ago. She suffered all kinds of problems, but the biggest one, the one that has pretty much ruined her life, was her pelvic injury." Jesse looked back at his beer. "Ever since the crash she hasn't been able to have sex, penetration, without pain so intense she couldn't take more than a few minutes. That's where you come in. If anyone can help her learn how to find pleasure in her pain, it's you."

"Ah." Bryan rubbed the space between his eyebrows. "Jesse, I'm a sensual sadist, not a doctor. How am I supposed to help her?"

"Six months ago she had surgery to try and reduce pain while restoring sensation. It worked, sort of. She can take penetration now, but it is still painful. She says it's a bearable pain, and she might be able to learn to enjoy sex again if she could find someone to teach her how to make her body convert it to pleasure."

"Are you sure this woman isn't in the lifestyle?"

"Yep. I told you. She's brilliant. She had a problem, so she researched everything she could on it. Damn persistent woman too. When you meet her—"

"*If* I meet her."

"Look, Bryan. She's only twenty-seven years old, and if she can't figure out how to get past the pain, she will never get married, never have children, and will have to live with being betrayed by her own mind and body."

Bryan knew the other man was giving him a guilt trip, and damned if it didn't work. He could no more ignore a submissive who needed his help than he could drive by the scene of an accident without stopping. "When can I meet her?"

"Now?"

He gave Jesse a slow blink. "She's a club member?"

"Yes."

"Have I met her before?"

Jesse cleared his throat. "Well, no. She got approved last week." He fiddled with his bottle between his legs as his lips moved.

Bryan sighed. Jesse was the worst liar. "What are you holding back?"

"Well, she kinda went looking around here with Sunny and watched you do a scene. From what Sunny said, my friend saw you, and that was it. Once she had you in her sights, she wouldn't consider anyone else. So if you meet her and don't feel a spark, be easy with her and try to help her find someone who could help her."

After tossing back the rest of his stout in two big gulps, Bryan stood and set the empty bottle down. Excitement started to fizzle through him, and he actually felt awake for the first time in months. Knowing she'd seen him doing a scene and had been attracted to him was not only a nice boost to his ego but a necessary step if he was going to dominate her in a sexual way. Without any chemistry between them, any attempt at BDSM play would be a complete and utter disaster. The spark had to be there to make it work sexually, and that was as true in BDSM as it was in any vanilla relationship.

He smoothed the front of his black suit and straightened his cuffs. "You said she saw me do a scene, but that really doesn't mean anything other than enjoying watching me. Does she have any idea what she's in for? What Dominance and submission is really about? Fuck the sadist and masochist stuff for now. I need to know if she has any idea what it means to submit."

"Academically, yes." Jesse stood as well, stretching out his back. "Before you meet her, I should mention one thing."

"What's that?"

"Her name is Kira Harmony."

Bryan tried to put the name of the popular actress and the woman Jesse had described together. Even he knew who Kira Harmony was, and he rarely paid attention to anything. Kira's exploits were known the world over, from partying with princes to skydiving over the Grand Canyon. She'd starred in a number of action movies, a few of which he'd seen. A very pretty woman with auburn hair and big golden-brown eyes. Too thin for his taste, but he'd wait and see what the past four years had done to her.

Rubbing his face, he blew out a tense breath. Bloody fuck, did the paparazzi still follow her around? He'd left England to avoid the paparazzi and had worked hard in the States to fall out of the public eye. While he knew no photographers or media got anywhere near Wicked, thanks to its influential members, he didn't always want to scene at the club. He worried if he invited her to his home, she'd come with some camera-flashing baggage.

If he helped this woman, he could be exposing himself and his family to further embarrassment. All it took was one photographer, one tabloid to recognize him, and he was sure that fucking video of him whipping that evil bitch, then fucking her would surface again. His humiliation at being blackmailed would be plastered all over the world. Sometimes he wished he'd just paid the bitch the money, but at the time, his stupid, naive principals had demanded he do the right thing and turn her in. Unfortunately, as soon as he did that, the video went up briefly on the Internet, and every news agency had latched onto it with glee. The resulting scandal had destroyed his life back in London and cost him his family. He didn't know if he could go through that again. Except this time it would drag down an innocent woman with him if he was photographed with Kira. The very thought made him ill.

He should stay as far away from her as possible.

Her image came to mind, some picture he'd seen in a magazine. He remembered her because of her flaming red hair. He'd always had a thing for redheads, to the point of obsession, and she was about as ginger as one could get. Pale skin, freckles, and long red hair. Too bad she was so skinny. He liked a woman with meat on her bones, softness to cushion him, padding to grab on to.

"How sexually experienced is she? I don't want to scare her right out the gate by doing something too edgy."

Jesse blew out a harsh breath. "She's only slept with two men. The one who took her virginity and the one who broke up with her after they tried to have intercourse last year."

Bryan gave a sympathetic wince. "Ouch."

"Yeah. Kira said she tried, she really did, but the pillow didn't muffle her crying when they had sex, and he freaked out and left her. After that, she started dating women but didn't find anyone that would work as a long-term relationship."

"Is she bisexual? Would she better off with a Mistress?"

"No, women are just safe for Kira right now. She can have sex with women without hurting, but she's way more into men than women, so it's been a meeting of her physical needs. From what she said, she's bisexual, but like eighty percent guys, twenty percent women."

"This is a big bloody mess you've thrown in my lap."

The muscles of Jesse's jaw tightened. "Look. She's a good woman. I'm not asking you to go shag some hag."

Bryan couldn't help but smile at the big Texan's unintended rhyme, then sobered. "Let me meet the girl. I can't promise you anything, but at the very least, I'll speak with her. If there is no spark between us, I can't force attraction, but I will try to help her find someone she may have a better connection with."

Jesse stood and let out a relieved breath. "Thank you. I owe you one."

Standing, Bryan gave him a nefarious grin. “Yes, you do. When your little Dove gets back, perhaps we could arrange for her and Kira to spend some time together. I wonder if they both have pretty pink cunts.”

Jesse groaned and cupped his crotch. “Putting images like that in my mind when my girl is across the ocean. That’s cruel.”

“I am a sadist. Comes with the territory.”

Kira crossed her legs and ignored the dull ache in her pelvis. Her hips still complained about being in a sitting position too long, but at least her tailbone no longer hurt. Being able to wear high heels again was an amazing feat in itself. She could probably return to acting if she wanted to, but without the thrill of doing her own stunts, it was boring. She glanced down at her cute gold pumps and smiled. New shoes, new body, new life.

Now she needed to get her ability to have sex back, and she’d be good to go.

The room at Wicked where she waited was pretty awesome. She sat in a small foyer/seating area with furniture that looked right out of the time of Julius Cesar. The room itself was built to look like a walled Roman garden, complete with torches and the sound of crickets and other night creatures. Beautiful potted plants graced the courtyard, adding a hint of lushness to the stone walls. Overhead a pretty sunset faded into the night, visible through a lattice festooned with blooming honeysuckle.

The attached open space behind her made her blush. It had to be an orgy room. She couldn’t think of any other reason why the entire floor of one room had been made into a gigantic, black silk-covered bed. There were various pillows strewn about, and actual shackles were hanging from the walls. More chains hung from the ceiling, and in the very center of the room a strangely shaped dais of blue velvet rose from the floor. She wondered if it was some kind of sex chair. One that would allow different, funky positions.

Shifting slightly to ease the pressure off her right side, she stared at the door and tried to be patient. From what Hawk and Jesse said, Bryan was one of the best sensual sadists out there. If he couldn’t help her, they didn’t know who could. So even though she was as nervous as a virgin at a porn convention, she made herself stay still and wait.

Besides, she'd masturbated at least a dozen times to her memories of watching Bryan last week at Wicked.

The discomfort of her body was nothing compared to the hot mess in her mind. She waffled between wanting to run, wanting to throw herself on Bryan the moment he walked through the door, and pretending to be sick so she could leave with her dignity intact if he didn't like her.

Well, maybe not intact, but at least she could hold her tears in until she was alone.

Hell, she didn't even know Bryan, and yet was considering having sex with him. Just about the most intimate thing one human being could do to another. She didn't cheek kiss people she didn't know, let alone suck their dicks.

Her empty sheath clenched, and she winced, anticipating pain. Instead it was only a mild soreness. Nothing like the cramps she'd had before her last surgery. Even wearing a tampon had been too painful, and the thought of trying to have someone shove their dick in there made her wince. God, what if the sadist wanted to have sex with her right away? What if he liked her pain so much he wouldn't listen to her if she said no? Unease crept down her spine. Yeah, Jesse had told her Bryan was geared more toward sadistic sexual torture than physical torture, but fuck, she didn't know if she wanted anyone to torture anything on her. Then again, she didn't need him to hurt her. Her body already did that on its own. Most people didn't understand how good it felt to be somewhat normal.

She desperately wanted to be normal again.

Taking a deep breath, she tried to let the negativity out. In this world a person attracted what they gave out, good or bad, and she'd like to stay on the right side of karma.

A soft chime sounded, and Kira stood and smoothed her dress over her hips. Her big hips. One of the results of her injury had been inactivity, but she continued to eat like she burned twenty-five-hundred calories a day. As a result she'd put on weight, a lot, like, a dangerous amount that hurt her healing bones. She'd managed through exercise and eating kinda right to get back down to a size 16, but it was a far cry from the size 4 she used to wear. Swallowing hard, she hoped Bryan wasn't disappointed by her.

Jesse walked in with Bryan, who had to be the most fuckable man she'd ever seen. All sinfully good, dark looks and more charisma than JFK. Seriously, he was the kind of guy who could enter a room and every woman turned to take a second look. Trying to roll her tongue back into her mouth, she mentally scolded herself. It didn't matter if Bryan was a Jedi between the sheets. She wasn't screwing up her body for anyone.

Their eyes met, and everything inside her tightened. The first rush of desire, electric and fierce, actually knocked her back a step. Her heel wobbled at her awkward move, and she almost fell but got her balance in time. Embarrassment burned through her, making her face heat with a rush of blood while her body was still deep in lust.

Great first impression. He looked like a sex god, and she looked like a spaz.

He didn't walk across the room toward her. That would have been too mundane. This man with his piercing, dark eyes and sin-black hair prowled across the room. It wasn't an exaggerated movement; it was a change in his demeanor. As his gaze held hers, his full lips curved in a smile. She knew women who would kill to have lips like his, herself included. She'd been cursed with her mother's pretty but thin lips.

He stopped about six inches from her. Inside her comfort zone but not pushing her into the red, panicky area yet. His impeccable suit clung to his lean, powerful figure. The scent of his masculine, delicious cologne wafted toward her, and she took a deep breath, enjoying how it reminded her of the ocean in Norway.

Cold, crisp, and potentially deadly.

Giving her a very visible once-up, once-down look he tapped his lips and stepped back. Looking up at her face, he smiled. "Well, eating pussy certainly has been good for you. Seems to have mellowed and filled you out." He had a wonderful English accent that made even his insult sound sensual.

She gaped at him, unsure if he was trash-talking her or being a dick. Either way, if he thought she was the kind of girl who wouldn't talk shit right back, he didn't know anything about women. "I see you've been fasting."

His eyes widened the tiniest bit, and she swore he wanted to laugh, but his expression remained closed. Her pussy continued to tighten as her gaze locked with his.

There was something so...so...intense about him. The complete attention on her, to the point of utterly ignoring Jesse, was at once hot and rude. Her hormones made her want to fall to her knees right now and beg him to take her, but her pride managed to overrule her body.

At least for the moment.

Giving the sadist a pointed look, she stepped around him and walked over to Jesse, glad she had her old swaying stride back. Well, she had a little—a lot—more junk to sway now than she used to, but she knew how to work a set of heels. Besides, if the sight of her clothed didn't interest him, she highly doubted the sight of her naked would.

She really, really wanted him to be interested in her.

If his barely audible growl was any indication, he liked what he saw. Or he was going to bite her. One of the two.

She gave Jesse a quick hug and a kiss on the cheek. "Thank you for bringing him here, Jesse."

Jesse glanced over her shoulder and nodded before looking at her. "Time for me to go."

Confused, she took a small step away from Jesse. She wouldn't look at that devilish man behind her, but she could almost feel his body, his energy reaching out to her. Heat crept up and down her back, like a whisper of fingers brushing her skin. Afraid of what she'd do when she was alone with the handsome Master, which probably included a hell of a blowjob, she gave Jesse a pleading glance. "But you just got here."

"Darlin', it isn't me you're here to see tonight."

"Oh, okay." Feeling very vulnerable, she swallowed hard and nodded. "I... Thank you, Jesse. No matter what, I appreciate you doing this for me."

Giving her a grin, he ruffled her hair like a bratty older brother. "No problem, kid."

With that, Jesse left, shutting the door behind them. Fake crickets continued to chirp, and she pretty much looked everywhere but at the other man. Not that it mattered; she could feel him getting closer. It was crazy, but his energy almost seemed to push at her.

"Kira, turn around."

"I believe you have me at a disadvantage, Sir. I don't recall your name."

Well, she knew who he was, but she needed to say something to even the playing field between them. The command in his voice ordered instant compliance, and oh how she wanted to comply. But she needed to keep her head on straight, her feet firmly on the ground, and her mind in the game.

The smell of his cologne enveloped her a moment before he moved her hair off the side of her neck. The move was so sudden, so controlled that she didn't have time to tense up. The tip of his finger stroked along her jaw and over to her neck. He continued to slowly caress the column of her throat, lingering touches that somehow mesmerized her. He pulled her tighter against him, and she leaned her head onto his shoulder, enjoying his touch. The fact he didn't grope, didn't rush, and didn't hump her ass allowed her to breath.

His lips brushed her ear, the soft ruff of his goatee tickling her neck. "I forgot to introduce myself, which is very poor manners. My name is Lord Bryan."

She giggled, unable to help herself. "I have to ask. Are you a like for real lord, or is that some BDSM thing?"

The deep vibration of his laughter rumbled through his chest, a dark, almost evil sound.

Fuck, that was hot. Just standing here with him felt so good it should be a sin.

He trailed his hand over her collarbone, then down to the first rise of her breasts peeking out of her flowing green dress. It had an empire waist and showcased her breasts while hiding the bump of her belly.

"Yes, for real. Through no fault of my own I inherited a title along with all the drudgery that comes with it."

"Better than inheriting a big ass."

She winced at her admission, and he laughed again. "You have a very pretty arse. Nice and thick but soft. The kind of bum I want to grab with both hands while fucking you."

Desire pooled in her belly, and she instinctively tensed. When nothing but warmth spread through her, stirring her sex, she let out a soft sigh. This was nice, really nice. Part of her mind argued they should talk first, do something other than this dangerous touching. She didn't want him to think she was easy.

He collared her neck with his hand, stroking her pulse with his thumb, and all thoughts of putting any distance between them fled. "You are not what I expected. Why did you seek me out?"

The formal tone to his speech made it almost flow like poetry. "I..." She screwed up her courage and told him what she hadn't told anyone else. "My doctors think a large part of my pain during sex is psychological. That if I can learn to not fear being penetrated, it would get better. Please don't tell anyone."

For a long time he didn't say anything, just continuing to stroke her and seduce her with his scent, his body, and his heat. "Your secret is safe with me. I would never betray your confidence." His tone changed, becoming a guttural purr that would have fit a tiger getting ready to leap on his prey. "Tell me. Am I what you expected in a sadist?"

"I had no idea what to expect." She swallowed, feeling the pressure on her throat from his grip, kinda liking how possessive it felt. "But, well, I don't think any woman could ever be ready for you."

He rubbed his lips against her cheek, speaking against her skin. "You say the nicest things, but I'm still going to keep you gagged most of the time."

That made her pull away, or at least try to pull away. He held her tight, and as his arms bunched around her with muscle, she knew there was no way she could escape. With deliberate intent, he pressed her back fully into his embrace so his pelvis brushed her ass. The sensation of his hard erection against her body had her near shaking with fear and arousal. God, she wanted him, but she was so scared of the pain. She'd only recently gotten to the point where she could masturbate with a very, very small vibrator.

The thought of taking anything bigger than her finger was terrifying.

Memories of being racked with cramps, curled up on her bed while her boyfriend threw on his clothes and walked out filled her mind, adding a new shame to her fears.

Holding her tight with one arm, Bryan moved her hair again. "Easy, girl. We aren't going to do anything that will bring you any more hurt than you're ready for. By the time I'm done, the thought of having a cock inside of you, making you ache, will get your pussy as wet as can be, allowing me to slide into you up to the hilt with one long stroke."

Words failed her—something that rarely happened—and she made a little groaning noise when his teeth grazed the side of her neck. He bit hard enough to sting, then sucked at the hurt, bringing blood to the surface, making her burn. No one had given her a hickey in forever, but fuck if it didn't feel good.

Pulling away, he nuzzled the spot. "I like your skin. It's so pale and perfect."

"Freckles," she said in a breathy voice as he resumed biting on her neck, now in a new location.

He pulled back. "Pardon me?"

"I have freckles. My skin isn't perfect."

"I'm actually surprised at how nice you look. You've stopped trying to be a strawberry blonde, have gained some generous curves—"

"Hey, did you just call me fat?"

With a low growl he gripped her hips, but his touch was gentle, a restrained violence. "I called you a woman. A beautiful, lush woman. Now strip."

She looked at him over her shoulder. "Pardon me?"

"Your clothes. Take them off. I want to see your body."

"Wait, I haven't agreed to anything."

"Neither have I."

Balking, she crossed her arms under her breasts. "Why do you want to see me naked?"

He moved back behind her, his hands sliding over her shoulders, slowly lowering the straps of her top. "Because I think you're beautiful. And I need to know if you can bear my touch and follow my commands."

"Can't you touch me through my clothes?"

"Yes, but you won't come."

While her hormones did a happy dance, she tried to ignore the sudden throbbing of her clit. "Who says I want to come?"

He laughed, an honest and true sound. Feeling stupid, she tried to pull the strap to her dress back up. Before she could secure it in place, his hand moved over hers, easily pinning her arm to her chest. "While I do love a redhead's temper, I can assure you any orgasm I give you will be beyond anything you've experienced."

Everything south of her belly button tightened, and her arousal soaked her panties. "Really?" She'd meant for it to come out sounding sarcastic, but instead she sounded breathy and almost hopeful.

"Really."

She frowned, so many emotions and sensations swimming through her that she had a hard time cataloging them all. "I don't know. I…I want to, but I hardly know you."

"Honest answer."

He jerked the arms of her dress down, capturing her wrists in the fabric and revealing her emerald-green bra. He paused and examined her, his gaze roaming her skin like a caress. "Stunning."

She tried to push him away, desire and the glow of his compliment tangling with her fear. "What are you doing?"

"What you're too afraid to do." He cupped her face and gently stroked her cheeks. "Kira, anytime you want things to stop, to slow down, simply pick a magic word, and I will make you feel as safe as I possibly can."

His unexpected humor and the kindness in his voice startled her. That and the fact that she wanted to see if he was as good as his bragging. God, she hadn't been this attracted to anyone in what seemed like forever. Her emotions were as intense and varied as a teenager's, while her woman's mind could conjure up all kinds of delicious things Bryan could do to her, with her.

"Magic word?"

"Yes, a special word you won't say in everyday conversation. It can't be 'stop' because at some point you might want to yell 'don't stop' as I'm flogging you and making you come over and over again. It's called your safe word, and the instant you use it, everything stops and I take care of you."

"Oh God." She tried to turn in his arms, to look at him, but he held her in place. "Okay, safe word. Pookie."

"Pookie?"

"Yes."

"Huh. Very well. Now, you need to stop fucking around and strip."

Once again he moved away from her, but this time her dress was dangling from under her breasts where the small elastic band in the fabric kept it against her. His words irritated her, brought the stubborn and competitive side of her nature out. Her mind argued that turning around and staring him down while she stripped wasn't very submissive, but she didn't care.

Spinning on her heels, she tossed her long hair over her shoulder and defiantly lifted her chin. While she had the hots for him, that did not make her a sure thing. Well, actually she was a pretty sure thing, but that didn't mean her feminine pride wouldn't insist on a little bit of insolence. When she got a good look at him, at how he was looking at her, all thoughts of defiance melted away in a tsunami of heat.

His gaze locked on her body with such lust that everything inside her at once tensed and relaxed. Her pussy hurt but in a good way. In a way that made her want to be filled. And if anyone could teach her how to coax her body into accepting a man, it had to be him. Her mind waved the white flag, unable to resist his charm and the pleading of her hormones.

She picked up the edge of her dress and pulled it over her head, her breasts bouncing as they slid free of the elastic. While she didn't have DD-cups, she was certainly better endowed than her previous A-cup size. Tossing her dress on a nearby stone bench, she avoided his gaze. Now that she was down to her underwear, it was much harder to continue. Her thighs touched, and she had a definite pooch of a belly, even while sucking it in. Not to mention her big ass. If she was back in Hollywood, they would have been appalled at how out of shape she'd gotten.

The tabloids would have had blown-up pictures of the cellulite on her thighs all over their Web sites, along with the caption of Guess Who Got Fat!

Actually, she wasn't that out of shape. She exercised and ate relatively well, and her body had decided to become curvy, just like her mother and grandmother.

She hoped he liked curvy.

He didn't say anything or even move. He was like a shadow at the edge of her vision.

With trembling fingers, she took off her bra, sliding it down her arms and revealing her breasts. The nipples were tight and long, and she worried if he liked big nipples. Feeling unsure, confused, and no longer aroused, she crossed her arms over her breasts. Taking off her panties was too much, too exposing. She couldn't do it.

Moving like a ghost, he came closer. The front of his suit coat and shirt filled her vision, and his body heat licked against her. "Do you want me to take them off?"

She nodded and shivered when his hands skimmed down her arms.

"You have beautiful breasts. If you agree to be my submissive for the duration of your training, I will enjoy punishing them."

"Punishing?"

"Put your arms behind your head. And before you sass off, save us both time and do as I say. If you can't follow a simple command, you need to get dressed, walk out that door, and never come back."

She stared up at him, not believing his nerve. When he merely gazed back at her with bored indifference, she grudgingly did as he asked. He stopped her and rearranged how she had her hands so she was lifting her hair off her neck in a graceful arch.

Making a pleased sound, he brushed her cheek with his knuckles, causing her to want to turn toward his touch.

"You have a lovely neck, long and elegant. It is one of your best assets." His tone became lower, deeper. Heat teased her body. Being near him was like admiring a fine work of art and having the art admire you back. "And now, since you were such a good girl, I will show you what I mean by punishing your breasts."

Before she could prepare herself, he slapped her breast. Not hard, but it was still a slap, and that was kind of insulting. She'd taken and given plenty of punches and kicks during her time as a stuntwoman and action star. That was different. Slapping was like...punishment pain. An almost scolding gesture that conveyed his power over her. No one had ever done that to her. She glared up at him.

He wasn't even looking at her face, instead fully focusing on her breast. Then he slapped the other one, and a stinging warmth suffused her flesh. Grabbing both of her nipples, he pinched and pulled hard enough to bring her up on her toes. Electric arousal burned through her, merging with her pleasure but not mixing. Instead she was slammed between pain and pleasure like a Ping-Pong ball.

It became a game in her head, a dare to see how much she could take. In a way this feeling of enduring was like the survival sports she'd used to love. Rock climbing and being almost to the top, her muscles burning and shaking but pushing herself a little bit harder to get the reward. In this case the reward was finally being able to love someone with all her body and heart.

He held her there, straining on her tippy toes. "If at any time you have pain from your body that is bad, the kind that could lead to reinjuring your pelvis or is an indication of something wrong, you will tell me right away. Am I clear?"

Sensations spiked from her breasts to her clit and back again. Gentling the pressure on her nipples, he tugged and rolled them between his fingers. A different kind of energy flowed from him now, not as sharp but more confining.

"There now. That's a good girl."

He stopped touching her altogether, and she watched him wet his fingers before grasping her nipples again and rubbing gently. Amazing pleasure suffused her until she thought her legs might give out. She groaned when he stroked the sensitive tips of her breasts. His mood shifted, and he grasped her nipples, squeezing hard enough that it was all hurt and painful pleasure. She looked up at his face, and as he stared into her eyes, something way down deep in the darkest reaches of her psyche began to wake. Her pussy clenched; then her honey wet her inner thighs.

Of fucking hell, why hadn't she tried BDSM sooner?

"Feel that? How the pleasure is different than what you normally feel when someone plays with your breasts? The pain has sensitized you, made you more aware of your body, conscious of how good it can feel once you push past the pain to the pleasure. Submit to me, Kira, and I will make you feel things you never even imagined were possible."

CHAPTER THREE

The moment Bryan released Kira's nipples, he shifted his arm around her back, ready to catch her if she fell. Her shriek became muffled against his chest as the blood rushed back into her nipples and her hands moved between them to cup her abused nubs. He couldn't help but smile, pleased by the way her hips pressed against his and the unmistakable scent of her wet pussy reached his nose.

Her beauty appealed to him in some way that was like all the notches in a key finally fitting the lock and turning it. Things he'd never considered as striking now enraptured him. The way her freckles spread over her shoulders and lightened as they neared where her panties covered her bum made him want to trace each dot with his tongue. Speaking of her arse, it was a work of art. A nice, big, fat bottom that deserved his worship. He was going to make that healthy bum pink, then red, and finally when she was begging for her release, he was going to make her come by fucking it.

Hell, he wanted to fuck her right now. If she was any other submissive, he would have been buried up to his balls with her screaming his name. Chiding himself for acting like an eager baby Dom, he took a deep breath. He'd have to go slow with her. She was as green as the grass and as skittish as a fawn. That meant small toys, fingers, and tongues at first before moving on to anything more substantial.

Like his aching cock.

She moved closer to him, and he found himself wanting to soothe her. While he was tempted to coddle her, something unusual unto itself that he'd think about later, he knew it was past time to see all her body as he'd commanded. If she was truly hurting or terrified, he'd slow down, but if she was scared, she would soon get over it. If there was one thing he knew how to do well, it was coax the response he wanted out of a woman's body.

Dropping to his knees before her, he grasped her hips and rubbed his face against the softness of her round belly. "Place your hands on my shoulders."

She complied, a needy sound accompanying her squirming beneath his hands. Usually he found such lack of self-control a turnoff, but Kira had no idea what the rules were—yet. Her movements were natural, unstudied. An expression of her desire. He'd teach her protocol and, along the way, mold her into the kind of submissive men dreamed about, he dreamed about.

He nibbled his way to her belly button, pausing to dip his tongue into the hollow, then bite along the edges. There was something very erotic about biting for him. The sight of his teeth marks on a woman's body, the subtle crunch of skin almost breaking beneath his teeth made his dick ache. That was another reason he liked curvy women—there was more to bite. He didn't have to feel like a dog trying to get some meat off a dry bone.

Amused at his thoughts, he refocused on the task at hand. He'd give her a little bit of pain, watch her responses, and push her comfort zone while learning what aroused her. Kira needed to know pleasure from him first. To see what kind of ecstasy he could give her as a reward if she behaved.

Unfortunately—and fortunately—he didn't think that was going to happen very often. No matter who she ended up with, Kira would always be a handful. It would take a great deal to make her bend to anyone's will. But he had a feeling that once she accepted a Master, that lucky man would be her one and only. Until he got her to acknowledge his Mastery—and mean it—he'd have a hell of a fight for dominance on his hands. Especially since she had an Irish temper to match her flaming-red hair.

He'd always loved a challenge.

Kissing his way over her hip, he took his time to brush his lips against each freckle. They were actually rather cute. Gave her an innocent air he wanted to corrupt and defile in the most delicious ways. Speaking of delicious, her cunt smelled divine. Musky like a woman but with a hint of almost sweet to it.

Threading his fingers through the hips of her panties, he slowly drew the green silk down her legs. When she lifted her foot to step out, he lightly smacked her hip and earned an indignant yelp. "Stay still. I want them around your ankles so you can only open your legs as much as your panties allow."

He leaned back so he could inspect her and sucked in a deep breath. She had one of the prettiest pussies he'd ever seen. A very thin strip of neatly trimmed strawberry curls exposed the rest of her shaved cunt to his sight. Small but with extremely puffy outer lips, her clit hid between her swollen labia, barely visible. His cock tried to punch a hole in his pants, and he made a vow he would not give up until those plump lips were being spread by his thrusting dick.

Unable to resist, he leaned forward and sucked one outer lip into his mouth, nibbling on it while she gripped his shoulders and gasped. A hint of her liquid arousal met his tongue, and now it was his turn to groan. She tasted as sweet as she smelled.

Eating her would be like eating candy.

He pulled back and blew a warm breath on her mound. "I can see why the girls like you so much. Your pussy is as sweet as can be."

She gave a breathless laugh. "Vegetarian. We taste sweeter."

"Interesting. Kira, I want you to start playing with your nipples, as hard as I played with them. If I feel like you're doing a half-arsed job of it, I'll stop, and you will not like that one bit."

She licked her lower lip and looked down at him with passion-glazed, dark eyes. She was such an unusual combination, warm sherry-brown eyes, soft auburn hair, and those freckles. As long as she didn't speak, she could carry off the virginal-young-woman look rather well.

At the first stroke of her nipples, she thrust her hips at his mouth. Eager for a better taste, he delved between her labia, seeking out her clit. The hard little nub brushed his tongue, and she groaned. "Oh, Bryan, that feels so fucking good."

Well, looks like it wouldn't be hard to get her to talk dirty. That would help in the long run. Communication was essential between a Master and submissive. Even though this was only temporary, he still wanted a connection with her.

But right now he just wanted her to come.

Pulling her sex open with his thumbs, he began to rhythmically lick her pussy from her perineum up to her clit. One of the things God had blessed him with was a long tongue, and he knew how to use it. He almost fingered her but stopped himself and caressed her inner thigh instead.

Looking up, he caught her standing still, her hands cupping her breasts and her face slack with pleasure.

Displeased, he gave her inner thigh a hard slap that made her moan. "Play with those pretty fucking tits, love, or the next slap is going to be on your clit."

Groaning deep in her throat, she began to rub her palms over her nipples before twisting them like he had. He used his thumbs to hold her open again and got to enjoy the sight of her pussy clenching down on an imaginary cock, seeking something to grip. Poor girl. It must really be frustrating to want and not be able to have.

Leaning forward, he placed his mouth against her clit and let her labia go, enjoying how the ultrasoft skin surrounded his mouth. He began to swirl his tongue around her clit, judging from her reactions how she liked it. Her scent enveloped him as her taste flooded his tongue, making him want to fuck her in the worst way.

She hunched over, her hands scrambling for his shoulders. He began to massage her bud with his tongue, a rolling motion he'd learned from a Swedish submissive he'd met while riding his motorcycle through Denmark. Much like when someone did that to his balls, Kira didn't stand a chance. She gave a long, breathy moan, then clutched at his hair, grinding her pussy against his face.

Feeling primal, on the edge, he nipped at her clit, and she began to orgasm against his mouth. She kneaded her fingers against his skull like a kitten's paws as she came, her breath bursting out in harsh pants. For as loud and vocal as she was before her orgasm, when she came, she was incredibly soft, quiet, and oh so fucking sexy. More of her honey leaked out, and he eagerly ate it up, reveling in the delicious taste. If he had a cunt like this available to him at all times, he would start every morning with her for breakfast.

She tried to push him away, but he sharply nipped her labia. "You're going to come again."

"Oh, no." She gave a shaky laugh. "I can only come once."

He ignored her halfhearted attempts to pull back and began to lick around the entrance to her sheath. She tensed, then let out a soft sigh when he did no more than tease. Soon her movements became restless, and he slapped her inner thigh again but didn't stop eating her. She seemed to respond well to the slaps, even tilted her hips forward after each blow and made these little hungry moans that drove him crazy. He varied the strength of his strikes, focusing on her response and altering his techniques in order to pleasure her as much as possible.

Keeping up that pattern—spanking her, then sucking on her clit, then spanking her again—he soon had her jittering against him. He rested his hands on the warm surface of her reddened skin and began to pinch and further stimulate her. Her pussy convulsed against his mouth. The urge to see her orgasm this time suffused him, so he leaned back and held her labia open. "Make yourself come."

When she hesitated, he slapped her pussy, and she screamed. He soothed the abused skin with long swipes of his tongue, then pulled back again. "Do it."

This time she didn't hesitate. She reached between her thighs and rubbed her clit with a hard, circular motion that would quickly send her over the edge. He didn't bother to hide his growl of desire at her efforts to please him. She began to play with her nipples again, which were now thick and hard, begging him to chew on them, to make her squirm and whimper even as she came all over his fingers.

Her breath caught, and he watched with fascination as the first contraction hit her pussy. Her slick, reddish pink flesh began to pulse gently as her inner muscles squeezed and released. Not ripping down his pants and shoving his cock into her as he normally would with a submissive was torture.

When her last contraction passed and her legs began to shake, he stood and pulled her against his chest. "What's more comfortable for you? Sitting or lying down?"

She looked up at him, her eyes glazed like she'd been drinking all day. "Lying down."

Moving slowly, he eased her into the adjoining open space which held the enormous black silk bed. After settling her among the pillows, he removed his shoes and tossed them in the corner before joining her. She smiled and wiggled on the silk, totally unashamed in her nudity.

As usual, a really good orgasm or two had a way of making a woman relax and embrace her sexuality.

He leaned on his elbow and looked down at her. She hesitantly reached for his face. Grasping her hand, he placed it against his cheek, then let go. Her soft stroke helped to soothe his inner beast, allowing him to regain control of himself.

Somewhat.

"Do you swallow?"

She blinked, some of the fierce intelligence coming back to her eyes. "No."

"You do now."

Her look of shock was almost comical. "I beg your pardon?"

"I swallowed you, every delicious fucking drop. You will do the same for me."

She flushed and began to inch her hand down his torso. The way she licked her lips making his already hard dick hate him for what he was about to do. Capturing her hand and holding it against his stomach, he shook his head. "No, not tonight."

"Seriously?"

"Extremely. Your Master's seed is a reward, not a given. After you leave, I'll wrap my hand around my cock and come long and hard, thinking about you."

Her eyelids half shut, giving her a sensual look. "Can I watch?"

"No." He couldn't help but grin at her disappointed pout. "But you can think about me when you're home. I'm assuming alone?"

She stiffened. "Yes, alone. Do you really think I'm the kind of girl that would do that?"

He shrugged. "At Wicked, you never know."

She started to push away, but he gently dragged her back. "Easy, love. If this is going to work, you can't run every time you get your knickers in a twist. Because I'm going to twist them up a lot."

She grumbled but allowed him to tuck her against his body. She fit quite well, tall enough so they naturally curved around each other. He usually only dated short women, but it was nice to have more to touch, to hold on to. With a soft sigh, she pulled one of his arms around her and began to stroke his hand.

"Thank you."

He smiled at her pensive tone, glad she couldn't see his face. "Why do you sound like you're sorry when you say that?"

She seemed to shrink down into herself. "No reason."

His Dom sense honed in on her, feeling something was not quite right. "Kira, be honest with me." She stiffened against him but didn't say anything. "Now."

"I feel like shit because I can't make you come, okay!" She grabbed a nearby gold-brocade pillow and held it against herself in a death grip.

Fuck, she was a complicated woman. Keeping up with her mood changes would be a challenge. "Perhaps I wasn't clear. Even if we could fuck until I passed out from dehydration, I wouldn't with you, not tonight. You aren't ready."

She turned, tears trailing down her cheeks. Poor girl. She appeared to be one of those submissives who would come down hard after an orgasm. He made a note to have plenty of warming blankets, chocolate, and other comfort objects for the next time they met. Now, he just needed to convince her there would be a next time.

Closing her eyes, she tucked back into that almost fetal position. "It's okay if you want to leave. I understand."

He wanted to ask her what the hell she was talking about, then remembered Jesse mentioning that the second man she'd ever had sex with had dumped her after she wasn't able to take his penetration. Suddenly angry at the callous asshole who would leave a vibrant woman like Kira in such a hurt state, he forced her to look up at him. "I'm not going anywhere, and neither are you."

She reached out to his hand with the tips of her fingers, sighing when he curled his hand around hers. "Okay."

"You could at least pretend to believe me, woman."

Her soft laughter seemed to wash away some of her sorrow. "Okay, oh Masterful Lord Bryan. I believe you." She glanced up, her eyes a little red from crying. "When can I see you again?"

"Would you feel comfortable coming to my home?"

"Um... No offense, but I really don't know you that well."

"I completely understand. But I would ask that you talk to Jesse and Hawk about me, Sunny too. You can trust that bratty little sub to tell you the truth."

She gave him an offended look. "Hey, I like Sunny."

"I like her too—her honesty is refreshing—but that girl would benefit from a good spanking."

Kira wiggled her bottom and looked at him through her lashes. "Will you spank me?"

He grabbed a handful of her plush bum, then squeezed hard. He was fucking ravenous for her, and it was getting harder and harder to maintain control. Shit, he couldn't remember the last time he'd been this turned on without any actual sex. It was bloody annoying how hard it was to maintain his self-control over a woman he just met. In an effort to cool down, he smiled at her and said in a teasing voice, "Only if you're a good girl."

The sudden heating of her gaze brought a renewed surge of blood to his already aching dick.

She traced the side of his neck, her fingertips tickling over his pulse. "What's your phone number?"

"Do you need me to write it down?"

"No, I'll remember it."

He told her and made her repeat it back to him. "Text me, and I'll give you my e-mail address. I'd like you to do me a favor."

"What's that?"

"I want you to e-mail me your sexual preferences and fantasies. Things that make you instantly hot. All the forbidden and taboo pleasures that you've never admitted but fantasize about. I want to make your every desire, your wildest fantasies come true. But I can't do that unless you're honest with me."

Flushing, she looked down at his chest. "That's kind of personal."

He laughed and gently slid his hand between her legs, stroking her soft flesh until she moaned. "Darling, I haven't even begun to become personal with you yet. If you're going to submit to me, I need you to trust me. Yes, trust is something that needs to be earned, but please believe that I would never reveal your secrets."

"I'll think about it."

He traced his thumb over her now hard clit and loved the way she bit her lower lip. "When you think about it, think about me doing all those lovely, dark, forbidden things to you, with you. Think about how much better they will be when I'm in control of your pleasure."

A rush of wetness dampened his fingers where they were stroking her pussy, and a savage satisfaction gripped him. He slowly withdrew his hand and licked his fingers clean while she rubbed her pelvis against his with a little needy moan.

"Can you do that for me?"

"Yes, Sir." She smiled up at him, her earlier energy returning. An electric buzz tingled over his skin. She stretched, then winced.

Instantly concerned, he helped her sit up. "Are you all right?"

"Yeah, just old lady aches and pains." The small muscles around her eyes tightened, and she took a deep breath. "Trust me. I'd endure a hell of a lot more for what you did for me tonight."

"Good, because I plan on putting you through hell and bringing you out the other side to heaven."

"Arrogant, aren't you?"

"It's not arrogance when it's true."

CHAPTER FOUR

Bryan stood in front of the giant antique Moroccan mirror in his bedroom and took his jacket off for what had to be the tenth time. On his bed, scattered over the navy-blue silk comforter, were six more jackets, four pairs of pants, and three shirts he'd tried on and discarded. In a pile on the chair near his mirror were a variety of ties, suspenders, and cuff links.

Lawrence, his butler and surrogate father, was going to choke Bryan when he saw the mess he'd made of his closet. They'd been together since Bryan was four years old. When Bryan had been banished to the United States by his family after the sex tape scandal, Lawrence had followed him across the pond. His mother, the esteemed Lady Sutherfield, had sent Bryan seven hundred and fifty thousand euros in order for him to establish a financial consulting business in the States. At least that was what his parents told their friends. In truth it was hush money, payment for leaving without yet another stain to their illustrious name.

Closing his eyes, he forced his mind to stay in the present and not dwell on a time when he'd felt like a broken man. Things were different now. Not only was he older, but he also had turned that seven-hundred-and-fifty-thousand-euro investment into his own multimillion-dollar financial empire. He'd cashed in early on the fact that more and more people were going to be looking for a financial consultant as the US economy weakened. Unlike most of his colleagues, he offered services to those making under fifty thousand dollars a year. True, his lower-end clients didn't get the in-depth attention that his wealthiest clients received, but they did get sound financial advice that helped them increase their own wealth. His company had a close to 100 percent retention rate for their customers, which meant when the client got wealthier, so did the company.

Bolstered by the thought of how many people he'd helped, people his parents would have seen as being beneath them, Bryan took off the jacket and tossed it onto the bed, deciding it was too formal for the mood he wanted to set tonight with Kira.

At the thought of the beautiful ember-haired woman, his lips curved into what was no doubt a stupid grin. When he thought about their time together, he'd become aroused to the point of jerking off and even more excited about seeing her again. She would be here soon, so he should stop fucking around with playing dress up like some teenage girl going on a date.

Striding over to the seating area tucked into a Moroccan-tiled alcove, he grabbed the printout of Kira's e-mail and read it again. To his delight she'd gone beyond just listing her sexual preferences. She'd been rather honest about what turned her on, what she thought she might like, and what she was absolutely no way ever interested in. Or, as she put it, he was more likely to poop canaries than she was to ever want needle play.

While the imagery was somewhat vulgar, he found her quite funny. It was hard to keep a straight face around her, but he couldn't let her use humor to try to break the mood between them. He needed her to be out of her mind with pleasure, literally. If the pain associated with penetration was mostly mental, he'd have to somehow get her to check out and just feel.

Not an easy task but also not impossible. He'd just have to try to get her deep into subspace, something that would take time, but he wouldn't rush this experience with her. Kira deserved to have some joy in her life, to let her Master take her pain away. He'd fulfill all her desires, give her everything she could ever want or need.

She'd included four very detailed fantasies, including one that involved spanking. Tonight he planned on making that particular dream come to life, to show Kira that even as her arse burned from his hand, her pussy would burn hotter.

Multiple partners also seemed to be a running theme in her sexual interests. Fortunately she hadn't indicated any interest in having more than one man at once, but she'd certainly had a bunch of fantasies about being with a man and another woman. While he noted that she went into great detail about her interaction with the other woman, there had been no mention of Kira's male partner touching anyone but Kira. In his experience some submissives became extremely possessive of their Doms, while others were fine with open swinging. He had a feeling that Kira was more on the jealous side, so he'd act with caution and make it all about her pleasure. There were a few submissives he had in mind, a couple of lesbian submissives he knew who would love to be with Kira and wouldn't pose a threat to his bond with her either. One of his personal favorite kinks was to watch two women play with each other.

The thought of his beautiful Kira getting her pussy eaten while he tortured her nipples made his dick stiff as a fucking board.

Taking a deep breath to clear his head, he set the paper down and decided to just stick with his black pants and a white dress shirt. If things went well, he wouldn't be wearing them for long. He wasn't going to try any vaginal penetration with her yet. He would experiment with one of the things she'd indicated she was interested in trying but had never actually done. She'd put down that she'd always wanted to try anal sex. Bryan couldn't wait to share that painful pleasure with her. The thought of being the only man to take her back there, to give her the sensations of her first anal orgasm had him gritting his teeth. While he wouldn't be using his cock—he'd use a small anal plug instead—he still couldn't wait to see her little arsehole stretched.

Would she scream? Would she cry out for more as she came all over his tongue with the toy shoved up her ass? His whole body ached with the need to fuck, and it took him a bit to come back down from that high state of arousal.

Mastering his own lust was going to be a challenge. He would have to keep himself on a very tight leash. Kira was absolutely beautiful when she orgasmed, and he'd like to see her do it over and over again. He needed to get her to associate pain with pleasure, so tonight he would arouse her to the point of being mindless with pleasure and then add a sting. If he did it right, if he was patient and really paid attention to her signals, he should be able to give her a nice endorphin-packed orgasm.

The thought of touching her, kissing her, sliding her body against his had his erect dick begging him for some relief. He couldn't put his finger on it, but there was something about her that just flat-out did it for him. Sure, she was a beautiful woman. He'd been with plenty of beautiful women and never had this soul-deep reaction, this craving for their presence. Being near Kira, feeling her energy, had been an absolute delight. It had also been absolute torture to not avail himself of her willing mouth, but she needed to know without a doubt that his pleasure wasn't an issue. If she was aroused, he was aroused. Simple as that. All he needed was her trust in order to take her from ordinary arousal to painful ecstasy.

The best kind.

Another thing he'd bet no one had done for her before.

In an odd way, that made him feel even more protective of her.

His cell phone rang, and he pulled it out of his pocket, noticing Lawrence's number. Once Lawrence had turned sixty, Bryan had insisted that he carry around a cell phone to call when he needed something instead of trying to find him in the gigantic Victorian mansion. It had taken some time, but the butler now texted him the information. Unfortunately, Lawrence also had an odd form of texting shorthand that made no sense to anyone but Lawrence.

Gst hz rived.

It took him a moment, but then he figured out that Lawrence was telling him that Kira had arrived. He tossed the phone onto the table and moved quickly to his bathroom, brushing his teeth and double-checking his appearance. Finger combing his hair, he gave himself a once-over and nodded at his reflection.

His submissive was here, she was counting on him, and he wouldn't let her down.

Kira pulled her opalescent white McLaren F1 through the now open wrought-iron gates to the entrance and into the massive circular drive before Bryan's fabulous home. No, wait, home wasn't the correct term. This was a manor. While her town house in the city kept her more than comfortable, there was something to be said for estates. Bryan's boasted a gorgeous Victorian mansion, probably built in the 1850s. She was glad she'd taken the chance on coming here tonight. True, she'd questioned everyone about Bryan and had been assured over and over again that he was a good man, but how well did anyone really know anyone else? Just in case, she'd left a note on her kitchen table at home about where she was going and who she was going to be with. Paranoid? Yes, but a little extra safety never hurt.

As she slowly made her way up the drive and more of the home came into sight, she smiled at the obvious love and care that had gone into the stately mansion's upkeep. She'd gone through a phase where she'd been obsessed with everything Victorian, reading all she could find on it, and that information helped her appreciate his home. In her opinion, learning something new was always beneficial, no matter what the subject. While she hadn't gone to college, she'd traveled the world and educated herself with whatever struck her fancy. It led to a rather esoteric knowledge database, but she kicked ass at Trivial Pursuit.

When she eased her car around the winding curve leading to his home, she slowed down to take in the details of the trim and the warm color choices of the exterior. Brass lanterns hung on either side of the large front door, illuminating the second-story wraparound porch for a few feet in either direction. A white painted set of curving stairs led up to the second-floor entryway, while the first floor was a series of French doors with heavy cream drapes blocking the view. An enormous boulder sat between the two stairs, and a natural looking waterfall tickled down the boulder into a hidden drain. Small water plants added bursts of color to the fountain, and Kira rather liked the contrast of old-world architecture and the naturally raw water feature.

Pulling up behind a black Aston Martin One 77 with its sleek racing curves and low-to-the-ground body, she wasn't surprised at all that Bryan liked speed and sporty cars. She could just see him, hitting the gas so the car flew and G-force pressed his body back into the seat.

It had been two days since she'd met Bryan—they'd both been busy with other obligations—and she found herself excited to see him. For one thing, she'd certainly made more of an effort to look pretty. Bryan was almost unfairly handsome, and in order not to look like a hag next to him, she'd put large, loose curls into her hair. Tonight she wore a black dress with a plunging backline. A silver chain set with onyx and white sapphires dangled down her back in a manner so the chains looked like corset stays. Beneath she wore a pair of black garters and a black bra but no panties. He seemed to really like her pussy, and she sure as shit liked what he'd done to it, so why not display it a bit.

Besides, it was the closest thing she had to a BDSM outfit. She'd need to go shopping soon. Even if things didn't work out with Bryan—though she really hoped they would—she wanted to have a wardrobe of appropriate clothing to wear to Wicked. The bar was amazing, and she couldn't wait to see more of it, but hopefully this time with Bryan at her side. The thought of being seen with him, being marked as belonging to him sent a rather primitive sense of satisfaction through her. He was fine, so, so fucking fine. Whatever did he see in her?

Screwing up her courage, she checked her pale rose lip gloss and made sure her mascara hadn't smudged. She wore waterproof mascara tonight, just in case she sweated or cried.

Anticipation coiled through her belly, making her nervous and excited at the same time. His oral sex skills had been beyond amazing, and though she'd had some small bruises from his bites the next day and her nipples hurt, she'd still walked around with a goofy grin. Even before her accident she'd never managed to have more than one orgasm at a time.

Bryan was some kind of pussy whisperer.

The dress swung around her thighs as she grabbed her purse, then shut the door. A moment later, the porch light came on, and she glanced up at the house as she made her way across the driveway to the winding stairs. The detail work on the railing, with its curves and floral carvings, were beautiful works of art. She made it to the landing of the front door and was getting ready to knock when it opened from the other side. An elderly gentleman in a dapper black suit and red tie smiled at her and gave her a small bow.

"Ms. Harmony, I presume?" He had the same English accent as Bryan but a little stuffier and very formal.

She smiled and gave him a small wave. "Yes, that's me."

"Please do come in. Lord Sutherfield will be down in a few moments and has asked if you would wait for him in the Green Room."

"Of course."

She walked past him and let out a soft sigh at the sight of the foyer of this grand home. All dark wood and sixteen-foot ceilings with muted artwork on the walls. To the left the sliding doors opened onto a parlor, and to the right, a study. The furniture was either period or excellent reproductions, and she wandered over to look at the carvings on the staircase railing.

"This house is lovely."

"Thank you, Ms. Harmony. My name is Lawrence. May I get you some light refreshments or a spot of something to eat?"

"No, thank you."

"If you will please follow me, I'll take you to the Green Room to wait for Lord Sutherfield."

She followed Lawrence through a long hall and into a lovely room that must have been a trophy room at one point. It had the huge, open walls suitable for mounted heads, something a man of means in those days would have had. Now it held a staggering array of stunning Impressionists' artwork. The green silk wallpaper and thick green oriental carpets explained the name of the room, and a green onyx fireplace sat against the far wall.

Moving in a daze, recognizing some of the pieces from her studies and travels, she almost bumped into one of the couches and laughed. "Oh my."

This wasn't a room. It was a museum.

Lawrence's chest puffed with pride. Having grown up in wealth, she was accustomed to having servants, and her maid was also one of her best friends. Lawrence had the feel of a family servant about him, and she wouldn't have been surprised if he hadn't been with Bryan since his birth. Wouldn't be unusual among the British elite.

"Oh my indeed. This is but a portion of Lord Sutherfield's collection. He inherited many of these pieces from his grandparents but also bought quite a few of them. He has a great eye for beauty."

Taking her time, she examined a painting to her left. It depicted a woman brushing out her long, beautifully rendered red hair. Her back was to the viewer, and her hair pulled up over her head as she brushed, exposing the smooth line of her spine and plump buttocks. Her pose was very similar to the one Bryan had made her hold at Wicked while doing marvelously arousing things to her breasts.

"Degas?"

"Ah, it appears you know your art, Ms. Harmony."

"I used to travel a great deal. Something would capture my imagination, and I'd be on the next plane out, reading about the subject as I flew to whatever destination struck me."

She let out a long sigh, wishing she could sit on a plane long enough for overseas flights. Oh, she could take a private jet, but that was too expensive to hop around the world like she used to. Besides, she had no one to travel with her. She had plenty of friends, but she wanted something more. A lot more.

And Bryan was going to help her get it.

Speak of the devil, Bryan's sinful voice washed over her in a caress of warmth, making her whole body tingle. "Where was the first place you went?"

Lawrence stepped over to the side and bowed, giving Kira a small smile before he left and shut the door behind himself. She wanted to run up and cover Bryan in kisses, but a sudden onslaught of shyness struck her. Turning around, she pretended to look at a Cézanne instead of drooling over him in a pair of black slacks and white button-down shirt. Currently the top two buttons were undone, showing a nice, muscled chest. Her body gave a hard throb, and desire soaked her panties.

"The first place I went was Africa."

"Really? What part?"

"Kenya."

Once again the feeling of the electricity passing between them alerted her to his presence. He reached around her waist and drew her back against him. His heat enveloped her, and the scent of his crisp cologne stroked her senses. It was pathetic how easily she became putty in his hands. She tried to rally the will to resist him, but it was impossible.

"How old were you?"

"Eighteen."

She could feel his chuckle more than hear it. "Brave little thing, aren't you?"

Taking a deep breath, she turned in his arms and looked up into his beautiful dark eyes. She was about to find out just how brave she was. "Lord Bryan?"

His brows raised the tiniest bit at her use of his title, but she remembered he'd wanted her to back at Wicked. "Yes?"

"Would you please kiss me?" Heat flared through his gaze, and his pupils dilated. Before he could speak, she rushed to add, "How you want to kiss me. How you would kiss your submissive."

He stepped back a pace, and she followed, not wanting any distance between them. Holding up his hand, he nailed her to the spot with his gaze. "No, Kira. You have to earn my kiss."

A sweet rush of desire spun through her veins like sugar candy. While his look was completely serious, there was a slight challenge in his eyes, like he was daring her. Curiosity prickled her mind, and she lifted her chin. "What do I have to do, Lord Bryan, to earn your kiss?"

"Strip."

She glanced at the closed door. "Umm, what about Lawrence and whoever else is here?"

"The house has been cleared for the evening, the curtains drawn. No one will see you, enjoy your beauty, but me. You are mine, Kira, and I will allow no other to covet what is mine."

His primal declaration set her on fire even as she scowled at him. "Then you're mine as well."

"But of course."

Thrown off stride by his quick answer, she tried to regain her mental footing. "Well, good."

"Kira?"

"Yes?"

"That's yes, Lord Bryan."

Swallowing her pride, she nodded. "Yes, Lord Bryan?"

"Since you seem so hesitant to follow my orders and remove your clothes, I think you need a little motivation. Bend over the arm of the couch with your bum in the air. If that position is uncomfortable, we'll work around it."

"Wait, what?" She glanced at the couch, and heat flamed through her cheeks.

"What's your magic word?"

She let out a little sigh of relief at the reminder of her safe word. He said everything would stop the instant she said it, and she had to trust him to uphold his end of the bargain.

"Pookie, my lord."

"Good. Now do as I ordered or get out and don't bother me again. If you are serious about submitting to me, then you need to stop questioning my every command. Try to trust me, love, just a little bit. I promise you won't be sorry."

The tremble in her legs worsened, but she did as he asked. The sincerity in his voice eased her fear a little bit. The thick green velvet-covered arms of the couch were oversize and plush. She leaned over, afraid that in a moment she was going to fall, but the arm provided a comfortable place to rest against. Panic started to tighten her gut, a fear that he was going to shove himself into her. She tried to trust him, she really did, but she hardly knew Bryan.

Before her fear overwhelmed her courage, she used a technique she'd learned as a stuntwoman. Clearing her mind as much as she could, she picked one of her five senses and expanded it. Taking a deep, slow breath, she pulled the scent of the couch into her lungs. There was a faint whiff of something to the fabric, almost like pipe smoke, and she wondered if Bryan smoked a pipe.

How very Sherlock Holmes of him if he did.

A moment later, Bryan stroked his way up her legs, pausing to play with the top of her stockings, before pushing her dress up around her waist. His pleased, guttural murmur when he saw that she wasn't wearing panties beneath her garters made the lower half of her body flush with need. He continued to touch her, his hands more than big enough to grip her ass in a way that had her squirming.

"Five spanks for not doing what you were told."

"Wha— I mean, okay. Yes, Sir. Roger that."

He cleared his throat, and his voice held a touch of amusement. "The proper response is, 'Thank you, my lord.'"

God, he didn't really want her to say that, did he?

It was one thing to accept his spanking, a whole other thing to thank him for it. But if she didn't do what he said, he would kick her out. She knew he meant it just like she knew he was the right one to help awaken her sexually again. But fuck, actually submitting rankled on her nerves.

"Thank you, my lord."

He gave her butt a vicious pinch that stung like a bee sting. "Next time say it without the 'fuck you' tone of voice." He then pinched her other cheek, making her wiggle. "When I spank you, you will say, 'Thank you, my lord' with every spank. For every one you miss, I will hit you extra hard the next time. And trust me when I say I can make it hurt."

His voice dropped an octave on the last word, and her sex throbbed. Shit, who woulda known she would find being put in her place such an incredible turn-on? "Yes, my lord."

"You have my permission to moan but not scream. If you can't do it on your own, you may scream into the couch."

Internally she had to laugh. She'd survived just about the worse blunt force trauma wounds a human being could have and live. If he thought a little spanking was going to make her cry, he was delusional. Rather than risking him hearing the insolence in her voice, she nodded.

Without preamble, he laid the first smack on her ass. She knew she'd fucked up. It hurt, a lot. The next one came even harder, hard enough to shove her on the arm of the couch. "Ow! I mean, thank you, my lord."

The next spank was gentler, but it hit the crease of her right leg where it met her ass cheek, and stung like a mother. "Thank you, my lord."

The next two came in rapid succession. She choked back a cry when they hit the same place. "Thank you, my lord."

The warmth of his breath against her already heated skin was uncomfortable, but his goatee scratching against her stung. Then he licked over her bottom and began to gently probe between her rear cheeks with his wickedly long tongue. Hell, that man could give Gene Simmons a run for his money.

Suddenly thrown back into a state of sexual craving, she moaned and arched her hips, trying to give him better access. In response, he nipped her hip, and she stilled. He scraped his nails down her butt. She shuddered, a confusing blend of pain and pleasure overloading her mind. Her entire being focused inward, concentrating on his gentle strokes and probing at her anus.

Swimming in a pool of heat and desire, she was totally unprepared for the next slap. That made it hurt all the more, and she struggled to thank him. By the time he'd worked her up to the tenth spank, her voice was raw with unshed tears. "Thank you, my lord."

He massaged her ass, gripping it hard and digging his fingers in. It felt so fucking good and mingled with the burn. The edge of his pants pressed against her, and he reached between her legs, fondling her aching pussy. "Oh, sweetheart, you are so wet for me. Did you like being spanked?"

She moaned when he slid a finger between her labia and began to pet her clit. "I don't know."

"It is very simple question, love. Did being spanked bring you sexual arousal?"

She didn't know why he was bothering to ask her. The evidence of her arousal was coating his fingers, and her nub quivered beneath his knowing strokes. Sucking in a deep breath, she then let it out and whispered the truth. "Yes, it aroused me."

"Your honesty pleases me, Kira."

The warmth in his voice, the genuine pride in his words made her all glowy inside. Slowly, the heat from her spirit merged with the burning desire of her body, and she rocked herself against his fingers. He held fast, making each movement of her hips tug at her clit trapped between his fingers. With his other hand, he gathered some of her abundant honey and smoothed it between her ass cheeks.

Before she could muster enough brain cells to protest, he teased at the opening with his thumb, making her whole body tense. She'd never had anal sex before, at least not with a man. Somehow she didn't think having his dick in her ass would be the same as a small butt plug. The thought of taking him, of touching him, and tasting him had her worked up into a frenzy of need. She wanted to touch him in the worst way, to bring him pleasure.

"Please, my lord. Please let me touch you. I want to make you feel good."

"Earn it." He began to rub his thumb in tight circles around her clit and at the same time sink the thumb of his other hand into her bottom. "Come for me."

It only took a few more strokes from Bryan to pitch her into the fire of her release. She burned from the inside out, the contractions of her pussy reverberating through her ass and back again. Bliss slowly replaced the harsh pleasure. A sweet, floating release that gently surrounded her with happiness. She barely stirred when he pulled her dress back down and moved to the couch. Before he sat, he lifted her around the waist and pulled her down with him, arranging her so she cuddled against his strong, muscled body. The ecstasy began to recede, and a darkness slipped into to her soul, a sense of shame that she'd liked being dominated, had liked being hurt. What kind of sick woman would actually seek this out and enjoy it? What was wrong with her?

"Kira, give me your hand."

Blinking back tears, confused as to why she was suddenly so emotional, she did as he asked. Instead of shoving it down his pants, he placed her hand over his heart. It was an incredibly intimate gesture, and when she looked up at him, his concern made a few tears slip free. Distressed, she tried to wipe them away, then choked on a cry when he leaned down and kissed them from her cheeks.

"Hush, sweetheart. This is all so new to you. I'm here. You're not alone, and I will take care of you. I'm so proud of you, my good girl. You responded beautifully, and you endured for me in a way that almost had me coming in my pants."

She let out a watery chuckle, his words lifting her as much as the steady beat of his heart beneath her hand. "I was wondering if I even turned you on."

"Why in the hell would you say that?"

"Well, because, you know, it must not be too difficult for you if you haven't let me touch you." Suddenly shy, she closed her eyes and turned her head against his shoulder. "I promise I can make you feel good."

He let out a frustrated sigh. "Woman, you already make me feel good. The gift of your submission? It is a drug that makes me fly like no other."

She kept her hand on his heart, stroking the inch of his chest that she could reach from the opening of his shirt. "Will you ever want me to please you? I mean sexually, physically."

He grew quiet, pensive. "Why is my pleasure so important to you?"

"Because...well, because you made me feel good. Isn't that what you're supposed to do? Return the favor?" She looked up at him, capturing his dark gaze with her own, shaking at the strength and power reflected in his eyes. Next to him she felt so...small. Not something she usually felt at five-ten. "You amaze me, my lord, and I'm afraid I'm a lousy submissive."

He gave her a long, penetrating look that made her feel as if he could see into her soul. "If you want to please me, all you have to do is what I say. Simple as that. Now strip."

She hesitated only for a moment before pushing herself off his lap and standing before him. He looked so cool and controlled while she felt like a hot, sweaty, emotional mess. It didn't seem fair he should be perfect and unaffected. So she decided to see if she could change that, if he really did see her as desirable, as he'd said.

Leaning down, she slowly removed her modest heels and placed them next to the couch. Looking up through her lashes, she noticed he was completely focused on her, still and contained as only a predator could be while examining their prey for the best place to bite.

And holy shit, may God have mercy, did she love his bite.

With a little bit of wiggling, she managed to slowly roll her dress up, exposing her body to his perusal. Unease about her weight made her movements slow, and once she finally had her dress off, standing there in her garter and bra, she looked away, afraid of the disappointment she might see in his gaze.

He made no reassuring sounds. In fact as far as she could tell he hadn't moved an inch. With trembling fingers, she unhooked the back of her bra and shrugged it off, placing it on the pile with her clothes. When she went to reach for the clasp on her garter belt, his rough voice stopped her.

"Leave it on." The tightness of his tone made her look up, and she caught an almost savage hunger shining in his eyes before his features once again smoothed out. "Turn around and lift your hair off your neck. I want to see the color I put on your pretty arse."

She turned, feeling naughty, but in a good way. So good that she felt like giggling while she pulled her hair up, mimicking the woman in the Degas picture. Bryan's soft inhalation sent renewed warmth through her, awakening her body once again. Giving him a coquettish look over her shoulder, she asked, "Does my lord approve?"

It was getting easier and easier to refer to him as "my lord." First, because he actually was British elite, and second because there was an aura about him that commanded her respect. That didn't mean she was going to be curtsying to him anytime soon, but calling him by that title helped her to give some control to him. She guessed a part of her would always be the princess waiting for her handsome prince or, in this case, her handsome lord.

"Very much." He stood, an elegant uncoiling of muscle and grace. "Follow me."

He turned without so much as a backward glance, secure in the knowledge she would do as she was told. While his presumption irked her, in this case he was right. She followed at his heels like an eager puppy, wanting to see what he had in store.

Hopefully more orgasms for her and at least one for him. Seeing him come undone as she pleasured him was now one of her new life's goals.

They left the Green Room, and he took her through the house, passing various unlit rooms, and went down a staircase. Artwork hung on every available inch of the walls. She almost ran into his back a couple of times while admiring a painting or sculpture and not paying attention to where she was going. Just those brief touches had her pussy slicking her inner thighs with her arousal.

He stopped before a nondescript door and removed a key from his pocket before turning it in the lock. The bolt slid back with an easy *click*, and he opened the door, gesturing to her.

"Ladies first."

Apprehension mixed with anticipation, a combination that reminded her of the feeling she had before pulling off a particularly hard stunt. It made her feel so very alive. Bryan made her feel so very alive.

Scared shitless but alive.

She paused before him and placed her hand on his shoulder for balance before leaning up and kissing him on his smooth, shaved cheek next to the scratch of his goatee. "Thank you, my lord."

His dark eyes briefly warmed, but his expression remained stoic. "Get going before I paddle your bum."

She smiled at him, and the answering curve of his lips delighted her. "Yes, my lord."

There were stairs leading down into darkness. She hesitated on the threshold. "My lord, I'm not sure if it's safe for me to take the stairs in the dark."

"Trust me, Kira. Take the first step."

Feeling foolish for fearing a fall down the stairs like some old woman afraid of breaking her hip, but still scared nonetheless, she took a deep breath and placed her foot on the first step. The moment she did, a mellow, golden light illuminated the way down from recessed fixtures hidden in the ceiling. Not wanting him to think she was hesitating because she didn't want to see what he had in store for her, she made her way down the rest of the stairs, then paused and gaped.

Holy fucking shit. It was like a perverted sex-toy showroom.

The section of the basement they were in had to be the size of half the mansion. The sheer amount of gleaming chrome, black leather, chains, and wooden structures made it hard to actually see anything. It was like looking at a jar full of jelly beans, unable to focus on the individual colors.

Bryan stroked his hand down her back, smoothing her hair over her shoulder. “Welcome to my dungeon.”

CHAPTER FIVE

Drawing in a lungful of the almost edible caramel-based perfume she wore, Bryan found he was nervous about his next move. He chided himself that he never got anxious, that he didn't care if she took his temporary collar or not. It was merely a formality, something that would be a symbol of his commitment to her as her trainer.

Nothing more.

He nuzzled against her neck, enjoying the smooth silk of her hair against his lips. Bloody hell, she intoxicated him. Enveloping himself in her energy was an amazing experience, something he could easily become addicted to if he wasn't careful. "Before you can enter, there is a price."

She leaned back into him, crossing her arms over her chest. He didn't think she was cold—he kept the room at a comfortable seventy-seven degrees—more of a defensive posture. Not that he minded the position; it pressed her lush buttocks against his aching cock. He reached into his pocket, then pulled out the diamond-encrusted black leather collar. He ran his thumb over one of the spikes coming from the side and tried to untangle the diamond chains and pendant without her noticing his movements. He had a rather vivid and pleasurable mental image of attaching a leash to the glittering collar and taking his pet for a stroll through Wicked, letting all the other Doms see the beauty who belonged to him, however temporarily.

Originally he'd intended to give her the regular black leather collar he used for his submissives. It was pretty, with gold embellishments, and he had a jeweler he trusted craft it. When he'd gone into the jewelry store today and was taken back to the private viewing room, Bryan had found himself wandering over to where the more elaborate and extremely expensive collars shimmered on beds of black velvet.

He'd examined them all, the jeweler eager to talk about each piece. At first he tried to tell himself that he was browsing, simply admiring the art. Something to think about in the future when he settled down with a nice, well-mannered, and safe submissive. Certainly not for a woman he'd only met once but had thought about constantly since the moment their eyes first met. Kira had the most beautiful eyes, a lovely golden brown that seemed to reflect her joyful soul.

He gave up the farce when he'd told the jeweler her neck measurements from his hand around her throat. In the end he chose a black leather collar with four platinum spikes on each side. The center was fastened by a diamond circle holding the separate pieces together, and from either side of that diamond circle a platinum chain hung down, suspending an elaborate topaz pendant circled with pavé diamonds. When he'd first seen the collar, it had reminded him of a piece of jewelry one would find on a princess. He wanted Kira to have a beautiful collar that she would be proud of, something she'd wear and cherish. The thought of her feeling it around her neck for the first time, and being the first man to ever place a collar on her graceful throat, made him aroused to the point of his cock aching.

She shifted against him. "What's the price?"

"That you wear my collar; that is, my training collar."

"Okay."

He grinned, bemused by her uncharacteristic acceptance, and kissed the side of her neck. "Okay? You don't want to ask any questions first?"

She shook her head. "No. I trust you."

Thrown off stride yet pleased, he placed another kiss against her neck, then a bite. As his teeth sank into the skin where her shoulder and neck connected, he enjoyed the way she groaned and pressed harder against him. Damned if her skin didn't taste faintly like sugar.

He never knew he had such a sweet tooth.

Reluctantly pulling back from her offered flesh, he tried to gather his wits. As tempting as it was to just put the collar on, she had to understand the implications of the act, to know what it would really mean. This wasn't just a BDSM prop to him, but a promise to always take care of her and put her needs first.

"If you accept this collar, it means you are giving over control to me. You no longer call the shots. You don't have to worry about what to do or what to say. I will make you do and say exactly what I want, how I want, for however long I want. And before you open your insolent mouth, I'd like to remind you that I can paddle your bottom until you come and then you'll beg me to beat you some more."

Her body trembled against his, her breath quickening. "I believe you, my lord."

She was fucking beautiful when she allowed herself the pleasure of submitting.

"Lift your hair."

Her movements were clumsy, a little unsure, but soon her actions would flow with utter relaxation. She was nervous now, and he understood that. Trust was something that had to be earned, and he intended to never give her a reason to doubt him. And once they had the trust needed to really start to play rough, he'd be able to put her into something close to subspace by just bringing her down these stairs and putting on her collar.

There was a poetry to a submissive's body when she was getting near subspace. A languid, easy grace that captivated him. While he hadn't gotten Kira anywhere near deep subspace yet—they still had too much to work on—he had a feeling she would be poetry in motion.

Keeping his movements slow and controlled, he allowed her to savor every sensation that came from being collared. True, this wasn't a permanent relationship collar, as binding in its own way as a wedding ring, but even placing his training collar on her was an act of ownership that he cherished. For however small of an amount of time, she agreed to be his, and he would take the best care of her possible.

He forced his thoughts away and focused on her, on the drag of the diamonds over her skin, the cool kiss of the leather that would soon warm and become supple. No expense had been spared in the making of this collar, and he had to say it was money well spent. The contrast of pale skin, black leather, and the sparkle of diamonds made his breath catch.

When he began to fasten it, her arms moved, then jerked back in place. "My lord, may I look?"

"Not yet." Her spine stiffened, and he couldn't help tormenting her. "I may blindfold you every time you enter this room, never allowing you to see yourself or me."

"That would suck donkey dick." She made a high-pitched noise and then cleared her throat. "My lord."

Now he really did need to blindfold her, because holding back his laughter at the way her chest and neck flushed scarlet was extremely difficult. "Do you know what we do with sassy mouths around here?"

She looked over her shoulder at him, her beautiful sherry-brown eyes conveying a depth of emotion and need that called to his Dominant soul. Poor girl. Her desire was so easy to read. With her half-parted lips and dilated pupils, he would have known she was aroused. Not to mention the fact he could smell her wet cunt.

"No, my lord."

"I stuff things in it and make the submissive suck."

She arched her back slightly, offering herself to him. "Please let me suck your cock."

"No."

She grumbled. "Would it help if I told you I can suck a watermelon through a garden hose?"

He took a step back, putting his mouth into the crook of his arm to hide his laughter. Dammit, she was so unlike any woman he'd ever topped. Free-spirited and sweet, an addictive combination. He couldn't remember the last time he'd laughed this much, and he found that thought impossibly sad. Sobering, he stepped closer and played with the edge of her garters where they curved over her arse.

"You can let your hair down."

The brush of her silky strands against his face was something he savored. Part of rising into his top space involved a deepening of appreciation for physical sensations. Both for himself and for his submissive. Her pleasure was his pleasure, but her pain was also his pleasure. The trust she placed in him to not abuse her, yet give her enough pain with her arousal to begin to train her body to confuse the two, was staggering. He would do his utmost to make sure this scene was the best it could possibly be for both of them. And right now the strands of her hair falling across his face was heaven on earth.

Fuck, he needed to stop acting like a besotted plonker and do what he had to, to make her feel whole again. She wasn't here to be his plaything—well, she was—but she was relying on him to help her heal, and he was messing up with all this lovey-dovey bullshit. Kira didn't need to be courted. She needed to be fucked.

That meant it was time to be cruel in order to be kind.

Indulging himself, he grabbed a handful of her hair and proceeded to drag her across the room by it.

"Ow!" She started to reach up, then wisely kept her hands down and followed him as best she could in her hunched-over position.

He made his way to the corner that held shelves and cupboards of toys. Everything here was new, purchased specially for Kira. He didn't want anything touching her that someone else had used, no matter how sterilized it had been.

He released her hair, and she straightened, rubbing her scalp.

"Kira, you do remember your safe word, correct?"

"Yes, my lord."

"Very good. Place your elbows on the countertop and spread your legs."

That lovely blush suffused her body again, and she slowly, grudgingly did as he asked.

Irritated, he walked behind her and slapped her bum hard enough to sting. "I see you still have a problem remembering orders."

"I did— I mean, I'm sorry, my lord."

"Close your eyes."

He turned his back on her, sure she was looking, but removing the items he needed from a lower cupboard prevented her from seeing them. Because of her sass, her resistance to his will, she'd earned herself a larger toy than what he'd been going to start with. Still a small beginner size, but slightly larger than what he'd first intended to use.

It was going to hurt, and she was going to come hard and long.

He turned and noticed she had pulled her hair over her face, a psychological shield against him. That was fine; he didn't have to see her face to know what her body wanted. Moving slowly behind her, he put the toys into his pants pockets and began to remove his shirt.

Tossing it over to the side, he then stood behind her, in the position he'd be in if he wanted to fuck her like this. He adjusted himself, then pressed his cock, still contained behind his pants, between the generous cheeks of her arse. She stiffened, and he stroked his hands along her hips, over the edges of her garter, and across her buttocks. When he didn't move, she began to slowly calm, and by the time he leaned forward and placed his bare chest against her back, she was relaxed enough to moan in pleasure.

"Feel that, love? The way electricity sparks between our bare skin. It's a special chemistry we have together because right now you belong to me. Your body, your soul knows it and tries to draw me closer."

He began to kiss her back and rubbed his lips over her adorable freckles as he continued his way over her spine, paying special attention to every scar and bump he found on the way down. So many, of various ages and sizes. If it had just been the scars from her accident, he wouldn't have been worried, but this amount of damage was an indication of someone who took unnecessary risks with their body. An adrenaline-junkie submissive was a dangerous combination, especially with the element of sadomasochism thrown in. He'd have to watch how far he pushed her, because he had a feeling she'd let him accidentally hurt her before she gave up her adrenaline high.

When he reached the top of the crease of her buttocks, he placed a chaste kiss there and stood. Her disappointed moan was music to his ears, the sound of a woman needing to come.

But he wanted her to burn hotter before the gift of her release.

Grabbing the lube first, he then poured a generous amount into the cupped palm of his hand. He started at the top of her bottom and trickled it down his fingers over her skin, sensitizing her, making her pay attention. Getting her hyperactive mind to rest was hard work, but she was worth it.

He knelt behind her, running his hand over the crease, brushing his fingers between her bum cheeks while totally avoiding her pussy. And what a pretty cunt it was. The healing bruise of a bite mark shadowed one plump lip, and he couldn't help but lean over and kiss her labia, then gently lave it with his tongue. Kira arched against him, her needy whine playing havoc with his self-control. A touch of her sweet arousal hit his taste buds, and now it was his turn to groan as he pulled himself away.

He'd have his reward soon enough.

Picking up the small but sturdy stainless-steel anal plug from where he'd set it, he debated on whether to warm it up or not. He certainly wasn't going to stretch her first. No, he was going to push it into her body while playing with her pretty little clit and make her scream.

"Kira, lay your face on the counter and reach back with both hands to your arse. I want you to pull your cheeks apart for me and show me that pretty anus."

After a moment's hesitation, she did as he asked, her hands gripping her bottom so hard her fingers left red marks.

He'd intended to shove the anal plug in, to make her take it, but instead he found himself slowly swirling the tip against her puckered entrance, warming it and her up. Fuck, he couldn't be cruel to her like that. He tried to rationalize it was because a virgin arse was something to be savored, not rushed, but truth be told he didn't want to abuse Kira's trust.

He just wanted to hurt her until the lines between pain and pleasure blurred to the point where they became one and the same in her mind.

Reaching between her legs with his other hand, he then scooped up some of her arousal and spread it over the anal plug, mixing it with the lube as he eased it in her tight back passage inch by inch. She began to make little mewling sounds of distress, and her hips shifted to avoid the toy.

"Move your hair off your face." She did but kept her eyes closed. "Push back, sweetheart. If you push back, I'll reward you for your good behavior."

She nodded, and her face scrunched up. When her hips started to move toward him, he placed his hand between her legs and stroked the underside of her clit, rubbing at where the base of the sensitive nub went into her body. With a long, low groan, she pushed herself back on the toy, moving his fingers closer to her clit. Right when the biggest part of the anal plug stretched her, he paused, enjoying the sight of her distressed rosette trying to accommodate the plug.

He finally swirled his thumb around her clit with a gentle pressure and slammed the toy the rest of the way home. She yelped and went up on her tiptoes.

"You can let go of your cheeks now."

She did and moaned. "That stings."

"What hurts more? Your need to come or your arse? Concentrate on your body and ignore what your mind is telling you."

She drew in a deep, shuddering breath. "The need to come, my lord."

"Do you want me to make you come, Kira?"

"Please, my lord, so very much."

He patted her pussy, enjoying how his hand slid across her swollen flesh. "Good girl. Stand up and follow me."

Without looking back, he led her toward another section of the large room. If he turned her the right way, she would see the mirror on the opposite wall, but from this angle, all she would see was him and the prayer bench. The bench itself was an antique made of dark walnut covered in red and gold brocade from an estate in England. It was padded enough so she should be able to remain on her knees for a good amount of time, but he needed to keep an eye on her old injuries.

He reached around and traced his fingers against the outer curve of her breast. The softness of her skin felt like heaven beneath his fingers so he spent a few moments touching her, stroking her, and making her purr. He loved how cuddly she got, and placed a gentle kiss on her temple before taking a step back and firming his voice.

"Kira, kneel on the bench. If at any time your hips begin to lock up or it gets painful in a manner that might lead to injury, you *will* tell me right away. I cannot stress enough how important it is that you communicate your needs to me."

She moved past him and carefully knelt, then grimaced. "It doesn't hurt my back or hips, my lord, but it does shove that steel beam further into my butt."

He moved over to her and swept her hair back. "Sweetheart, that's a starter size. If you want a steel beam in your arse, I'd be only too happy to oblige." He lifted her breasts so they sat perched, displayed and plumped up, on the top portion of the kneeler.

She gave a soft laugh. "I keep wanting to put my hands in a praying position, but I'm afraid God will strike me dead."

Trailing his fingers over the tops of her breasts, he then walked around to the front of the bench and took his time enjoying the view. The mixture of apprehension, fear, and vulnerability in her face sent a hard surge of blood to his cock, and he let her see his passion. She slowly looked him over, her gaze tracing his skin like a burning ember, taking in his hard nipples, down to where the hair on his stomach disappeared into the waist of his pants. Her soft, pink lips parted, and she took an unsteady breath.

She licked her lips. "Um, may I speak, my lord?"

"Asking my permission? You must be scared."

A hot flush stained her cheeks. "I wanted to say that I like your body, my lord. Very much."

Anticipation tightened his gut. Such a darling girl. He couldn't wait to defile her.

"Open your mouth, love."

After an initial hesitation, her golden-brown eyes searching his face, she did as he asked. What a pretty picture she made. Hands clasped together, breasts presented for him, and that smart mouth open to receive him. He traced her lips with the tip of his finger, reawakening her nerves, moving her mind back to her body.

Placing one finger in her mouth, he grunted when she immediately began to suck on it. "Taste that? It's the sweetness of your pussy."

She groaned and sucked harder, sending blasts of lust through his body and making his already hard cock throb. With his other hand, he began to twist and pull on her nipples, forcing her to absorb the discomfort. Much to his delight, the harder he pulled, the harder she sucked, almost like his finger was a pacifier to soothe her.

No man on earth could resist the temptation of her eager mouth.

Withdrawing his finger from her moist heat, he then began to undo his pants with one hand while continuing to torment her breasts with the other. Her breathing sped up, and she focused on his crotch even as her face tightened at the pain. She was beautiful in her suffering. The flush of red to her cheeks, the way her mouth softened, then drew tight. But most of all he treasured the dreamy quality that began to enter her gaze.

When he had her fully under, deep in subspace, she would barely be aware of the world around her, including the pain of sex that might be mostly psychological. He mentally flipped through all the devices, the painful pleasures he could offer her in this room. Even if he spent every waking moment of the rest of his life down here with her, he would never get enough of her submission.

He'd promised his good girl an orgasm, but he'd bet his family estate back in England that she'd never come like he was going to make her come.

"Open my pants and take my cock out."

She smiled at him like someone had given her a pony for her birthday. Her joy affected him on an emotional level. Could he be falling for this woman whom he hardly knew? The very idea was so unlike him, so outside of the realm of how he lived his life that he dismissed it right away.

He controlled everything, including his heart.

"Yes, my lord. With pleasure."

That bit of sass only made it all that much sweeter when she reached inside his pants with an almost greedy expression. He'd bet right now the pain in her bum, the discomfort from her nipples, everything had faded beneath her need for him. The thought of being able to take her beyond herself was a heady thing, a power he craved. When she was with him, she would have nothing to fear because he would make every bit of misery into joy through the strength of his will.

Her eyes widened when she found he wore no underwear. The moment her smooth fingers wrapped around his shaft, it was his turn to growl and flex his hips. Working her up to the point of madness was a double-edged sword because he ended up just as needy, as fucking savage as she did. Except while she could revel in the feelings, he had to keep a tight leash on his own emotions and body in order to prolong and intensify the experience for her.

"Bryan, I mean, my lord, I didn't know you were pierced." She ran her thumb over the thick hoop going through his urethra and the head of his cock. An intense tingle flooded his pelvis, and he swallowed hard. With a gentle touch, she pulled his dick out and made a happy, almost purring sound. "Uncircumcised as well. I've never been with a man like you."

Leaning over, he gathered a handful of her hair and held her still. "Open your mouth."

She blinked, her eyes burning from within like amber lit by flames. She opened wide for him, and he almost came all over her face right then. Such a tempting sight, lush and feminine yet with an inner strength he loved to tame.

With slow movements, he began to sink his cock into her eager mouth. All too soon he hit the back of throat, and she gagged.

"Do you know how to deep throat?"

She shook her head, then sucked him hard enough to make his toes curl.

Using her hair as an anchor, he began to slide her mouth up and down his shaft, pausing at the tip to let her play with the hoop. She reached up to touch him, and he shoved her mouth down on him until she gagged again. "Play with your nipples for me, girl. Hard, like I would."

Her moan vibrated against his flesh, running through the piercing and making it hum like a tuning fork. She began to wiggle against the bench, her cries increasing in strength and intensity as her busy fingers stretched and pulled her now red peaks. It pleased him to see she was taking his directions seriously, pulling hard on those tips and making herself hurt for him. His body tightened, and he fought the need to come. Despite her not being able to deep throat him—his favorite way to fuck a submissive's mouth—her talented tongue drove him to distraction.

No wonder the ladies liked her so much.

The mental image of his Kira licking another submissive to orgasm had him pulling out so the tip of his cock stretched her mouth. She was going to make him come, he was too close to the edge, but he'd be damned if she didn't go over first. Reaching into his pocket with his free hand, keeping his other buried in that amazing hair of hers, he found the slim remote to the anal plug and turned it on.

Immediately she yelped and tried to pull back, but he kept his hand fisted in her hair and pulled her closer until the ring on his dick pressed against the back of her throat. "Feel that? The lovely little plug stretching your bottom can do a variety of things. Including giving you a mild electrical shock."

Her hands fluttered toward his hips, but he smacked them back down. "If I see you remove your hands from your tits before you come, I will shackle you to the wall and jerk off in front of you, leaving you with nothing but need and no relief."

Shaking her head, she took in a deep breath through her nostrils and resumed her torment. With a smile, he turned on the vibrator inside the anal plug. Her low, deep groan was music to his ears. Because of her position on the kneeler, the vibrations would easily travel down to her aroused clit, resounding through the plump, delicious lips of her labia. Fuck, he wanted to sixty-nine with her, to spread her pussy over his mouth and drink her down.

As he rocked his hips, he gave himself over to the sensations of her eager sucking, her little whimpers and moans as he played with the vibrations going through her bottom. Easing his grip on her hair, he let her set a rhythm while he told her how beautiful she was, how precious to him. And by God, she was precious to him. Never had he been with a woman who took such joy from pleasing him. Oh, he'd been with submissives who were so well trained that it was a pleasure to be with them, but with Kira, he wasn't just another Dom to help her get into subspace. His feelings, his pleasure was important to her, and despite the discomfort he put her through, she was only too eager to bring him to completion.

The edge of her teeth gently scored him, and he swore. The way her sucking became disjointed, yet more intense along with her now thrusting hips, let him know she was close to her own orgasm.

"Give over, love. Come for me, and I'll pour myself into your mouth. And you will drink down every fucking drop like a good girl should."

Her mouth went slack around him, and she trembled, her eyes closed and her hands gripping the edge of the bench. He briefly considered pulling out just in case she bit him while she came, but there was no way he could resist the lure of her mouth. Hopefully she'd continue to be outspoken and sassy in the future so he could shove his cock down her throat on a regular basis.

Her moans increased, and he reached down, rolling the hard tip of her nipple between his fingers before using his nails and pinching down. That seemed to be the edge she needed because her muffled wail filled the room even as she sucked frantically at him.

Oh fucking bloody hell.

With a roar of his own, he shuttled his cock in and out of her mouth, reveling in the scent of her pussy, the grip of her hands on his hips, her pants and whimpers. The burn exploded from the base of his spine, traveling up through his balls before shooting out of the head of his cock, pouring cum into the hot, wet cave of her mouth. She stilled and swallowed, taking every drop like she'd been told.

After the last spurt had been sucked, he reluctantly pulled away from her. She stared up at him, dazed and with a very satisfied smile curving her lips. "Good job, Kira. You've pleased me very much."

She licked her lips. "Thank you, my lord."

Tucking himself back into his pants, he nodded to her. “You can stand up now, and we’ll get that anal plug out of you.”

He immediately noticed how slowly she moved, how her face tensed in anticipation of pain. “Love, I promise I’ll be so gentle you won’t feel anything but pleasure. It won’t hurt as much coming out as going in.”

She gave him a strained smile and stood, then cried out and slumped against the kneeler.

“Kira?” He moved quickly to her side and pulled her up, supporting her body with his. “Are you all right?”

CHAPTER SIX

Kira wanted to scream in frustration. This evening had been so good, so perfect, and her fucked-up body had to ruin it. She knew she'd pushed herself too far, should have let him know the bench was hurting her hips, but she didn't want to stop. He'd been close to coming and so had she. Plus, she'd wanted to please him so badly, to show him that his time with her wasn't one-sided, that she could give him back some of the amazing sensations he gave her. Plus the fucking awesome adrenaline surge that came with the orgasm had dulled the pain to the point where she really hadn't noticed it.

Trying to keep her voice smooth, she pushed at him. "I'm okay."

With a low snarl, he said, "Put your hands on the kneeler."

She complied, wincing as her lower back seized up. A moment later, he pulled the anal plug from her bottom and she shuddered, confusing sensations of pleasure and pain mixing with the fading rush of endorphins. His warmth briefly left her back, but he quickly returned.

"You promised me you would use your safe word to keep me from damaging you."

"I'm fine." She tried to rise on her own, and her back seized again in a way that pulled an unwilling groan from her. "Just give me a second, and I'll be right as rain."

Cursing, he helped her stand and kept an arm around her waist. "Kira, stop lying to me. I hate it, and I'm already more than a little fucking pissed right now, so I suggest you stop trying to bullshit me and tell me the fucking truth."

She took a deep breath and let it out, hating to have to admit to a weakness. "I'm a little sore."

"Where?"

"My lower back."

They slowly walked across the room, Bryan letting her set the pace. Thankfully she didn't have those horrible cramps that kept her doubled over in agony, only the feeling of a shard of glass stuck in her tailbone. Probably pinched a nerve or something like that.

"Really, it's no big deal."

By now they'd reached the stairs. He was quiet, a tense storm waiting to break. When she glanced up at his face, the rage and the disappointment she saw tore at her soul. But what hurt the most was the hint of guilt she saw in his gaze.

"Kira, hold on to the wall. Because of your lies, your blatant disrespect to my wishes, you've lost the right to wear my collar."

She did as he asked, suddenly meek and afraid. When he unbuckled the collar, she had a very real fear he was going to kick her out, that things were over between them. After all, she had broken her promise to him to tell the truth.

Fuck, what was wrong with her?

All she knew was that when she was on her knees before him, reveling in the sensations he was giving her, she felt more alive than she had in a long time. It almost reminded her of the sensation of riding a big wave on her old surfboard, a pure rush of intense emotion combined with physical sensation. But unlike surfing, where she had to keep her mind focused, with Bryan she'd been able to let go and just exist.

No one had ever been able to make her feel that way before.

"Please, Master. Please don't give up on me. I'm so sorry. I wanted to make you come. Please don't make me leave."

"Don't you understand? I can't keep you safe, can't trust you if you won't be honest with me about your body. What if I'd really messed something up, Kira? What if I'd reinjured you? Don't you know that would kill me?" He met her gaze, and her heart lurched at the absolute seriousness in his gaze. "For a sadist to scene with a submissive who won't use her safe word is a travesty waiting to happen."

He jerked the collar off, giving her only a glimpse of black leather and sparkle before he shoved it in his pocket. Even in his anger, he was a magnificent specimen of male flesh, all cut muscles, defined abs, and those hard nipples that drove her crazy with need. How could she let herself fuck up something so potentially good? He leaned back against the wall and stared at her, his dark eyes blazing with emotions that stripped her raw, whipped her soul until she bled.

With a grunt of effort, she began to lower herself to her knees, desperate to earn his forgiveness. "Please don't leave me, Bryan. This is all so new to me. I didn't know that it would be this bad. I thought I could handle it, and I didn't mean to lie to you, honestly. Please don't go. I'm sorry I disappointed you—"

Before she'd made it two inches, he was at her side, lifting her back up. "How badly do you hurt? You better be fucking honest with me, love."

"I"—she swallowed hard—"I think I might have pinched a nerve in my lower back."

He closed his eyes and pressed his forehead to hers. "Do you need to go to the hospital?"

"No." He lifted his head and gave her a skeptical look, his jaw and body tight with tension. "No, really. I'm okay. I'll go to my massage therapist tomorrow, and she'll fix me up. This isn't the first time this has happened."

He took in a sharp breath, his nostrils flaring. "What is the most comfortable way for me to carry you?"

"I don't need to be carried."

"Really? Then take those stairs on your own."

She glanced at the stairs, knowing he'd see in an instant the pain they would cause her. "Umm, give me a minute."

Gritting his teeth, he placed his hand around her neck, reminding her of his collar and making her sad all over again that she'd lost the right to wear it. "If you ever want to earn my trust, you must stop lying and telling me half-truths. Would you like it if I lied to you about being in pain?"

Chagrined, she shook her head. "No, I'd hate it."

"Exactly. Now, tell me the best way to help you up those stairs."

She looked at the dozen steps leading up to the main house. "If you let me hold on to the railing on one side and your shoulder on the other, that should do it. I'm not sure if carrying me would make my back better or worse because of how my spine would move."

His jaw tight, he nodded and slung her arm over his shoulder. Slowly, surely, they took each step. The whole way he was beyond solicitous, coaching her when she faltered, praising her when she took a step. His words flowed over her, wrapping her in warmth even though she was still naked except for her garters and stockings. By the time they made it to the top, her body was covered in a fine sheen of sweat and her lower back ached.

"Thank you, my lord."

"Kira, I'm so fucking pissed at you right now." He brushed back a strand of hair off her cheek, his gentle touch at odd with his words. "I would highly suggest that for the next few hours you do everything I say."

"But I thought you wanted me to leave?" Her voice trembled on the last word, and she tried to push away, to keep him from seeing the tears. Now that the endorphins were fading, she felt vulnerable, cold, and very alone. Her back ached, her bottom hurt, and her soul was an icy ball in her chest.

"Just because I'm angry doesn't mean I want you to leave." He cupped her chin, the gentle touch undoing her. Tears flowed down her cheeks, and he brushed one away with his thumb. "That doesn't mean I will tolerate such lies from my submissive, but I will work with you on being honest. We're still very new to each other."

"I'm so sorry. I didn't mean to make you angry." She shuddered when he gathered her into his arms, warming the ice in her veins.

"I know, love, I know." He sighed and rubbed her back. "Can you walk?"

"Yes, but slowly."

He led her through the quiet mansion, and she wondered what time it was. Reality had a way of slipping by when she was with him. It was kind of disturbing how lost she became in Bryan, how his charisma, his pull became the center of her universe. She hadn't felt that way since...well, never. Bryan made all the previous relationships she'd had feel like practice for the main event. She tried to steel her heart against him, to tell herself that his concern and caring were merely that of a Master to his submissive. For all she knew, she'd feel like this with any Master.

Not just Bryan.

He stopped before they reached the main foyer and opened the door to a small, elegantly appointed sitting room. A white marble fireplace dominated the far side of the room, and a pretty lounge area with comfortable cream and gold furniture used up the majority of the space in the center. The air held the faint scent of lilacs, and she spied a giant vase full of the flowers on an elegant table near the window.

"Would sitting or lying down be more comfortable?"

"Really. You don't have to make all this fuss over me."

He gave her an exasperated look. "Answer the question."

"Couch, please."

After making sure she was comfortable, arranging pillows around her, and bringing her a blanket, he stood over her with a foreboding expression darkening his face. "Stay here. If you move one inch, I'll let every Master at Wicked take a turn paddling your arse."

She swallowed hard, not liking the idea of any Dom but Bryan touching her. She trusted him to not hurt her beyond what she could endure, but the thought of strangers hitting her made her ill. "Yes, my lord."

He nodded and tucked the blanket more securely around her. Picking up a remote from the table situated between the couch and chairs, he pressed a button, and the gas fireplace across from her flickered to life. He gave her one last warning look and left.

As she curled into the soft cushions, she stared at the flames and tried to get her rambling thoughts under control. She felt so used up, like she'd run twenty miles, then done a thousand jumping jacks. The nerves in her spine twitched, and she tried to shift to a more comfortable position. It was funny how the pain Bryan gave her could feel good, while the pain of her injuries just fucking hurt.

She was so tired of hurting.

Well then, why did she keep doing stupid shit? Things she knew pushed the limits of her endurance and health, but challenges she couldn't say no to. Her teachers at the stuntman school had warned her time and time again about taking too-big risks, about pushing her body too hard. She'd laughed it off, feeling young and invincible. Besides, her fearlessness had gotten her coveted acting roles her fellow stuntwomen would have killed for. If she'd been careful, she would be just another chick wearing a wig and taking the fall for someone else. But was that feeling of invincibility she chased after her drug of choice? Was she blind to what her relentless pursuit of the next dangerous high had done to her life?

Was that what she was doing here with Bryan? Chasing another adrenaline high? Trying to compartmentalize her feelings and emotions, she examined her actions during her time with him. Sure, when she'd first stumbled across the idea of retraining her body to handle pain, it had seemed like going to an experienced sadist had been the best idea. Like going to any professional when she needed help. But she hadn't known what it would be like to do a scene with a Dom. No, not just a Dom, with Bryan.

A man she knew nothing about.

His touch was painful magic, a pleasure so deep and soul altering that she felt like his stamp would be on her forever. After two times together, without sex, she already felt as if she was under his thrall. His disappointment in her had cut to the bone, almost as deep as her ex-boyfriend leaving after she'd tried so hard to give him what he wanted. A knot twisted in her stomach as she wondered how long Bryan would hold out before he wanted to have true sex with her. Her vagina clenched at the thought, not with desire but with fear. The cramps she got from penetration were terrible, the closest thing to labor pains a woman could have without actually having a baby. She couldn't imagine how Bryan could possibly help her overcome them.

Shifting so she could see the door when it opened, she tried to calm herself, but the little spider of panic was beginning to spin a web in her mind. Bryan's dungeon had been so big, so vast, there was no way she was the first woman to be there. And he was sinfully hot. When he got tired of her inability to put out, she had no doubt there would be throngs of submissives waiting to do what she couldn't. Beautiful, skinny women who could fulfill his every need. Not fat redheads with more issues than Carter has pills. A mental image of Bryan fucking some nameless female in his dungeon made her heart clench.

Disquieted by the thought of Bryan, a man she barely knew, having that much control over her emotionally, she debated sneaking out of his house before he got back. That way she could nip this stupid emotional bond in the bud and find some Dom who wouldn't tempt her to want things she couldn't have. Some Master who would teach her how to manage her body and then they would both be on their separate ways. Then she could find some normal, safe guy and get married and have 2.5 kids while living in the suburbs. Not a dark, dangerous, and utterly captivating lord she could easily become lost in.

Groaning softly, she sat up and looked down at the comforter enveloping her. Well, she really couldn't drive like this, but maybe she could step out and call a cab or something. Yeah, she'd go back to the trophy room, get her stuff, and make it out before Bryan was any the wiser. She wasn't sure how much time she had left before he got back, or that matter for how long he'd been gone.

Where had he gone? Maybe he was so disgusted with her that he would return with a couple of aspirin and send her on her way. Shit, she'd rather have that than the lecture she had a feeling was coming. Then again, would he lecture her if he didn't care? No, that was grasping at straws. He'd lecture her because he probably got off on it, not because he was really worried. Or if he was worried, it was the concern someone would have for one of their pets when they got hurt. Not the worry of a man caring about his woman.

No, she didn't have to sit here and listen to him yell at her like she was some child. He could kiss her big ass. She was a grown woman, and no man would make her feel like anything less.

After pulling the comforter around her, she slowly made her way to her feet. Little shards of broken glass had taken up residence in her hips, and she tried to tell herself she was fine and nothing would happen if she took a risk with her body for the sake of her pride.

For a grown woman, you sometimes sure act like a child, her mind whispered.

Ignoring her conscience, she started to walk toward the door, but before she'd taken two steps, it opened. While he was gone, Bryan had taken the time to put on a new button-down shirt, much to her disappointment. As he entered, a tall woman with blonde hair dressed in black slacks and a white classic silk shirt followed him. She had a giant black zippered case over her arm and an intense energy about her that went well with her bright blue eyes. Both the woman and Bryan gave Kira a quick head-to-toe inspection, and their mouths tightened in an almost identical line of disapproval.

Bryan closed the door quietly after himself. "Going somewhere? I believe I told you to stay put, Kira."

Busted, she flushed and shook her head. "I was wondering where you went." Trying to salvage her dignity, she tightened the comforter around her and lifted her chin. "May I ask who this is with you?"

The woman set the giant case down next to the chair near the door, then came forward with her hand extended. "My name is Jennifer Barnette. It's nice to meet you, Kira."

Extending her hand as much as she could while still maintaining her grip on the blanket, Kira shook the other woman's hand. "Umm, nice to meet you as well."

Jennifer smiled. "I'm a physical therapist who specializes in therapeutic sports massage and a friend of Bryan's. He called and asked me to come look at your back and see if I could bring you some relief."

Kira wasn't sure if she should be pissed with him for assuming she'd be okay with some stranger working on her, or happy that he cared. She looked over Jennifer's shoulder at Bryan and let out a low breath. "Thank you."

He raised one eyebrow in a devilish way that managed to look arrogant and hot. "Thank you what?"

Feeling very uncomfortable, she glanced at Jennifer, then back at him. There was no way in hell she was calling him by anything other than his given name in front of a stranger. "Thank you, *Bryan*." The emphasis she put on his name was kind of snotty, but instead of looking pissed, he grinned and winked.

That, man confused the shit out of her.

Jennifer laughed. "Before you earn yourself an ass beating, I'm also a Mistress at Wicked, so don't worry about following your Master's protocol in front of me."

Sure she was going to die of embarrassment, she looked at the floor and muttered, "Thank you, my lord."

He snorted. "You could at least pretend to be intimidated."

"You could at least pretend to be humble."

Jennifer laughed and moved across the room to her case, which Kira now recognized as a portable massage table. "Bryan, can you clear me a space please? Then we'll get her fixed up enough so that you can take care of her sass."

While Bryan moved the table and chairs around, Jennifer unfolded her table and put on a small waist apron with bottles of oil in the pockets. Kira stayed out of their way, more confused than ever. If Bryan had gone all lord and Master on her, she would have been able to shore up her emotional defenses. This nice, almost playful man was a side she hadn't seen from him before.

"Bryan, help your girl up on the table. I'd like her on her stomach first."

Clearing her throat, Kira tried to hide her flush as she said, "I'm nude."

Jennifer smiled. “Darling, beneath our clothes we’re all nude. Now up on the table with you. No more dillydallying.”

With some effort, maneuvering, and lots of blushing, she made it up onto the table. Her back seized, and Jennifer instantly placed her hands on Kira’s lower spine. “Easy. Just relax.”

Bryan pulled up a chair so he sat at the head of the table. With a gentle touch, he gathered her hair and swept it over to the side. They began to touch her together, Jennifer soothing her muscles while Bryan ran his fingers through her hair. The scent of apples filled the air, mixed with cinnamon as Jennifer began to rub oil into Kira’s tailbone area. Ever so slowly, the tense muscles around her spine softened, and she let out a grateful sigh. “You know, it’s easy to forget how good feeling normal is.”

Jennifer traced a fingertip down a scar going over Kira’s hip. “I don’t think I’ve ever seen a woman so beat up.”

Before Kira could answer, Bryan spoke. “Kira used to be an actress and one of the best stuntwomen in the world.”

“Wait… Is she Kira Harmony?” When Kira moved to look at Jennifer, the other woman gave her ass a brisk slap. “Stay still. Let your Master answer for you. The only thing you’re responsible for is laying here and enjoying.”

Grinning, Kira did as she was told. If there was any doubt in her mind that Jennifer was a Mistress, that imperious command erased it. Besides, Jennifer had moved on to her legs now and was doing something heavenly to her thigh muscles.

Bryan continued to stroke Kira’s hair, the touch soothing and slightly arousing. She couldn’t help but associate his touch with pleasures of a more carnal nature. “Yes. She got injured on set in a stunt gone wrong. A motorcycle accident.”

Kira tensed at the mention of the accident, memories gaining strength. The pain had been so intense, so all-consuming that she’d thought she would go mad as the emergency response crew worked to stabilize her. Before her accident, she’d never understood how someone could hurt so much that they couldn’t even form words, but now she knew all too well how an injury could be so agonizing that all she could do was moan and beg God to make the excruciating agony go away.

Bryan leaned down and whispered in her ear. "Love, if you don't snap out of that bad memory, I'm going to ask Jennifer to give you an internal massage that will have you squirting all over the room."

Kira coughed at the graphic image. "You need therapy."

He laughed and kissed her cheek.

Jennifer began to work her fingertips around the back of Kira's knee. "That must be what all this scarring is from. I'm guessing she broke her pelvis, maybe her tailbone as well, along with a couple ribs." Briefly Jennifer stroked Kira's left shoulder, tracing over the surgical scars. "This injury looks to be around the same time."

It was actually rather nice to not have to go through what had happened that terrible day for the billionth time. She would have thought the memories would fade by now, but they remained bright and painful. She could almost feel the agony she'd endured on the ambulance ride to the hospital, her body shattered but her mind still all too aware.

"Shh," Bryan whispered into her ear, his beard brushing her sensitive skin. "I told you, no bad thoughts. One more time and you're going to get an anal massage as well. Did I mention Mistress Jennifer's specialty is fisting? She knows how to make a woman's muscles relax enough to take her whole hand. I've seen her fuck her submissive, Shy, with her fist. Trust me when I say you are not ready for that."

Kira froze, her ass and pussy tightening until her back twinged.

Jennifer made a tsking sound. "Stop scaring the poor girl. Kira, I assure you, your ass is safe with me. Idiot men."

"Sometimes I really wish you were a submissive so I could beat you."

"Ditto."

Bryan and Jennifer laughed, and the tension eased, allowing Kira to slowly drift back down again. Bryan resumed stroking her hair. She felt so utterly pampered, spoiled even. It had been so long since anyone had shown her so much affection. She was starved for it.

Jennifer switched topics to Wicked, and the two Doms began to talk about mutual friends, who was dating whom, what parties were coming up, and other mundane things that became extraordinary because of the subject. After following their conversation for a bit, Kira began to drift, lulled into relaxation by Bryan's scent, his touch, his presence. On a primal level, she felt extremely safe around him, despite the fact he'd put her through some pretty harsh shit downstairs.

Harsh and wonderful. Oh my fucking God, had it been good. The memory sent a warm wave of lust through her, and if she wasn't so relaxed, she would have tried to kiss Bryan, to let him know how much she appreciated his care. And that he'd decided to give her a second chance.

"Kira, darling, let Bryan help you turn over."

She muttered a sleepy protest but did as they asked, vaguely uneasy about the other woman seeing her breasts and pussy but feeling too good to really give a shit.

"Mmm, I can see why you're so besotted with her, Bryan. She is lovely. My Shy would adore her."

Bryan laughed, a deep sound that rubbed over Kira's skin like fur. "Isn't she? Such creamy skin and a lush body." He threaded his fingers through Kira's hair, gently tugging it from beneath her head. "And so responsive."

Jennifer traced a spot on the side of Kira's breast, the touch sensual but not intrusive. "Nice marks."

"Thank you."

After that their conversation turned toward politics, then on to mutual friends. Jennifer massaged every inch of Kira's body, from her forehead all the way down to her toes. By the time the other woman was done, Kira was a big, boneless mass of purring pleasure. Doing anything, even blinking, was beyond her at the moment. She drifted in a dreamy state of relaxation, enhanced by Bryan's constant soothing touch.

Jennifer saying her name got her attention, and she tuned back in to their conversation.

As the other woman gave Kira a foot rub to die for, Jennifer asked, "Do you think she'd want to play with Shy? I must confess, I would love to work them over together with you."

"I don't know. Kira is bisexual, but I don't think she's ever done anything with more than one person at a time. Plus, she is very, very new to the scene. I don't want to push her too fast."

"Lord Bryan going easy on his submissive? I thought I'd never see the day."

He chuckled. "Trust me. I'm going easier on her than she does on herself."

"Mmm." Jennifer found a tense muscle in the arch of Kira's foot and began to work on it. "I can believe that, especially for the new subs who are eager to please. They try to go above and beyond what you're asking of them, not realizing the best way to please is to do as they are told."

"Exactly. Case in point, the girl that you're currently working on who crippled herself giving me a blowjob. I owe you for coming out here this late at night."

Jennifer laughed, a low and husky sound. "No worries. You know it's only a fifteen-minute drive for me. Besides, Shy is visiting her parents in Maine, and I could use the company. But, if your girl is interested, I would love to do a scene with you and both of them at Wicked when Shy gets back. Just think, the two of them strapped next to each other while you work them over with fire and me with ice."

Bryan's fingers briefly tightened before resuming their caress of her throat. When he spoke, his voice had a delicious rough edge to it. "I'll speak with her when she's awake. I don't know if she's ever been with more than one person at a time, let alone you and Shy."

That did make Kira open her eyes, and she cleared her throat. Her voice still came out whisper soft as she said, "I'm interested if my Master is interested. I've actually been with two other women at once."

Bryan stood and moved over next to her, looking down with a bemused expression but a rather lustful gleam in his eye. "Really?"

Enjoying his surprise, she gave him a lazy smile. "Mmm-hmm."

Jennifer laughed and gave Kira's nipple a pinch that made her hips twitch. "It's always the quiet ones that shock you. I think she's just about done. Kira, do you still hurt?"

Unable to stop the giggle bubbling through her, Kira shook her head. "No. You are magic. Thank you so much."

"You are most welcome." She patted Kira's stomach with a gentle touch. "Bryan, can you have Lawrence return my table to me tomorrow? I want her to rest for a few more minutes. Make sure she drinks lots and lots of water to flush out all the toxins the massage released into her system. And some Tylenol or something before bed should help her sleep through the night and wake up good as new tomorrow."

"Thanks again for coming out and taking care of my girl, Jennifer."

"Anytime. I'll let myself out."

Letting her eyes close, Kira abandoned herself to the happy warm-and-fuzzy feeling drifting through her limbs. She couldn't remember the last time she'd felt so well cared for. While being independent by nature was great for helping her achieve her goals in life, it was nice to be the one being taken care of for once. Usually she was the one making sure everyone else was okay, thinking of herself last.

Bryan briefly left the table and came back with the comforter. He bundled it around Kira and gently lifted her into his arms. She wanted to protest that that she was too heavy, but oh God, it felt good to be held by him. Moving to the couch, he put her down and stroked her cheek.

"Think you can stand up for a second?"

When none of her muscles or nerves protested her movements, she stood and sighed. "That was awesome."

He pulled a thick black robe off the arm of the chair and helped her slide into it. The soft, plush fabric chased away any chill, and she inhaled the scent of his cologne that wafted from it.

"In the future, if you need to take a second to talk about something during a scene, all you have to do is say the word yellow. It's not your safe word, so I'll know you don't want to stop playing altogether, but I will know that you need to talk about something that may be hurting you or something you may have an issue with. Hopefully we can avoid a repeat of the way tonight ended."

She looked at him through her lashes. "I rather like the way tonight ended."

Shaking his head, he cupped her cheek and stroked her face with his thumb. "I'm serious. Seeing you hurting like that, knowing I was the cause and could have possibly reinjured you..."

The sadness in his voice sent a pang of guilt through her. "I'm sorry, Bryan, I really am. I promise I'll use yellow in the future." She leaned up and gave him a gentle kiss on the lips. "Thank you for tonight. It, and you, were amazing."

He gave her a brilliant smile that chased the lingering sadness and concern from his gaze. "Come on, love, it's late. Let's get you home."

Stretching her arms above her head, she let him belt the robe around her. "Let me get my stuff and I'll be off."

He shook his head and pulled her toward him, tucking her neatly against his body in a hug. "I've already had my driver bring the car around. I don't want you driving this late, especially not after a night like tonight. You seem a little sub drunk to me."

"I can drive myself home, Bryan. I'm not an invalid. And what about my car?"

"I'll have your car brought by in the morning. Look, I know you're a perfectly capable modern woman who can leap tall buildings in a single bound, but indulge me in this. The thought of you driving home alone right now would give me gray hairs."

"You sound like my father. Every gray hair he had he blamed on me."

The vibration of his laughter ran through her body like a tuning fork, bringing a pleasant rush of heat to her sex. "That I can believe. Now, let's get you home."

CHAPTER SEVEN

Just as Kira took her first sip of coffee, the doorbell to her town house rang. Her brain kicked into gear and reminded her she'd promised her sister they would go shopping for their parents' anniversary gift today. Cursing, she looked down at Bryan's robe and tugged it closed, hoping her sister wouldn't notice how the oversize robe dragged across her feet. When Kira woke up this morning, she'd been unable to resist the temptation of wearing Bryan's clothing and smelling his scent on it.

Bright, late-morning sunlight streamed through the windows of the first level of her home in Georgetown, illuminating the mishmash of art and furniture she'd collected in her travels before her accident. She loved her home, and even though she didn't really need four bedrooms and three baths, when she'd purchased this place seven years ago, it had been with the dream in mind that someday she'd return home to DC to start a family after she left Hollywood.

Unfortunately sometimes dreams had a way of not coming true.

Shaking off her melancholy, she tapped the security code into the pad next to the red painted door and opened it, revealing her older sister. Impeccably dressed as always, Mary Kate was four years older than Kira but acted like she was her mother. With her red hair upswept into a fashionable coif and her mint-green pantsuit flattering her lean figure, Mary Kate sighed and shook her head.

"You forgot, didn't you?"

Sticking her tongue out, Kira stepped aside. "Come on in."

The two women made their way back into the pale silver kitchen with its modern decor, and Mary Kate put her purse on the slate countertop. "So what were you doing last night that had you sleeping until almost noon?"

Using the coffeepot as an excuse to turn her back and hide her furious blush, Kira reached into the cupboard and pulled down a blue ceramic glazed cup for her sister. "I was out…with a guy."

"Really? Like on a date?"

While Kira didn't know if she and Bryan were actually dating, she nodded. "Yep."

After both women had settled at the kitchen island and sipped from their respective cups, Mary Kate leaned closer. "What is that on your neck?"

"What?"

Reaching forward, her sister tugged at the collar of the robe. "Right there. It looks like a terrible bruise. What happened?"

Oh, she knew what happened. That was the spot where Bryan had bitten her. It ached when Mary Kate's fingers brushed over it. "You know me. I wasn't paying attention to what I was doing and I hit it on an open drawer while putting clothes away."

Satisfied, Mary cupped her cheek before drawing back. "I swear one of these days I'm going to put you in a giant hamster wheel to keep you safe."

"Don't you think it would scare the kids?"

Mary Kate grinned. "No, because I'd put Brad and Lisa into one as well."

They laughed, and her sister lifted her chin. "So, who did you go out with last night?"

"Oh, a guy I know." She prayed her sister wouldn't push it, but Mary Kate pushed everything.

"Come on. Give me some details. I'm an old married woman who has to live vicariously through you. Where did you meet him?"

"Umm, at a club."

"What does he do?"

Stumped, Kira stared at her sister. She had no idea what Bryan did, other than being a lord. In fact, she didn't really know anything about him. When they were together, their physical attraction was so intense and all-consuming that she really didn't think about anything but what he was going to do to her, make her feel. A lump of disquiet twisted her belly, and she shook her head. "I don't really know."

Mary Kate frowned and set her coffee cup down. "Kira, what are you doing staying out all night with a man you barely know?"

"Jeez, Mom. I didn't know that at twenty-seven years old I'd get the third degree about who I date."

"Don't be defensive with me. I'm worried about you." Mary Kate sighed. "First, you don't date anyone for two years. Then you start dating only women. That was no big deal because they were all nice girls and they made you happy. Then you started dating what's his name, the pro-hockey player, but that didn't work out because he was an ass, followed by a yearlong dry spell. Now you're dating a guy again, and I get the feeling you're hiding something from me. Can you at least tell me his name?"

"Bryan Sutherfield." She took a quick breath and decided to tell Mary Kate his full name in an effort to get her off Kira's back. "Lord Bryan Sutherfield."

For a moment Mary Kate stared at Kira, the coffee cup suspended halfway to her mouth. "Really? A lord?"

"Yes, really truly."

"And you met him at a club?"

"Yes."

Mary Kate pursed her lips and stared out the kitchen window looking out over the tiny enclosed patio. "That's going to be a heck of a long-distance relationship."

"Actually, I think he's an ex-pat. He has a gorgeous home outside of DC." She tugged Bryan's robe tighter around herself.

"Why would a British lord become an ex-pat? Doesn't he have all kinds of lord stuff to do? Like go to balls and such?"

"I-I don't know."

Kira frowned and took her untouched cup back to the coffeepot for an unnecessary refill. Mary Kate's questions bugged her. What was Bryan doing over here? Would he be returning to England at any point? The thought of him being across the ocean sent a pang of hurt through her heart, and she chided herself for getting so wrapped up in him. Okay, they had amazing sex, but it wasn't like they were really dating or anything. In a way, he was more like a glorified booty call.

"Shoot, look at the time. Now go upstairs and get dressed; I need to be back by three to take Lisa to her karate lessons, and I'm not shopping for our impossible parents who own everything by myself."

Relieved Mary Kate was going to let it slide, at least for the moment, Kira hustled across the kitchen to the elevator in the hallway. As she rode up to the third floor, she tried to get rid of the niggling feeling something was wrong. Not that Bryan didn't have every right to live anywhere and everywhere he wanted, but why was he in the States? His home had the look of someone who'd lived there at least a few years, and Jesse had mentioned he'd known Bryan for three years.

When she came out of her walk-in closet, buttoning her high-necked silk blouse, she shrieked and jumped about a foot when she saw Mary Kate sitting on her big sleigh bed.

"Shit. You just scared a good six months off my life."

Instead of laughing, Mary Kate gave her a very somber, worried look. "Please don't be cross with me, but while you were getting dressed, I decided to look Lord Bryan Sutherfield up on my smartphone."

Rolling her eyes, Kira dug through her jewelry box, looking for her jade bracelet. "I'm supposed to be shocked you snooped?"

"Come here."

Disconcerted by the grave tone of her sister's voice, Kira slipped the bracelet on, then made her way across her bedroom and took a seat next to Mary Kate. "What's up?"

A red flush spread from Mary Kate's neck upward, the line where her foundation started becoming more obvious. "I know why he left England."

Trying to calm the panic in her stomach, Kira shifted so that she was more fully facing her sister. "Why? Did he kill someone? Am I dating a fugitive?"

"Honey, does he hit you?"

Shock froze her in place, locking her mind and only allowing her to whisper, "What?"

"Oh God, he does. Kira—"

"Wait, wait. I never said he hit me." That was true. He'd spanked her and slapped her breasts but never hit her. "Besides, don't you think with my fifteen years of karate I'd lay any man on his ass who lifted a finger against me?"

Letting out a long sigh, Mary Kate nodded. "You're right. It's just...well, here. You read it."

Mary Kate handed Kira her phone. After taking it, trying to ignore the slight tremble in her hands, Kira took a deep breath and read the screen. It was some trashy English tabloid, the kind of vicious gossip magazine she never looked at. Scrolling down, she read the headline, and her heart slammed against her ribs.

MORE DETAILS ON THE BARON BRYAN DE SADE'S SEX TAPE

A stinging sweat broke out over her, and she vaguely hoped she didn't get her silk shirt wet. Scrolling down, she read a sordid tale of how five years ago Bryan's girlfriend had tried to blackmail him with a video of them having very kinky, BDSM sex together. Bryan had gone to the authorities, but by then, it was too late. She'd put the video up on the Internet, where it went viral. At the bottom of the article that basically made Bryan seem like some sadistic monster, Kira came to a clip from the sex tape.

It wasn't good quality, a grainy picture from a distance of a shirtless man striding around a blonde woman tied to a whipping post. When he turned enough so the camera could capture his face, Kira's heart sank at the sight of a younger Bryan giving the woman his sinister smile, the same one he gave Kira. The other woman was naked, covered with long welts all over her fair skin, and manacled to the whipping post. Bryan touched her face and stroked her hair, and Kira wished she could make out what he was saying.

Seemingly satisfied, he moved back behind the woman and bent to pick up something off view of the camera. When he came back into the frame, he held a long whip he expertly snapped. The scene cut off, some nonsense about what happens next being too graphic for the public, but oh God, she knew all too well what it was like to be beneath his sadistic touch.

When she looked up, Mary Kate gave her a very somber look. "There's more. All kinds of articles about it. While I feel bad that he was blackmailed by some gold digger, at the same time, I don't want him around you. He's dangerous."

"No. He's not." She handed Mary Kate back her phone. "So he had kinky sex with her. Big deal."

Mary Kate's lips thinned into a white line. "He's *beating* her and getting off on it. This isn't a little spank on the butt. He's whipping her. What kind of monster would do that?"

"He's not a monster."

"How would you know? You just told me downstairs you don't know anything about this man." Mary Kate put her hand to her mouth, her dark eyes going wide. "Blessed Mother, did he give you that bruise on your neck? Kira, is he hurting you?"

"No! For fuck's sake, Mary Kate, he isn't doing anything to me I don't want him to do." Tears actually filled her sister's eyes and took away some of Kira's anger. "Look, I know you're concerned about me, I really do, but this is my life, and I get to make the choices of how I live it."

"Look, I know how much you love to take risks, to court danger. For you that's your drug of choice. But this is different. This isn't jumping out of a plane over the Grand Canyon. This is an abusive man who could really hurt you, maybe even kill you."

Standing up, Kira brushed off her pants and avoided her sister's gaze. "He is not a monster."

"I didn't say he was."

Before Kira could respond, the chime for her front door rang. Glad for the distraction, she strode over to the intercom next to her bedroom door and pressed the Speaker button. "Who is it?"

"Hello, beautiful. I brought your car back."

Her heart leaped in her chest even as her stomach filled with a nauseous mix of acid and weariness. "I'll be right down."

Mary Kate stood. "Is that him?"

"Yes, and I swear if you make a scene, I will be really, really pissed at you for a long time. I'm a grown woman who can make her own decisions."

Glaring at her, Mary Kate placed her hands on her hips. "You're also my baby sister."

Sensing a fight brewing and not wanting to leave Bryan standing on her front steps, she took a deep breath and tried to rein her temper in. "Just please try to not judge him until you meet him. I promise, I swear to you, that he has been nothing but everything I need."

Mary Kate gave a jerky nod. "Fine, but I want to meet him."

It would do no good to forbid her sister to meet Bryan. She'd come along anyway and cause an even bigger scene. Mary Kate was as protective as a mama bear, and the last thing Kira needed was for Mary Kate to call their parents and tattle. "Fine. But not one fucking word to Mom and Dad. I'm trusting you, Mary Kate."

They made their way together down to the entry level, and Kira took a deep breath before opening the front door. On the other side stood Bryan, looking as handsome as sin in his black dress slacks and white button-down shirt. His face lit up when he saw her, a glow burning deep in his brown eyes. "Good morning, love."

Mary Kate pushed her out of the way with her hip. "Hello, I'm Kira's sister, Mary Kate."

Bryan's eyebrows rose a tad at her open hostility. "Pleasure to meet you." He held out his hand to shake Mary Kate's, and she hesitated before giving him the briefest of shakes. Obviously confused by her sister's aggression, he handed Kira her keys. "I used the code you gave me and parked your car in the underground garage."

"Thank you so much."

Fuck, she wanted to invite him in, to surround herself with him, to ask him what in the hell had happened back in England, but she couldn't do any of those things with Mary Kate glowering at him like a disapproving nun from their Catholic girls' high school. She gave her sister a pointed look but was ignored.

Mary Kate crossed her arms. "So, Bryan, what are your intentions with my sister?"

Shoving her sister back, Kira gave Bryan a smile that felt as false as pleather. "If you'll excuse us for one moment."

She shut the door in his face and turned on Mary Kate. "Knock it off!"

"What? I didn't say anything wrong."

"You sounded like Dad when he was about to give someone the third degree. Now stop it. You're embarrassing me."

Mary Kate's spine stiffened. "Fine."

Giving her sister one last warning glare, she opened the door again. This time the look Bryan gave her was laced with suspicion and concern. "Am I interrupting something?"

"Yes," Mary Kate said. "We are running late and need to get going."

Bryan stepped back and nodded. "I don't want to keep you ladies."

Pissed at her sister, confused by the revelation of his past, and unsure of her own feelings, Kira walked out and wrapped her arms around him, planting a big kiss right on his mouth. "Thank you."

Bemused, he stroked her hair back from her cheek, both of them ignoring her sister's obvious ire. "You're most welcome. Give me a call later."

She inhaled his scent, pulling the cool and clean fragrance deep into her lungs. When she was around him, all her doubts fled. While what they had was only sexual—and temporary—she couldn't help wanting to spend all the time with him that she could. Still, the images from the video kept playing through her mind, and she also couldn't help the sting of both jealousy and apprehension.

"I will. Thank you again, Bryan."

Mary Kate rudely took her arm and pulled her back up the steps. "Come on, Kira. We have to go."

Bryan's narrowed his eyes, but he nodded. "Talk to you soon."

He turned and took the few steps down to the street to where his driver was waiting. Before he got in, he gave Kira one more look, and her heart tightened at the glimpse of hurt in his eyes before he turned away and got in his car. As he drove off, she pressed her hand to her chest and wished she was leaving with him.

Five hours later, Kira sat cuddled up in her favorite teal suede chair, staring at her phone. She needed to call Bryan, she really did, but dammit, she didn't know if she should tell him she knew about his past or not.

After she'd returned from shopping, she'd spent some time reading articles about the scandal Bryan had been involved in. Evidently it had been huge news over in Europe, but at the time, she'd been recovering from her injuries, so she hadn't really been paying attention to anything other than getting better. For months Bryan's handsome face had appeared on one cover after another, usually poorly photoshopped to include cringing women with big, fake tits at his feet.

The paparazzi he'd had to deal with must have been insane. There were pictures of him each time he left his house. When he went to a restaurant to have lunch with friends, there was an image of the paparazzi pressed against every available window to the point where the police had to be called for fear of the glass shattering. She'd found an article where some reporter had stolen Bryan's garbage and gone through it bit by bit, cataloging the contents and speculating on its use as a possible BDSM implement.

Even worse, people came out of the woodwork to sell their stories to the papers. Oh, she doubted very much that most of them had even met Bryan, but there were a few that had the ring of a true story. She wondered if any of his friends had sold him out to the paparazzi. Having his life destroyed and dissected for public consumption must have been horrible, not to mention the shunning he'd received. The British aristocracy had basically disavowed him. Before the scandal, he'd been the dangerous party boy everyone loved. Afterward, he was a woman-beating pariah.

No wonder he'd come to the States and joined Wicked. At least there he knew his privacy would be protected. There were a few articles about him after he left for America, but new scandals had grabbed the headlines, and he'd fallen into obscurity.

She'd had more than her share of the media hounding her when she'd been a movie star, but much like Bryan, once the public interest in her had waned, the tabloids moved on to more popular targets. At the time, she hadn't minded the media. After all, any press was good press when she was trying to break into acting. Now, she was only photographed for the society columns at different dreadfully dull social events.

Chewing her lower lip, she scrolled through her contacts until she came to Bryan's. Even though she didn't want to, and would much rather pretend nothing had changed, she had to tell him. He was always going on and on about honesty, and if he knew something like this about her, she'd be hella pissed he hadn't let her know. Besides, as much as she hated to admit it, her trust in him had changed.

The whipping he'd given that woman had been fierce, far more than Kira could ever take. While she didn't watch the part where they'd had sex—the thought of seeing Bryan with another woman made her crazy jealous—she couldn't help but wonder if he wasn't getting what he needed from her. She still hadn't been able to overcome her fear of being penetrated enough to please him like a woman should please her man.

Now self-disgust mixed with her worry, and she pressed the button to call him.

After two rings, his deep, British-accented voice warmed her from the inside out. "Hello, Kira."

"I know you're the Baron de Sade." She winced, mentally kicking herself in the ass for her totally unsmooth move. "I mean—"

"I know what you mean." His voice was like ice, a bitter breeze across her soul. "Is that why your sister was so hostile towards me?"

"Yes." She curled up further in the chair until she was in a fetal position. "I'm sorry."

"As am I. It was a pleasure working with you, Kira. I hope you find a trainer who can help you."

"No! Wait! I don't want to stop seeing you."

Silence came from the other end, and she wondered if he'd hung up before he finally said, "Did you see the video?"

"Yes, well, not all of it. I couldn't stand to watch you have sex with her. You know, stupid female jealousy and all that." This had to be the most awkward conversation she'd ever had. "Look, Bryan, what happened to you was fucked up, and if I ever see that skank, I'll snatch her bald, but it doesn't change how I feel about you."

Some of the warmth came back to his voice, but it was still tight. "And how do you feel about me?"

Once again her big mouth got her in trouble.

"I, well, I like you. You know, like, for real like you." Silence from the phone. "You...you make me feel good. Safe."

He gave a harsh laugh. "You expect me to believe that?"

"Of course." She frowned and picked at the edge of the chair.

"Tell me. What did your sister say when she found out?"

Swallowing hard, she tried for a modified version of the truth, not wanting to hurt his feelings. "She was a little worried I was dating an abusive man."

"Exactly. To your sister, to everyone who loves you, I'm a dangerous psychopath who hurts women. They will and should do everything in their power to protect you from me." His voice grew tighter, more intense. "We should stop our training right now. I don't want to be responsible for driving a wedge between you and your family."

"You don't want to see me anymore?" She hated how wounded and little-girl-like her voice sounded, but damn, the thought of never being with him again hurt.

"I know what's best for you."

Some anger pushed back the hurt, her temper flaring. "That's rather high-handed of you."

"What do you mean?"

"Look, I agree that in the bedroom, dungeon, whatever, you hold the upper hand, but you don't get to decide what is right or wrong for me. I'm a grown woman, Bryan, and I've always been in control of my destiny. If you don't want to see me anymore, fine." Her voice broke on the last word, and she swallowed back tears. Not tears of sorrow but of anger. "But don't you for one fucking minute think that it's because I don't want to be with you. Your past doesn't change who you are to me now. Well, right now you're acting like an imperious asshole, but I mean when you're not being like this. I know you're a good man, and I trust you."

"I wish I could believe that. You deserve someone you can have a normal relationship with. A man you wouldn't be ashamed of."

"I'm not ashamed of you."

"Easy to say that now. But what about when you're out with me and someone takes a picture that ends up splashed all over the news? I haven't been out in public with a woman since I left England in order to spare her the humiliation of being the Baron de Sade's next victim."

"Oh, please. That's old news! Besides, I've already been there and done that. You're not the only one the paparazzi has stalked. I had pictures taken of me topless sunbathing and smoking a joint down in Brazil. If you think my parents didn't hit the roof about that, you're crazy."

"A youthful indiscretion is far different than being accused of being an abusive monster. Do you know what it's like to have everyone you know, people you've spent your entire life with, look at you with a mixture of horror and disgust? That is what could very well happen to you if we take this any further. I care about you too much to subject you to that, and it kills me that I can't protect you from the paparazzi. I won't let your life become evil-spirited gossip fodder for the masses."

He sounded so sad. She wished he was here so she could alternately hug him and choke him. "Don't you get it? I'm not some fragile flower that is going to wilt at the first sign of adversity. I can handle it."

"I don't want you to have to *handle* things. Your life is hard enough without adding my demons to it. I'll help you find a good sadist who will be able to get you past your block and be the kind of man you wouldn't be ashamed to be seen with in public."

"Please don't give up on me. I need you. I don't want anyone else as my Master. I want you."

Once again silence from his side of the phone, but she'd be damned if she was going to break it first. Yeah, she knew he was probably still a head case about being betrayed, but everyone had their issues from the past. At the end of the day, it came down to one thing: either a person was strong enough to let the past go and move on, or they were doomed forever to be stuck in an endless loop of memories. Shit, look at her. She'd been stuck in that loop but had made the decision to try to break free of her fear of sex by whatever means necessary.

"I wish it was that easy."

"It is. Please, my lord, please meet me at Wicked tonight. Just to talk in a neutral setting, nothing more. At the very least give us a chance to work on this. I need you, my lord."

His weary sigh let her know he'd agreed even before he spoke. "I'll see you there at nine p.m. Meet me in the public lounge."

CHAPTER EIGHT

Kira strolled through the front doors of Wicked after passing through the small security check, and a shiver of anticipation raced up her spine. Regardless of whatever happened between her and Bryan, she couldn't help the pulse of arousal as she crossed the threshold into what was basically an adult fantasy land. A large black onyx desk was situated next to the front door. The handsome African American man behind the desk with a name tag that said Tashawn smiled at her. "Good evening, Ma'am. Lord Bryan would like me to inform you that he is waiting for you at the Hall of Mirrors lounge. Is there anything I can do to further your experience at Club Wicked tonight?"

"Yes, I'd like to go barefoot. Could you please have someone put my shoes into a locker?"

"Of course." Tashawn looked over his shoulder to a room that was just out of Kira's point of view. "Jessica, we are in need of your service."

"Thank you, Tashawn." Kira slipped off her shoes. Her body still a bit stiff from last night, and she didn't feel like wearing her heels. While she could have gone into the women's sumptuous dressing room to change, she was too eager to see Bryan. Even though she was afraid he wouldn't want to see her anymore, the waiting was killing her. Patience was not one of the virtues that she was born with. Probably explained her need to rush through things that most people were afraid to do.

A lovely Asian woman in a frilly french maid costume came around the corner and took the shoes from Kira. She gave Kira a shy but flirty smile, and the soft scent of her jasmine perfume tickled Kira's nose. "Thank you, Ma'am. My name is Jessica, and if you need *anything* to heighten your pleasure this evening, please don't hesitate to ask for me."

There was no doubt about the open sexual nature of the offer, and it gave Kira's ego a much-needed boost. She smiled at the other woman and put a bit of heat into to it. "Thank you, Jessica."

The other woman curtsied low enough to show off her impressive cleavage before departing with Kira's shoes. Despite her nerves, Kira couldn't help but admire the lush sway of Jessica's bottom as she sauntered away. Kira could understand Bryan's urge to spank a full ass like that. Hell, she wanted to do it just to see what it was like. It wasn't like she suddenly wanted to be a Domme, but she'd always had a thing for Asian women, and Jessica was hot. Besides, thinking about something other than the conversation ahead of her helped calm her nerves a tiny bit.

Giving herself a mental shake, Kira looked away from Jessica's departing figure and tried to gather herself. The long, flowing royal-blue gown Kira had chosen was almost demure in cut but scandalously transparent. Held in front by a gold chain looped between two diamond pins, it covered her from her collarbone to her feet. Except she wore nothing beneath other than her skin-tone panties, which gave the illusion of being naked. She'd added rouge to her nipples to make them darker, and now they stood out plainly beneath her dress in the warm lighting of the club. Yes, it was far more outrageous than anything she'd worn here before, but she needed to pull out the big guns. Besides, she was wearing a mask, which resembled glittering ocean waves, and there was nothing about her that could be easily identified by the members of Wicked. Of course the staff knew who she was, and probably some of the members since she didn't keep her identity a secret, but she loved the feeling of being a mysterious woman in a mask. It was kind of like getting into character for a role she was playing in a movie by dressing the part.

The fabric molded to her legs as she strolled across the enormous entryway, the tiles were heated so her feet wouldn't get cold. That was one of the perks of belonging to Wicked. They thought of everything. Taking the archway to the right, she went down a long corridor with several hallways stretching off it. At the end, the golden light of the public bar spilled out over the black walnut floors.

Despite her best efforts to remain calm, by the time she crossed the threshold, her heart pounded against her ribs like a fist.

He was here already.

Well, she hadn't actually seen him yet, but she could feel him. A charge flowed through the sexually saturated air, a private touch for her soul alone. Either that or she was acting like a lovesick teenager. Both were equally possible.

Moving through the crowd, she was stopped by several Masters and Mistresses, each complimenting her on her outfit. While they were all polite, there was a carnal undercurrent to their words, a look in their eyes like she was a plump and juicy rabbit to their wolf when they saw that she wore no collar or any other marks showing she belonged to a Dom. Coming around the far side of the bar, she finally spotted Bryan sitting and talking with Jesse.

Ah, fuck. She didn't want Jesse to see her goodies. She knew him.

Before she could try and figure out what to do, Jesse spotted her and grinned. He put his fingers to his mouth and made a loud whistle of appreciation, the noise cutting through the crowd.

"Those are some of the nicest tits I've ever seen. Makes me want to tie them up and fuck them."

Bryan didn't turn, but his whole body stiffened. He must have given Jesse a look, because the other man winked at her and laughed at Bryan.

Somehow she managed to make it through the crowd without dying of embarrassment, but that was only because she intended to kill Jesse when she got to him.

Passing Bryan's stool, she stopped next to Jesse. It was nice having enough height so he didn't loom over her while sitting down. He still had that shit-eating grin on his face, so she decided to wipe it off before she beat him senseless. "Jesse, you're my friend, and while I value our friendship, I won't have you yelling things at me like I'm some kind of whore working on the corner. Your mama taught you better than that."

Jesse cleared his throat and actually flushed. "My apologies, Kira."

She smiled at him and bumped him with her hip so he'd know he was forgiven. "Thank you. I know you probably want to paddle my ass, and I would totally allow it if you, like, you know, needed to save your Dom reputation or something, but any punishment will have to first be approved by my lord."

Without another word, she turned to face Bryan, finding his kissable lips curved up in the barest hint of a smile. She moved as gracefully as she could to her knees, her damn hip giving her a little twinge. Once kneeling, she placed her hands on her thighs like she'd seen other women here do and thanked the good Lord that the floors at Wicked were clean enough to eat from.

For a long moment, neither man said anything, and she wanted to look up and see what they were doing but didn't dare. Damn, she'd probably screwed up really bad with Bryan. Submissives were supposed to be submissive, to take whatever a Dom wanted to throw at them. Well, that wasn't quite true. She could safeword anytime, and if public humiliation was on her hard list, any Dom she was with, who agreed to her terms, would have to abide by his word.

A few moments later Bryan stroked his hand over her hair, pulling her head closer until it rested on his thigh. All the tension she'd been holding on to slowly drained out of her and into the ground, leaving her almost light-headed with relief. Still, she needed to be the best submissive she could be, and her behavior with Jesse would be unacceptable with most Doms.

She needed to apologize.

The men were talking about the Redskins, and she waited for a lull in the conversation before tugging at Bryan's pants and peeking up at his face. "My lord?"

He looked down, his expression closed and the fine muscles around his eyes tight. Oh yeah. He was angry at her. She could feel it and wondered why he'd touched her with such tenderness if he was this mad. Then she looked closer and saw the sadness and uncertainty he was trying so hard to hide. Poor guy, he really did expect her to freak out and leave him at any second.

"What is it?"

"My lord, I beg for your permission to take a punishment for my rude behavior. Please let me make it up to Master Jesse."

The men exchanged a look, but she kept her attention on Bryan. She was trying to do the only thing she could to please and reassure him, submit to his will.

"Stand up and lean against the bar with your face down on its surface. If that position is uncomfortable for you, stand with your hands braced against the edge of the counter."

A tremor ran through here, part longing to please and part fear. What would Jesse want as a punishment? She knew Bryan's tastes in punishments ran to the darkly sexual, but she didn't feel right about Jesse touching her that way.

She wet her lips, conscious of the way Bryan watched her with an intensity that was almost unsettling. "I didn't know they allowed sex out here, my lord."

"They don't. Jesse is sticking to some stupid vow of chastity while Dove is over in Paris."

She let out a relieved sigh. "Thank goodness."

A way to fix this mess came to her, and she felt an instant sense of calm. She had a way to show him just how much she trusted him, how much she believed in him and his ability as a Dom. Despite his arrogant mannerisms, she had a feeling that the sex-tape scandal had dealt a blow to his self-esteem. How could it not? The entire world had watched him whip a woman and then have sex with her. Sure, asking him to whip Kira would be potentially dangerous, but she trusted Bryan not to hurt her too badly. The man who'd stroked her hair last night while she was getting a massage wasn't a man who would abuse her.

She took a deep breath and hoped she was doing the right thing, that he understood why she was asking. "My lord, would you please whip me for my insolence?"

Darkness flared within his eyes. "Jesse, would you excuse us for a moment, please?"

Clearing his throat, Jesse nodded. "Sure. I'll be right here. But if you're going to do a whipping demonstration on her, I want to watch. You're amazing with the single tail."

"Of course."

Bryan stood and helped Kira to her feet. Without another word, he led her through the public bar and into the private portion of the club. He took them to an area of isolated alcoves seated back into the walls beneath enormous mirrored arches. Turkish tile work covered the ceiling and walls, while brass lanterns with real flames hung from the ceiling, adding the scent of melted wax to the air. The curtains covering the alcoves were sheer, and if the people inside wished, they could turn on different lights, illuminating them behind a dreamy haze.

Bryan jerked aside the curtain of an empty one and motioned her to the pillow-strewn floor. Actually, it wasn't really a floor in the traditional sense. It felt more like some type of mattress. Mirrors covered the interior walls of the alcove, giving her a hundred images of Bryan as he dimmed the lights so they would be nothing more than dark blurs to anyone passing by.

Sexual tension filled the air like a switch being thrown, and she wished he would close the distance between them, then kiss her senseless.

"Kira, what are you doing?"

"My lord, I trust you. If you can make me orgasm with the whip, I'll know you can make me come when you take me, despite any pain I might feel. And I want you to take me, more than I've ever wanted anyone in my life. That scares me."

He moved a step closer, his handsome face all dark shadows and strong bone structure. "Why?"

"Because... Fuck it. Because I'm afraid you don't want to see me anymore, and that now that you know my feelings for you extend beyond just sex, you'll walk away." She turned but could still see him in the mirrors. "Look. You seem to think I should be freaked out by that video. Well, I am, but that's because seeing you with another woman like that makes me insanely jealous in some stupid, territorial way."

He laughed, his warmth brushing against her back but not touching her yet. "I must confess. The thought of Jesse spanking you made me want to stab him."

That made her spin on her heel so she could see his face. "Really?"

"Yes." He took a deep breath and stared at her for a few moments, then nodded. "Are you sure? You can back out at any time, and I won't think poorly of you."

"I'm sure." She ran her fingers down his cheek, stroking his goatee.

Grasping Kira's hand in his, Bryan pulled her after him as they left the alcove. Enormous wrought-iron chandeliers dripping with black crystals illuminated the long hallway spilling out into the main dungeon. A stark contrast to the luxurious Turkish harem area they'd left, and adding to the fear now tingling through her bones. He stopped and looked around before hailing a nearby submissive. The curvy Indian woman in a see-through red sari moved quickly and knelt before Bryan.

"How may this one help you, my lord?"

Bryan fairly vibrated with a dizzying mixture of command and power. The submissive at his feet certainly seemed to sense something. Her eyes widened, and her nipples stiffened. Despite Kira's fear of the pain to come, a dark rhythm began to beat in her own blood. What she was about to do, about to feel, was going to be intense. God, she'd missed this pulse-pounding adrenaline rush, the bitter foil taste of dread and excitement kindling in her blood. Add Bryan's energy to that, and she found herself near shaking in anticipation.

"Get my single tail from my storage unit. Fetch Master Jesse for me, and inform him I'll have a seat saved for him. Is the Russian Courtyard room open?"

The submissive stared up at him with wide eyes. "Yes, it is, my lord. May this one please ask if Master intends to do a public whipping?"

Now a larger dose of panic moved through Kira's body. The way the submissive was looking at her, in a mixture of awe and disbelief, she wondered if she'd bitten off more than she could chew. Nearby, she heard excited whispers spreading from one person to another that Lord Bryan was going to do a scene.

Fuck, she didn't know if she could handle people watching them.

Bryan nodded and gripped Kira's hand harder, like he sensed her sudden reluctance. "I am."

"Very good, my lord." The girl's tone fair tingled with eagerness. "May this one please be released to do your bidding?"

The whispers now rose to shouts as word began to spread through the club that Lord Bryan was going to do a single-tail demonstration with his new submissive.

Oh, fuckity fucking fuck. What had her adrenaline-junkie side gotten her into now?

"Yes, off with you. Oh, and tell Mistress Jennifer she may assign her submissive as a handmaiden if she wishes, and I need to talk to Master Rory about Jessica if she's available."

Bryan led her quickly through the halls of Wicked and stopped before a pair of double doors. They were made of heavy wrought iron and had a sense of great age about them. Bryan turned, and the heat in his gaze traveled through her soul and stroked the dark ember of lust back to life.

"Kira, you have your safe word. Do not be afraid to use it. I would never be mad at you for being strong enough to admit something is too much. Am I clear?"

"Yes, my lord." She swallowed hard and moved a bit closer. "I'm afraid you've stolen my courage. I'm finding it hard to open those doors."

Without preamble, he grabbed her by the back of the neck, hard enough to resemble the feeling of a collar, and pulled her into his kiss. Unlike his grip, the soft passing of his lips over hers was a delicious seduction. Eager for more, she opened her mouth for him and melted at the stroke of his tongue against hers. He took his time, seducing her and stroking her body with his free hand in a way that was both soothing and arousing. Slowly, carefully, he made sure every inch of her mouth had been touched by his tongue. Once she was horny enough to want to mount him right here in the hallway, her body and the public setting be damned, he pulled back and gave her his sinister grin.

"Go through those doors. There will be submissives there to prepare you."

"Prepare me?"

"You'll see. Now stop dawdling."

He gave one breast a slap, and she gasped at the sudden, harsh sting mixing with the lingering effects of his drugging kiss. Despite the pain—or maybe because of it—her nipples hardened into rock-solid points, and moisture slicked her swollen sex. He raised his eyebrows, and she quickly turned, not wanting to anger him and give him an excuse to punish her.

Well, any more than he already did.

Despite their weight, the doors opened easily on perfectly oiled hinges. The moment she stepped into the dim lighting, Bryan closed the doors behind her, locking her in. Startled, she backed up until her bottom pressed against the cool metal. She was in some type of circular stone courtyard, and a bright, full moon shone down from a ceiling far above, bathing the dark room in silver highlights and obsidian shadows. In the center of the courtyard sat a life-size white alabaster statue of a nude woman kneeling with her hands outstretched and her back curved into a graceful arch.

CHAPTER NINE

Nervous energy flooded Bryan as he paced around the staging room next to the Russian Courtyard. Jesse, the unhelpful bastard, had stopped by to tell Bryan he was playing to a full house. Every seat in the viewing gallery was taken and almost all the standing room. For a second Bryan wondered if the audience was there to see his skills as a Dom or to watch him whip someone again like he had in that fucking video that had ruined his life. One moment of recklessness when he'd let his ex-submissive videotape their encounter, not knowing she'd try to blackmail him with it.

Anger mixed with his nervous energy until he had to pace the room or go insane. Then he stopped himself and tried to consider this situation from an objective viewpoint. If he knew a scene was about to happen that would be a rare first time between a Master and his submissive, there wasn't a doubt that he'd attend.

His tension gripped his muscles because of the undeniable danger this situation posed to both himself and Kira. She had to trust that he wouldn't abuse her, and he needed to know that if it got to be too much, she would tell him and safeword out before any permanent damage was done, either emotionally or physically. Only that trust allowed him to do a little bit of edge play with her, where he pushed her farther out of her comfort zone than she'd ever been. Kira loved her adrenaline rushes, and add to that the endorphins he'd get going during her whipping...well, bloody fuck, she was going to fly deep.

He couldn't wait to give her this gift even as he worried about hurting her.

Mistress Jennifer, tonight clad in an elegant gold-and-black cocktail dress and thigh-high black boots, stepped into his way as he paced, forcing him to stop and look at her.

Arching one perfectly shaped brow, she gave him a wry smile. "You haven't heard a word we've said, have you?"

Across the room, Master Rory snorted. Tonight he wore his usual leather pants and tight black T-shirt. He was sitting on the small couch and sipping a dark lager that he lifted in Bryan's direction before he spoke. "Oh, I'm sorry. Am I really here? I wasn't sure if this was a dream, because I was talking and no one was responding."

Closing his eyes, Bryan tried to let go of his irritation. These were his friends, generously loaning him their submissives. He needed to pull his head out of his ass and focus. "I'm sorry. What was it you were asking me?"

Mistress Jennifer gave his shoulder a gentle push. "We said you're going to have to work on calming your girl down. We've already sent Jessica and Shy in with the express purpose of making Kira feel as comfortable and relaxed as possible. Now you need to do the same. Relax and let all that negative energy go."

With a chuckle, Master Rory leaned forward and set his drink down next to Bryan's single tail. "I'm sure Jessica will have Kira purring within minutes and more than ready for whatever you want to dish out. Jessica was working the door tonight as part of her service submissive training, and she made a note of who Kira was when she came in, to see if she wanted to play later. She's exactly Jessica's type."

Bryan managed to give the other man a small smile, and a bit of his stress drained away. At the very least he'd be able to give his girl some intense orgasms tonight, so it would be helpful to have the other submissives there just in case Kira went too deep. If that happened, she would take pain greater than anything she'd normally endure because of her mental state.

The soft scent of Mistress Jennifer's peach-based perfume reached him as she gave him a quick hug. "And you know Shy is an expert at talking dirty. She can make the filthiest suggestions sound like poetry."

Master Rory held Bryan's gaze, his expression completely serious. "I'm not worried about your girl. It's you I'm worried about. I've never, ever seen you this stressed-out before a scene. I've seen you work a submissive into a frenzy with your whip without breaking a sweat. Now you seem as tense as a cat in a roomful of rocking chairs. I'm just asking you to take a moment to center yourself, for your sake and hers."

Bryan was tempted to dismiss what the other man said; then he reminded himself that Master Rory was one of the club's resident experts on helping introverted submissives find the courage to embrace their sexual self and gain self-confidence. The man could read body language like no one Bryan had ever met, and seemed to have an instinctive feel for what a submissive needed. If he was telling Bryan he needed to relax, then Master Rory meant it.

The soft slide of Mistress Jennifer's hair tickled his cheek as she leaned over and rested her chin on his shoulder. In a very odd way, Jennifer had become almost a bratty older sister to him. She was one of the first Dominants at Wicked to approach him when he'd joined. More importantly she'd never asked about the scandal, something that at the time had been a miracle. He was the BDSM poster boy for a "cautionary tale on blackmail," and people couldn't resist asking over and over and over again what had happened. It got to the point where he'd just say *"I'm not discussing that"* and walk away. There was no doubt she knew about it, but she had the class and kindness to not mention it.

She gave him a light hug. "You'll do great. I have faith in you."

Rory stood and ambled toward the one-way glass on the door, blocking Bryan's view of the courtyard. "Your girl should be coming out anytime now. If she wishes to involve Jessica, let my girl know she has my full permission to do as she wishes. This will be the first time Jessica has done anything before an audience, but it is one of her greatest fantasies. If your girl is willing, I'd greatly appreciate it if you let Jessica play with her during the whipping."

"Of course, and thank you for lending your girl to me."

Rory smiled at him and winked. “I’m a bit nervous myself. Jessica has chosen to try out her seduction skills on Kira. Jessica has no idea just how appealing she is, and I hope Kira likes her. It would do Jessica a world of good to have that kind of affirmation.”

The thought of the pretty Asian woman who was currently training with Rory flitted through Bryan’s mind, instantly followed by the fantasy of watching her eat the fuck out of Kira’s pussy. Desire roared through his veins, and his cock went from semierect to achingly stiff in the space of three heartbeats. He loved watching women pleasure each other. The idea of kissing Kira with the scent of another woman’s pussy on her lips made him want to growl with lust.

Jennifer left Bryan’s side and strolled over to Rory, working her boots in a way any man would appreciate. “Shy would do better as moral support. You need to put her in a position where she can give Kira something to focus on and can alert you to any problems that you may miss.”

Anger mixed with anxiety made Bryan irritable. Was Jennifer implying that he didn’t know what the fuck he was doing? That he was some novice who didn’t know his own fucking sub’s signals? Kira would safeword out if it got to be too much. He had to believe she would. Still, the implied insult stung and pricked the bubble of his anger.

“Fuck off. I know my girl.”

Both Rory and Jennifer turned, each giving him a look that set his teeth on edge. Jennifer actually looked hurt. Bryan felt like a major asshole. They were just trying to help, and he was lashing out at them because of his own worries. Self-doubt wasn’t something he usually felt, at least not about situations involving BDSM, but right now, he was really wondering if he’d be able to get Kira to go into subspace.

It wasn’t that he doubted his skill. It was that he really, really cared about Kira, and that made this whipping different. This wasn’t a submissive he might casually encounter here and there at Wicked. This was the woman who’d turned his careful world upside down and made him feel madly, dangerously alive. She deserved the absolute best experience, and he was worried that she wouldn’t like it and would leave him. Yeah, lots of women said they wanted edge play, up until the point that the first sting of the whip landed.

He looked at Jennifer and Rory, making sure he met their gazes in turn as he said, "I'm sorry. That was unnecessary. Thank you for your help, and thank you for giving me your support. It means a lot to me."

Jennifer beamed at him, and his chest lightened. Beneath that icy Mistress persona, she had a very gentle heart and was easily hurt. "It's okay, sweetie. Love does strange things to us."

"I'm not in love," Bryan muttered, and Jennifer hid a giggle behind her hand.

Rory shook his head. "Take a deep breath and let some of that energy out. Trust me. I get this way before meeting with a new submissive for the first time. If your sub detects your volatile emotions, it won't help reassure her."

"Can I have a moment alone, please?"

They nodded, and each squeezed one of his shoulders as they passed. When the *click* of the door sounded behind him, Bryan went over to the table and picked up his whip, running his hand over the medallion on the hilt. He'd had his family crest put there in what at first was a sardonic joke over his parents' terror that their family would be forever associated with BDSM.

Self-righteous pricks.

Now, as he rubbed the raised surface with his thumb, he took pride in who he was and where he came from. While his parents weren't the best examples of humanity to come from the Sutherfield line, he had ancestors who were just as scandalous, if not more so, than he was. Yet generations later, it was their good deeds that lasted after they'd died, not gossip about a chambermaid getting knocked up or the fourth Lord Sutherfield having not one, not two, but three gay lovers who all lived with him at the family's hunting lodge.

He'd have to tell Kira tales about his family's history; she'd find it hilarious.

Warmth suffused him at the knowledge that she'd found out the worst about him and she still wanted him. Not just wanted him—needed him. Her trust in him was staggering. The warmth grew, invading his heart, chasing away all self-doubt.

With a smile he shrugged off his shirt and tossed it over a chair before moving to the door leading to the courtyard. He dimmed the lights to their lowest setting, giving his eyes time to adjust before he opened the door and began what he hoped would be one of the best scenes of Kira's life.

Movement came from the corner of Kira's eye, and she turned and found a beautiful, nude Asian woman wearing a sparkling crimson and black mask approaching her. She quickly realized it was the maid who'd greeted her at the door, and a warm rush raced through Kira. For a second she worried how Bryan might react to her desire for another, but hell, he'd sent her here. He had to know how she'd react. The memory of the first time she saw him, his raw hunger as he watched two women pleasure each other, made her bite her lip.

From the other direction came a lithe, almost pixielike blonde with perky breasts and tiny nipples. Unlike most of the women at the club, she wasn't wearing a mask, and Kira found it strangely intimate to look at her without the mental protection that little scrap of cloth brought. It somehow made the other woman more real. Both of them stopped a few feet away, and the blonde girl spoke first.

"My name is Shy. My Mistress Jennifer has instructed me to assist you in getting ready for your whipping."

The Asian woman took another step closer. "My name is Jessica. My Master, Rory, has requested I attend you as well." Another step, close enough so the silken ends of her long, dark hair brushed Kira's arm. "I begged him to after I saw you tonight."

Kira's gaze was drawn up as dim, golden lights began to burn behind the panes of three rows of windows. She thought she detected movement and said in a low voice, "Are there people up there watching us?"

Jessica laughed softly. "Yes, there will be an audience. Lord Bryan is a legend with the single tail but only rarely uses it. He must really like you."

Shy giggled and grabbed Kira's hand. "Come on, darling. We have to get you ready or my Mistress will beat my ass in a less than pleasant way."

They tugged her over to a small screened-off section of the room and quickly stripped her. Next they both grabbed bottles of lotion and proceeded to rub it into every inch of her body, their soft hands eliciting a hunger that was like a refreshing bath after the intense flame of need for her Master. Her hair was upswept and held off her neck by silver pins. By the time they doused her in a shimmering silver powder, her pussy had left a trail of wetness between her thighs.

Jessica groaned. "How I would love to taste you."

Shy gave one of Kira's nipples a hard pinch. "How I would love to suck on these, but our bodies and our pleasure belong to our Masters and Mistresses."

Feeling bold and incredibly aroused, Kira ran her finger between the swollen lips of her sex and gathered some of her honey. She held her fingertip out to Jessica. The other woman's nostrils flared. Raising the finger to her own mouth, Kira sucked her taste off and smiled at Jessica.

"Yum."

Shy shook her head and stifled a giggle. "Oh, you are bad. You better get out there."

Kira's playful mood vanished the moment she stepped into the viewing area. Naked, terribly exposed, she wanted to cover herself with her hands but remembered how Bryan wanted to see her at all times. Since he was the man holding the whip, she should probably obey him.

As if her thoughts had summoned him, he stepped up behind her, his bare chest pressing against her pale, sparkling skin. "You look beautiful, a daughter of the moon. I can't wait to bring some color to all that creamy skin."

"My lord." She leaned back into him, comforted by this familiar position as his body curved protectively around hers. Warmth began to ease her trembling, and she took a deep breath. The way he held her, the way he touched her, made her feel so cherished. She'd forgotten how nice it was to have someone want her like this. Well, she'd never actually been with anyone that aroused her until she was mindless with need. That honor belonged to Bryan alone.

Lord Bryan. Her Master…however temporarily.

Bryan nuzzled her ear, his short goatee tickling her skin. "I want you to go up to the statue in the center of the room. Grasp the statue's hands and use the curve of her body to brace yourself. Don't let go until I tell you." He slipped his hands between her legs and rubbed her swollen sex in a shockingly proprietary manner. "Hmm, I see your handmaidens got you nice and wet." He pressed one finger against the entrance to her sheath, making her jerk against him. "Which one would you like to have lick your pussy if I decided to let you have that pleasure with your pain?"

Her body went loose with desire at the sinful picture he painted. "Jessica, please."

"Rory's submissive? Good choice. She is an exhibitionist, so I may need to strap you down before she eats you into a coma."

There was nothing she could do but groan at his words and press her ass against his rock-hard cock. "My lord, I'll do anything you wish as long as the night ends with me being in your arms."

"Such a sweet girl. If you get scared or overwhelmed, I want you to keep that thought in mind. No matter what happens, you will end the night in my bed, exhausted and sent into a state of bliss, cradled in the arms of your lord." A bit of steel entered his voice. "Now, stop stalling and assume the position I told you to."

Almost faint with lust, she made her way quickly across the stone floor—well, as quickly as she could. The room itself was immense, and she realized Bryan would need a good deal of space to use his whip. The knowledge that she was soon going to be in burning amounts of pain dampened her enthusiasm, and by the time she'd placed her hands into the cool grip of the statue, her legs were shaking.

It made her more fall than lean onto the stone surface of the woman's arched body. She embraced the solid feeling of the cold alabaster against her heated skin. Her bottom half was exposed to the room, but at least she had a place to rest her face. Tightening her grip on the statue's hands, she prepared herself to take as much as she could for his pleasure.

Bryan's voice rang out behind her, obviously addressing the audience. "Shy will be joining my girl. She can talk an angel into sinning, so I expect my lovely submissive will find it all that much harder to keep from coming against my wishes. This is my girl's first time ever being whipped, and it is for pleasure, not punishment. You are in for a rare treat."

Kira raised her head as much as she dared and caught a glimpse of the slim woman approaching the statue. Shy brushed her hand over Kira's hip in a soothing gesture as she passed. Climbing the alabaster fall of the statue's hair on the other side of Kira, Shy leaned in and laid her hands over Kira's.

"Easy, pretty girl. You're fair going to shake off that thing, and then he'd strap you in place. Do you trust your lord?"

"Right now he's scaring the piss out of me."

"Look at me."

Kira raised her head, and Shy smiled down at her over the shoulder of the statue. "There we go. Oh my, pretty girl. You show everything on your face. It's either because you're new to the scene or because your Master likes to be able to see your feelings. Regardless, it will make watching you lose yourself in the whipping all the more sweet."

Kira laughed, a somewhat hysterical giggle punctured by the snapping of the whip, the echoing of that crack of air rebounding off the stone walls. "Well, if I pass out before anything happens, let me know how it went."

Laughing, Shy stroked Kira's hair off her cheek. "I promise you won't want to miss this. God, if I wasn't as gay as the day is long, I would *so* be into your lord. When he whips someone, it is beauty and power in motion, all focused on you. He can draw feelings out of you that you've never imagined. I'm here kinda like your seat belt, ready to catch you in case you go down too deep."

"What do you mean?"

Shy leaned closer, the soft mint scent of her breath brushing past Kira's face. "You'll see. Trying to explain it is like trying to explain color to someone born blind. You have to see it to believe it."

"Should I be reassured or scared?"

"You are a brat, aren't you? I bet you give your lord a run for his money."

Feeling chastised, Kira wiggled her bottom as she assumed a looser stance. Sometimes forcing the body to relax made the mind also stop freaking out. She'd had to do this once before, when she'd been doing a fight scene while skydiving. Her chute had failed; then she'd gotten tangled in her partner's harness. They managed to get unstuck quickly, but for about three seconds, she'd frozen in terror.

Taking in a deep breath, she let it out slowly and chided herself for getting so worked up. Adrenaline filled her, and she wanted to move, to run, to do something with all this energy. A soft whimper managed to escape her when her muscles refused to relax.

A sharp, extremely loud *crack* snapped through the air behind her, followed by one more. He was either trying to freak her out or warm up and freak her out anyway. Bracing herself, she widened her stance and tucked her head down a bit.

"Jessica, my submissive is far too tense. I need her relaxed before I begin in order to avoid injury." Bryan's voice dropped an octave, becoming a sensual growl that vibrated through Kira's soul. "I will enjoy the sight of you pleasuring her."

Shy moaned. "Oh my. This is going to be lovely. I hope you don't mind if I touch myself while they work on you."

Kira snorted softly. "I bet if you put one finger on your pussy without your Mistress's permission, you wouldn't be sitting for a week."

"Oh, I'd be sitting, but not in a good way. She'd strap me to a vibrating horse saddle and make me ride it until I was screaming with the pain of overstimulation. Then she'd make me lick her pussy, just like Jessica is about to lick yours. Lucky bitch."

Well, this certainly answered the question as to whether Bryan would approve of her playing with Jessica. Her lord was one of those men who loved women, loved to look at them, loved to watch them together. Kira shouldn't be surprised. Look at his art collection. All beautiful women over the ages, each an example of her times ultimate female beauty. Guess her Rubenesque body turned him on as much as his chiseled abs turned her on.

Tilting her head to the side, she caught a glimpse of the beautiful Asian woman before Jessica disappeared out of Kira's line of sight. Bryan remained out of her view, and she wondered if he was touching himself while he watched them, aroused by his submissive taking pleasure at his command. Right now she had no power in the decisions being made for her, and the thought gave her a delicious shiver.

Shy remained silent but had begun to lightly stroke Kira's fingers and arms, tickling touches that made goose bumps rise on her skin. Being the center of this much attention was overwhelming, and Kira clung to the stone, grateful for its support. Shit, Bryan hadn't even touched her yet, and she was so turned on she could come with a press of her legs.

Jessica began to kiss her way down Kira's back, pausing over scars and murmuring low in her throat. When she reached Kira's bottom, she made a pleased sound. "You smell delicious. Bend forward more. I want you to open yourself for your Master to see. He is watching you right now, transfixed by the sight of your beautiful body beneath my hands. Let's give him something to remember."

Kira bent forward, and Jessica held her pussy lips open. Shy made a whimpering sound and rubbed the tips of her breasts over Kira's fingers. Behind them Bryan groaned a moment before Jessica's tongue lapped at Kira's slit. Going on tiptoes, Kira struggled to keep from instantly coming. She had a feeling having any orgasm without Bryan's permission would be bad. Still, it was hard as hell to keep from undulating her hips against Jessica's skilled mouth.

Shit, could that woman eat pussy.

Long, slow licks followed by the other woman's tongue circling Kira's increasingly swollen clit had her dancing on her toes. Jessica would pause every few seconds to lean back, and Kira was pretty sure she was showing Kira's pussy to Bryan. Jessica began to massage the skin around her entrance, bringing more blood to that area and awakening new nerves. When her full lips wrapped around Kira's clit and sucked hard, Kira couldn't help but scream out her pleasure.

"Jessica, move."

Before she could mourn the loss of Jessica's mouth, a tiny bite of pain hit her right butt cheek, something akin to being stung by a bee. She almost lost her grip on the statue, but Shy was there, steadying her and giving her a much-needed anchor. Another stinging pop, this time on her left cheek. It was almost like getting bit by her lord, those sharp nips that hurt like a motherfucker but faded to warm pleasure when he finally touched her.

Two more pops coupled with a long, stinging stripe against her upper thighs. Oddly enough it wasn't a hard strike, more like a caress. Her fear drained out of her as he worked her body, the blows coming harder, her pussy getting wetter. Soon she was panting and crying out with each kiss of his whip.

Shy smoothed Kira's hair back again. "You look so beautiful. There isn't a man or woman watching this scene that doesn't want to be yours or possess you."

Kira imagined what they looked like to the people watching above, her pale skin now probably red and pink, his muscled chest flexing and straining with each strike of the whip. Shy's body arched next to hers, pale and tiny with a little heart-shaped ass. Kira wondered if Shy was as aroused as she seemed to be.

Dragging in a breath, she managed to whisper, "Are you wet?"

Shy gave her startled smile and laughed. "I'm wet enough to take my Mistress's fist right now."

Before Kira could formulate a response, the hits became more rapid, crisscrossing each other and adding an almost unbearable pain. He snapped her where he'd already struck earlier, and she screamed at the burning sensation.

Shy quickly spoke up. "Mercy, my lord. She'd hurt herself to please you."

Before the words had even left the other woman's mouth, Bryan's energy brushed against Kira a moment before his cool hand ran down her ass cheek. "Beautiful. And so aroused I can smell it."

"Please, my lord. I want you. Please make me come."

"Turn around and put your arms behind your head."

Moving was harder than she anticipated, first because her fingers felt stuck to the statue's grip, and second because she was very fearful of what he would do to her pussy and breasts. There wasn't a doubt in her mind he could resist the lure of kissing her flesh there with his strikes. The scent of the lotion and her perfume mingled with her sweat filled her as she took a deep breath and turned.

He was magnificent. There was no other word for it. The moment she saw him, a fierce pride and joy filled her that this man was hers as surely as she was his. If it took the rest of her life to get his collar back, she would do whatever it took. He wore his leather pants and nothing else, his bare chest slicked with a faint gleam of sweat. The savage twist of his smile undid her, and she licked her lips.

Looking away, he took a step back and cracked the whip, making her flinch. His first strike caught her unprepared as she glanced up to see if she could figure out how many people were witnessing this intimate moment between them. And it was intimate, if unconventional. She trusted this man to beat her with a weapon that could scar, maim, or kill her if used with the wrong intent. But he used it to bring her pain and then push her over into intense pleasure.

She wanted him, oh so much.

Shy grasped her wrists and pulled her back a little bit, holding her in place.

The sting on her hip merged with the ones on her ass until her front burned as much as her back. His last two strikes caught her right on the tip of each nipple, and she fisted her hands in her hair to keep from falling from the pain. A moment later he was before her, his lips latched on to her burning nipple, sending exquisite anguish and pleasure through her, overloading her mind and sending her deep within herself.

The cool stone of the statue hit her back, and she leaned against it for support as his gentle tongue laved the burning skin, making her whimper. Shy kept her stretched, open for his touch like Kira had no ownership of her body. Never in a million years did she think she'd be doing something so kinky, but fucking hell, it felt divine.

She snapped her hips forward when he switched to the other breast and sucked gently, sending a firestorm through her blood. She relaxed further, trusting them to hold her. Shy began to place featherlight kisses over her palms, each as soft as rabbit's fur. What turned Kira on the most, sent her the deepest into relaxation was the way Bryan was touching her. Fierce, but with reverence. He didn't just suck her tits. He lavished her breasts with his teeth and tongue. Her whole body contracted when he sucked hard, and she moaned. Normally all this stimulation and pain would have been too much, but here, in her dark place, she was cocooned and floating.

When his thumb brushed her clit, she thrust her hips forward, inviting him to stroke, to touch, to do whatever he wanted with her body as long as he made her come. Teasing her entrance with his fingers while his thumb ran circles around her clit, her sheath ached to be filled. She lowered herself the slightest bit, and the tip of his finger entered her, making her almost limp with pleasure.

He stroked her entrance, massaging her from the inside out, slowly working his way deeper. Anticipating the pain didn't kill her desire like it normally would because she was already in pain. The burn of his body rubbing against her various marks overloaded her nervous system, and when he added a second finger, she undulated against him.

Shy whispered right in Kira's ear, "Look at the way he touches you. Amazing. You mesmerize him with your responses, your body, with your submissive soul."

The thought of his affection for her being obvious to everyone but her ricocheted through her head and tore up some long-held beliefs. She wasn't alone in her feelings for him. Thank God, because she could easily see herself falling in love with Bryan. The I-will-never-leave-you kind of love.

"Oh, please. Please, my lord. May I come?"

"Not yet."

For an eternity he tormented her with slow and steady strokes of his fingers in her very wet pussy. Then he hooked them like he was making a come-here gesture inside her and rubbed the top part of her vagina hard. His thumb pressed down on her clit, and her body raced toward release. Unable to stop herself, she came apart with a scream, coming all over his fingers, gripping the digits with her delicate muscles, shaking apart beneath his touch.

Shy released her hands, and Kira wrapped them around Bryan, hugging him to her and rejoicing in the ability to finally touch him. She'd done it. She'd not only found pleasure from his whipping, but he'd also managed to penetrate her with his fingers. Her orgasm still hummed through her skin, moving through her muscles like slowly shifting sands.

Exquisite.

All the pain from the whipping, all the soreness in her tight muscles became a part of the orgasm, adding a sharp edge to her release that burned away all the tension in her body and mind, leaving her floating in a state of ecstasy. He braced her with his free arm and kissed her hard, sucking on her tongue, eating her fading cries from between her swollen lips. She was surrounded by him, inside and out, taken by this man in every sense of the word.

Everything relaxed, and she found herself sliding out of his arms.

With a chuckle he caught her and hauled her back up. "Whoa. Once you're recovered, I'm going to have to punish you for coming without my permission, love."

She could barely nod, her mind and soul disconnected from her physical form and mixing with his essence. Almost of their own accord, her eyes closed, and she gave up trying to think and let the darkness carry her away. She could lose herself in the sensations of her body, give up every ounce of control, because Bryan was here, and he would keep her safe.

CHAPTER TEN

On the wide and sumptuous four-poster bed, Kira snored softly, one arm flung out beside her head and her legs askew beneath a thin green silk sheet. They were in one of the club's safe rooms, soothing places where overstimulated subs could be taken and coddled. Bryan sat in a chair next to the bed, studying the woman who'd completely thrown him for a loop. His emotions seesawed between awe at her courage and fear for her safety.

He'd seen before Shy warned him during the whipping that Kira was reaching the point when she should have used her safe word, but his stubborn sub had ignored her own body's danger signs. Right now he should be walking out the door and finding some Dom to take over her training that could make her safeword out. Bryan wasn't sure if she wouldn't say stop with him because she did indeed trust him or if her adrenaline-junkie nature made her push herself past her comfort zone so often that she didn't really know when she was putting herself in physical danger. And he cared about her too much to push her to the breaking point, unable to abuse the gift of her trust. Yep, he needed to get out now while he could, for both their sakes.

Unfortunately his heart threatened to quit working every time he even thought about leaving her side.

They were in a fuck of a mess.

Glancing at his watch, he decided he'd let her sleep long enough. It was time to put another layer of salve on her welt marks and address the other elephant in the room. He'd managed to penetrate her with two fingers, and while that was nowhere near the size of his cock, it was a start. He should be happy about that. He couldn't help but wonder if he'd ever be able to have vanilla sex with Kira. He sighed and rubbed his face. After all the kinky fuckery he'd indulged in, who would have ever thought he'd actually crave the intimacy of traditional lovemaking.

That's not to say he wouldn't want her tied up while they did it, but he wanted that connection with her. He wanted her to see him not just as her Master and her man. He was falling for her, hard, but loving her would be exposing himself to the paparazzi again. He'd done some Internet searches on his lovely lady, and she was active in the charity scene. She even had a foundation, rewarding underprivileged children with the chance to go to high school abroad for a year. With running a foundation came the responsibility of fundraising, and if they started dating, he would be expected to attend with her.

How long would it take for the media to realize who he was?

Kira shifted and rolled over to her side, revealing the welts crisscrossing her fair skin. Now a new worry surfaced. Was he the monster the media said he was for enjoying the sight of his marks on her fair skin? Everything he'd been raised to believe said hitting a woman was wrong, hurting a woman a sin, but in his soul, it felt right. Not that he would go around randomly whipping women, but when he found a masochist who had chemistry with him, they were like a lock and key fitting together.

Pulling his head out of the muck of his thoughts, he picked up the jar of herbal salve and sat down on the bed next to Kira, the mattress dipping beneath his weight. She made a sleepy protest and rolled onto her stomach. He tugged the sheet down, revealing her back and the swell of her buttocks. More angry lines here and the starburst kisses of the tip of the whip. She'd bruise. He worried about her reaction when she looked in a mirror in a few days.

Most women would freak out at their body turning black-and-blue, but would Kira? She'd certainly been banged up enough during her stuntwoman days to know what would happen to her fair skin when she took some hits. Truth be told, he didn't like seeing how far she'd let him go. He'd only intended to give her a very light, superficial beating, but once they were engaged in the scene, his mind had shifted to a higher level where he wanted to push her a little bit more, prove to her that the pain was worth the pleasure, that he could make her feel good even as she hurt.

Before she'd passed out, he was pretty sure she was flying deep in subspace, and her orgasm had been spectacular. Hopefully it had been enough to start conditioning her to accept pain from him, to associate it with intense pleasure. The memory of the way she strained against him, the scent of her pussy and the feel of her sent a hard throb of need that tightened his balls. And her cunt, God, she'd been so tight and hot around his fingers. His dick ached with the need to fuck her.

He took a generous amount of the balm onto his fingers and began to spread it over her back in careful strokes. When he reached the top rise of her arse, he looked up at her face and found her watching him. Her beautiful sherry-brown eyes brightened, and a soft smile curved her lips.

"Hi." Her voice came out rough and husky.

"Hi, yourself." He began to massage the lotion into her abused buttocks, and his cock twitched at the softness and heat of her skin beneath his hands. "How do you feel?"

"Amazing and awful at the same time."

His gut clenched, and he forced himself to keep his hands moving. "How awful?"

"Nothing I can't handle."

Now he did pause and gave her undivided attention. "Kira, why didn't you safeword out?"

"What? Why would I?"

"Because I was getting near the point of no return with you." Her confused look made him want to tear his hair out, but it wasn't her fault she didn't understand. "Look, in my experience, there is a point during pain play where it becomes too much for the body to handle and you pass out. If that happens, it means I've totally ignored your needs in favor of my own pleasures, and for a Dom, that is unacceptable."

"But I wasn't anywhere near that point."

"Yes, you were. I saw it, Shy saw it, and I bet everyone in the gallery saw it as well."

"Don't worry. I can handle anything you want to do to me."

"That's the point. I don't want you to handle. I want you to enjoy. I want to be able to trust you enough to make you walk the edge, but I can't because you refuse to tell me when you're about to fall. In fact, I'm not even sure you know when it's too much for your body to handle. You've been pushing yourself from one extreme to another for so long that your body's normal ability to signal when it's in danger is ignored by your mind."

She started to push up and yelped when he gently smacked her butt. "With all due respect, Mr. High-and-Mighty, I think I know myself better than you do."

He was tempted to smack her bum harder this time, but they needed to talk about this and he wanted her to speak her mind. "Do you? Then answer me this, Kira. How many times has your foolhardiness put you in the hospital? How many times have your friends and family had to receive phone calls about you getting in some accident or another that could have easily killed you? How many times have your parents been unable to sleep because of their worry about you?"

Her wounded look hurt more than any whipping he'd ever had. "It's not like I do it on purpose. They're accidents. Accidents happen to everyone."

"Yes, they do, but they happen a lot more to people who don't recognize true danger."

Her hurt turned to defensive anger. "That's really ironic coming from a man who just whipped me. Maybe you're a prime example of my inability to recognize danger."

Fighting to keep his own temper under control, he moved down her body and started to work on her thighs. "Maybe I am. The question is are you strong enough to walk away from me?"

She turned beneath him, coming to her knees with a painful groan and facing him with the sheet pulled up to her chest. "Are you dumping me?"

He was all ready to say yes, to do them both a favor and end this now, but when he looked into her eyes, the thought of never seeing her again was beyond intolerable. "No." He sighed and scooted her closer so he could hold her stiff body. "I'm afraid that's no longer an option for me. But if you were wise, you would leave me."

"What do you mean?" She tried to push away to look at him, but he held her close, savoring her warmth and trying to keep from pressing too hard on her welts.

"I mean, love, that I'm at your mercy."

She socked him lightly in the side. "I swear to fucking God, Buddha, and Superman, if you don't start making sense soon, I'm going to take a whip to you."

"Perish the thought." He hesitated, then chided himself that if he ever wanted her to be honest with him, he had to make that first step. "It means, Kira, that I would do anything to make you happy. Isn't that what men do for women they fancy?"

"You fancy me?" Her voice grew thick on the last word, and she buried her face against the side of his throat, rubbing her lips back and forth along the sensitive skin over his jugular.

"No. I'm telling you that so I get the pleasure of having you constantly pass out on me." He ignored her unflattering muttering. "What I'm saying is I'd like to see how this goes, but I can't do that if I'm constantly worried that you're going to allow me to push you too far. I can't live like that."

She let out a long sigh and gently pushed back so she was on her knees again, facing him. She searched his face and finally nodded. "Okay, I'll try. But how will I know when it's too much? I mean, seriously, so far everything we've done together has been awesome from my side. Like better than drugs. If my friends back in Hollywood knew about you, I'd have to cut some bitches."

"Charming."

"Thank you." She titled her head. "So where does this leave us?"

"Well, I was hoping you might consider stepping out with me sometime."

A teasing grin curved her pretty lips. "Why, my lord, are you asking me on a date?"

"Brat. Yes, I'm asking you on a date." Fuck, if he didn't feel like a schoolboy asking a girl out for the first time.

She began to slowly take the pins out of her hair with her free hand, an exaggerated thoughtful expression crossing her face. "I don't know… I mean, it could be quite embarrassing to have to kneel next to your chair during dinner. What would the waiters say? Would they leave a bowl on the floor for me, or would I starve while you ate?"

"If you weren't so sore, I'd beat you."

She laughed and shook her head, the mass of burning-ember hair spilling down her back and over her shoulders. "But no, seriously. If we're out in public, would you expect me to treat you like my Master?"

"I'd expect you to treat me like your man."

"My man." She gave him a coquettish look. "I rather like the sound of that."

"Don't get too carried away. If you act like a brat in public, I will punish you for it in private."

She fluttered her lashes at him and let the top of the sheet slip a bit, then winced. "Ow. My nipples are on fire."

"How is the rest of you?"

Her gaze unfocused. "Good. I mean, I hurt, but nothing I can't handle."

"I don't want you to 'handle' it. I want the truth."

"That is the truth. Bryan, I'm not some delicate English rose. I'm more like a kudzu vine."

"A what?"

"It's a vine that grows down south in the States and is practically impossible to get rid of unless goats eat it. Look, my point is despite my being of the female persuasion, I'm not a girlie girl."

Her tough expression was adorable. "I find you to be very feminine, soft, and delicious." He traced his fingertips over the top of her breasts before she swatted them away.

"Hey now. We're having an adult conversation here."

The flush of her chest distracted him. "Mmm-hmm."

"I'm serious. I was a professional stuntwoman, Bryan. I'm tough. In fact I'd say I'm tougher than most men. I could probably kick your ass."

He rolled his eyes. "You're misunderstanding me. I know how strong and courageous you are. What I want you to understand is that you don't have anything to prove to me. It won't make me think any better of you if you endure being whipped to the bone. In fact, it would make me downright ill to hurt you like that."

Her shoulders slumped a bit, and she toyed with the edge of a pillow. Looking away, she said in a soft voice, "But I want to please you."

Women had to be one of the most frustrating creatures God ever made.

Or his ultimate joke on men.

He reached out and stroked her hair over her shoulder, knowing that at the very least the touch of a Master always brought comfort to a submissive. And Kira was submissive. Maybe not to anyone else, but to him she would surrender most of her control. Not all, and he didn't expect her to do that so early into their relationship.

"Kira, you don't have to guess as to what pleases me. Do as I say. And I say that if you don't start using your safe word, I won't scene with you anymore."

"You won't see me anymore?" Her head whipped up, and her beautiful eyes filled with tears.

"No, woman. I said I won't *scene* with you anymore. As in I won't play BDSM games with you, I won't allow you in my dungeon, and I won't allow you to put me into situations where I might hurt you because of your foolish pride."

"Oh." She scrunched her brows down and gave him an adorable irritated pout. "I don't have foolish pride."

He merely looked at her until she lowered her gaze. "Which brings us back to the present. Foolish pride aside, is there anything you need right now?"

For a moment she was silent; then she let out a soft huff of air. "Fine. My nipples feel like someone has taken a cheese grater to them, my ass feels like it was dragged across the pavement, and I have a feeling all of these welts you left all over me are going to make wearing anything that touches my skin for the next few days painful. But you know what? All of that is trivial compared to what you gave me."

"And what's that?"

She closed the space between him, wrapping her arms around his neck and letting the sheet fall. "An amazing experience. Beyond anything I could have ever imagined. But I have a question for you."

"Go on."

"Well, if you're asking me out on a date, meaning, like, we'll be dating and stuff"—she ignored his snort—"I'll be willing to make the terrible sacrifice of playing with women for your pleasure, but if I see one submissive touch you, I may need you to bail me out of jail for beating some skank ass."

"Charming again, but I happen to agree. Seeing you with Jessica and Shy tonight, watching how they enhanced your pleasure, it was very arousing for me. Consider yourself the lucky girl. The sole focus of everyone's attention. But if it had been another man touching you, I would have whipped the shit out of him."

"Good, so we're both territorial psychopaths, and I will make the ultimate sacrifice of being your sexual plaything." She nibbled on his neck, sending bright sparks of pleasure through is body. "But, my lord, I haven't been a very good submissive."

"No kidding."

"Hey!" She nipped his earlobe. "I'm trying to offer you an amazing blowjob and maybe something more here."

He stroked her face and shoulders, avoiding the hot skin where his whip had struck. "You can't offer something that isn't yours to give."

"Oh, so we're back in Master/slave mode now, are we?"

"Love, the instant you call me 'my lord,' I know you want to play. So don't use those words unless you're ready for the consequences."

Her body softened against him, making his balls tighten. "My lord, would you please use the hole of your choice for your pleasure"

Lust slammed, hard and fast, into him. He wanted to fuck her, he wanted to make love to her, he wanted to have sex until she couldn't walk straight, but he didn't want to hurt her. "Kira..."

"Please, just try. When you touched me after the whipping, it felt so good, but I wanted more. I wanted your cock inside of me, stroking me, making me come with you deep inside."

His muscles fairly shook with the tension of not taking her right there.

"No. That would be a reward, and I won't reward you for endangering yourself." She pouted at him. "I want you lying on your back with your head hanging slightly off the edge of the bed."

She gave him a curious look and crawled over to the edge. He moved quickly after her, sliding off the silk sheet and helping her carefully turn over onto her back. For a long moment he admired her body, the lush softness, the pink welts, the deep red nipples still hard and begging for his touch.

"Part your legs."

At the first glimpse of the pink within, he leaned over and laved her clit, quickly made the bud harden beneath his tongue. While pleasuring her, he pleased himself by touching the slightly raised welts, the differentiation between the heated skin and the cooler skin around the damaged areas. The harder he touched her with his hands, the more he ate at her pussy until her breathy cries echoed through the room. This was an important part of her training, making her body associate pleasure with pain. Almost like Pavlov's dog salivating at the sound of a dinner bell, her body would become aroused by his painful touch.

Sucking at her pussy lips, holding them between his teeth and biting down, he felt the telltale tension fill her frame, her shoulders lifting from the bed as the muscles of her stomach grew tight.

Pulling away, he blew on her exquisite cunt and smiled as she moaned. "Lovely."

The taste of her filled his mouth, and his cock ached to be sucked. Kira gave him an accusatory look that he ignored, but wisely didn't complain. Lifting her hair from beneath her, he let it flow down the edge of her bed. A few minor adjustments as to how far her head was tipped back, and he had her at the perfect angle for a good, deep throat fuck. In this position he didn't have to worry about her gagging as much, only cutting off her air.

Knowing Kira's propensity for courting danger, she'd probably like that too. He'd have to keep an eye on her to make sure she didn't pass out, a recurring theme in his life right now.

He tapped her lips. "Open up, love. I'm going to fuck your mouth hard and fast. This isn't for your pleasure. This is for your punishment."

A full-body shiver made her breasts wobble becomingly. "Yes, my lord."

She opened for him, and he paused to rub the precum on the tip of his dick around her lips, making them shiny and slick. The hot puff of air from her sigh made the nerve endings flare to life. Not giving her time to do anything more than tease the slit of his cock with her tongue, he slid into her mouth and paused.

He pulled his prick away, stroking it until a fat drop hung from his piercing. "Put your hand on my thigh. I'm going to cut off your air with my cock, and if you begin to feel faint, I want you to squeeze three times in rapid succession. Do it now."

She did as he asked, and he shoved his way down her throat. She coughed and clutched his thighs with both hands but didn't squeeze. While she struggled to take him, he reveled in the convulsions of her throat, gripping him in a manner similar to the strong contractions of a pussy when he'd fucked his sub to orgasm. It felt so bloody good, but he pulled back out and watched her take a deep breath and cough.

"Take my dick into your mouth and suck on the tip of it like a pacifier. It will help your coughing."

He dipped back down so she could wrap her lips around the head. The hot, wet suction and feeling of her tongue stroking rhythmically had his balls tight with the need to come. Every now and then, she'd become fascinated by the hoop going through the head of his cock, making his toes curl with pleasure.

Holy fucking shit, could his girl suck dick.

The need to rut, to plunge his hips became overwhelming, and he stopped her with a pinch to her sore nipple. "Open your throat for me, Kira. Let me in. Please your lord."

She nodded and opened her mouth wide. He slid in slower this time, toying with her nipple and making her hips lift and lower. The way she was rubbing her thighs together would lead to her orgasming soon, and that wasn't going to happen.

"Open your legs." He reached over and slapped her thigh, shoving himself even farther down her convulsing throat.

The hard suction of her mouth as he pulled back made spots dance around the edge of his vision. Grasping her face between his hands, he began to plunge in and out, giving her a moment to breathe in between each thrust, then removing himself completely and making her lick his balls.

Laving his sac, she then pleaded with him in a rough voice. "Please, my lord, please let me swallow your seed."

Unable to deny himself any longer without making his dick explode from too much blood filling it, he fisted the base of his shaft and began to thrust into her mouth again. With his hand in the way, he kept from totally cutting off her air while being able to enjoy the hot clench of the back of her throat for brief periods. Kira began to thrust her hips into the air as if someone were fucking her, and she gripped his thighs hard enough that he wondered if he'd be the one wearing the bruises for once.

In and out, the slick massaging of her clever tongue, the visual treat of her breasts jiggling with his thrusts, all those wonderful sights and sensations mixing together in a way that drove him mad with lust. Fuck, he loved real breasts. The way they moved made him want to take her all the harder. The bright red tips of her tits begged for his touch, and he grabbed a handful of her breast with his free hand, stroking his thumb over the nipple.

Now her hips snapped, and the groan that vibrated through her mouth and into his shaft undid him. He quickly removed his fist from around his cock and placed his fingers against her throat, a second before he pushed all the way in. The combination of her struggle to take him, the feeling of his cock against his fingertips separated only by the thin walls of her throat, and the scent of her need all blended together into an amazing electricity that burned. Everything inside him stilled, coiled like a spring, and then released in an explosion of lust. The first spurt of cum down her throat felt so fucking good. He rocked in and out with each blast, pleasure suffusing all the nerves and cells of his being.

Panting, he eased out until once again only the head was between her lips. She gently laved him, nuzzling his balls with the tip of her nose and making a happy, purring sound. He pulled himself away and almost stumbled as his knees wobbled. Laying back on the bed next to her, his semihard cock resting on his stomach, he let out an exhausted laugh.

"You could give lessons on how to suck a dick."

The mattress shifted as she crawled next to him and draped herself over his body. "My lord was pleased?"

There was no doubting the smugness in her tone, but damned if she didn't have the right to feel proud of her skills. "Yes, Kira. You pleased your lord very much."

She pushed herself up and smiled down at him. "Would my lord like to return the favor?"

"Nope." He laughed at her irritated look. "Are you free tomorrow?"

"I have some things to do in the morning, but my afternoon is free."

He traced his fingertip over her back, pleased to note the balm was doing its job and her welts had returned to smooth, if red, skin. "Come over to my house at 4 p.m."

She fluttered her lashes at him. "Are you asking me on a date?"

He pinched her butt. "Brat."

"Ow. Well, okay, but keep in mind that I'll be a little tender tomorrow."

"Mmm, I love it when you're tender. Makes everything that much more intense for you."

"Sadist."

"Yep."

CHAPTER ELEVEN

Leaning back against his motorcycle, Bryan let the sun's warmth beat down on him, loosening his muscles and relaxing him. Today was the day he'd make his first attempt to help Kira accept him into her body, and he wanted it to be perfect. He'd set up a surprise for her, something he hoped would bring her joy. They'd need to ride on his motorcycle to get there, which was why he was currently outside detailing his bike until it gleamed. He'd picked his black Harley-Davidson Low Rider, imagining how it would feel to have the wind in his face and Kira holding on to his back.

She'd blown him away last night, and every time he thought about it, he got that tightening in his chest.

If he didn't know better, he'd think he was falling in love.

Rubbing the seat of his bike, he turned that thought over in his mind, not sure if he liked it. If he fell in love with Kira, he'd be exposing himself to great risk. She was wild, unpredictable, and not someone he could ever imagine controlling outside of the dungeon. Not the kind of woman who would ever be satisfied playing it safe, that was one thing he was sure of. Kira always had been and always would be a risk taker, something he absolutely wasn't.

The memory of her fainting on him last night sent a bolt of muscle-tightening apprehension through him. She'd been flying way down in subspace, to the point where her mind checked out altogether. For a brief, horrible moment, he thought he'd hurt her, really hurt her, and he'd mentally crucified himself for it.

As soon as he'd carried Kira to the staging room, Mistress Jennifer and Master Oak, one of the many members who were also doctors, met him. They quickly determined that Kira was fine, just sleeping. She'd briefly surface if they forced her but only to swear at them for waking her up. Thank God, because if she hadn't, he would have been in a world of misery.

The ringtone for a text from Lawrence rang on Bryan's phone, and he pulled it out of his pocket.

Mz KH r lte. B hur soon.

His mind translated the other man's text to mean: *Miss Kira Harmony is running late. She'll be here soon.*

Lawrence had taken a liking to Kira and in his own subtle way let Bryan know it. He knew Lawrence wished Bryan had someone in his life, but up until this point Bryan hadn't found anyone that really clicked with him. That is until he met Kira. As polar opposites as they were on some things, like safety and self-control, something about her just fit with him. What had started out as helping a submissive had turned into a lot more. He wasn't sure if he liked how much of a hold Kira already had on his life after having only met, but damned if he wasn't looking forward to seeing her...more than he'd looked forward to anything in a long time.

A *ding* sounded through the yard, his alarm system's indication that someone had entered the front gate. Bryan tossed the rag down and stretched, then started toward the front of the house. Before he rounded the corner to the drive, he ran his hands through his hair and took a deep breath. He couldn't wait to touch her, suddenly starved for her company, dying for her kiss.

The drive came into view, and he frowned at the brief sight of a silver Mercedes Benz. When the car pulled into his drive, he looked through the windshield and saw an older man in the driver's seat while Kira sat in the back. The man got out and opened the back door, giving Kira a hand as she exited the vehicle. Today she wore a pair of jeans that made him want to grab her ass in the worst way, and a pretty button-down green top that contrasted perfectly with her burning-red hair. She briefly spoke with the man, who got back into the car and drove off.

Wondering what the fuck was going on, Bryan started toward his beautiful girl.

THE WARM SUMMER sunshine caressed the exposed skin of her face and arms, and she took a deep breath, feeling so incredibly alive. Her day had been terrible so far, and she was looking forward to forgetting about her driver's license getting suspended for too many speeding tickets. As state-of-the-art as her radar detector was, she'd been caught by cameras doing 102 mph on the freeway. That had put her over the allowed amount of points on her license in a year's time. The judge had been less than impressed with her reasoning that it was after two in the morning and the freeway was practically empty.

So now, or at least for the next three months, she was carless, and that absolutely sucked.

As she looked up at Bryan's house, she wondered what wonderfully wicked things they'd be doing today. Anticipation hummed through her, an impatience to not only see her lord but to serve him. Whatever happened tonight, she wanted to give herself to him in all ways.

To finally please him like a real woman.

Ignoring the way her stomach lurched at the thought, even as her pussy began to swell with desire, she started to make her way to the front steps. Before she reached the house, Bryan's voice rang out over the courtyard.

"Kira, over here."

He waved to her from the other end of the house, and the whole world seemed to brighten. Clad in a pair of worn jeans almost the same faded blue as the ones she wore, he looked good enough to eat. A dark brown T-shirt clung to his muscled form, and oh God, how she wanted to feel the fringe of his beard against her lips as they kissed. A smile lit him from within. It was nice to see she wasn't the only one acting goofy. Attempting to be cool, calm, and collected, she managed to keep from skipping over to him, but it was an effort.

Then he held open his arms, and she gave up all pretenses of being an adult.

Running into his embrace, she then threw herself at him and began to cover his chin and neck in kisses. With a soft laugh, he captured her face and held her still so he could give her a slow, thorough kiss that left her wet—well, wetter—and panting. The warmth in his gaze when he looked down at her made her heart pound.

"I'm glad to see you too, love." He released her and gave her a serious look. "Mind telling me who that bloke was driving you here?"

"My driver." She winced, knowing he wasn't going to like the answer. Not after all his talk about being reckless. "I...well, I kinda got my license suspended for three months for too many speeding tickets."

His nostrils flared, and he said in a low, dangerous voice, "What the hell are you doing speeding like that?"

Stung and feeling a tad bit guilty, she fired back, "What's the big deal? I know how to drive. I've never been in a car accident. Hell, the only reason they caught me this time is because of those sneaky fucking cameras they have now."

Cupping her chin, he made her meet his eyes. Oh, he was so angry, but his touch was gentle and beneath that anger was a great deal of worry. She should know what that looked like. It was the same look her parents had worn since the day she started to crawl. He took a deep breath, visibly struggling to swallow his anger. "Kira, this is not a movie. This is the real world, and in the real world accidents happen."

"But—"

His grip on her chin tightened just the faintest bit. "Listen to me. I don't doubt your driving skills. You are an amazing daredevil, and I'm in awe of your reaction time. I worry about the car being driven by some idiot on a cell phone. You're coming up on him at a hundred miles an hour, and he gets distracted, swerving into your lane at just the wrong moment. At lower speeds, you would have been able to avoid the crash."

Not liking that he was right, she jerked her chin out of his hand and took a step back. "I'll call my driver. Sorry to have spoiled your day."

He reached out a hand to stop her. "Don't you know what it would do to me if anything happened to you? You mean a great deal to me, but I don't know if I can be with someone who constantly puts themselves at risk. I lie awake at night worrying about you. Do you know how odd that is for me? I feel like some old woman fretting about her wayward daughter, and I don't like it."

To her shocked amusement, he ran his hands through his hair and grabbed tight, then let go. It was something she'd seen her father do on a regular basis when she was growing up. She called it his "Sonic the Worry Hog" look. Before she could stop herself, she giggled, and he looked up at her like she'd gone mad. "You find this funny?"

"I'm sorry. It's just that you totally reminded me of my dad for a second there."

He gave her a baffled look, his hair an unruly mess from his hands. "I'm failing to make the connection."

She sighed and closed the distance between them, resting her head against his stiff body. At least she had a lot of practice apologizing for worrying people who cared about her. "I didn't mean to stress you out."

The solid mass of his chest lifted beneath her cheek as he took a deep breath. "When I think of all the terrible things that could have happened to you, it drives me crazy. I can't keep you safe if you're so determined to get yourself killed."

She pulled his arms around her. In a fucked-up way, knowing he worried about her and wanted to keep her safe made her feel happy and loved. "Can we pretend everything is okay? I really want to spend the day with you, my lord, but I'll understand if you want a rain check. I am sorry and I do know better than to speed and I am aware of just how dangerous it is. I just get carried away sometimes."

His hold on her relaxed, and he cuddled her to his chest, kissing the side of her head. "You drive me bug fuck."

With a smile, she turned her face to his chest and nibbled on his pectoral muscle. "Then you should punish me for being such a naughty girl."

He barked out a laugh. "Remember you said that. I won't say I completely forgive you for being so utterly reckless, but there is no place in the world I'd rather be than with you today."

She looked up at him and fluttered her eyelashes, then took a step back. "So what do you have planned for us?"

He started following the curve of the drive around to the side of the house. "Come with me. I have a surprise for you."

Anticipating some type of kinky outdoor bondage arena, she followed him, then stopped dead in her tracks when she saw what sat in the drive that led to his ten-door garage.

A beautiful black motorcycle.

She froze, fear roaring down on her. Phantom pains shot through her pelvis, ribs, arm, and shoulder. Nausea pushed a burst of bile up her throat, and she staggered back a step, unable to take a breath. True, the motorcycle in front of her was a touring bike instead of the street racers she used to favor, but that didn't matter to her mind.

"Come here, Kira."

She tore her eyes away from the bike and stared at Bryan, praying he wouldn't want her to go for a ride. His dark brows drew down, and he held out his hand. Reluctantly she grasped it, absently noting how warm his hand felt.

Pulling her closer and turning her away from the motorcycle, he rubbed her back. "Bad memories?"

Unable to speak, she nodded and rested her head on his shoulder, letting him support her, because she would end up on her ass soon if her legs didn't stop shaking.

"Talk to me, love. Have you been on a bike since your accident?"

"No."

"Not once?"

"No."

"Oh, sweetheart. I'm sorry. I should have asked you first. Please forgive me."

"Nothing to forgive." She swallowed hard and tried to still the panic by forcing her mind to think about something else. "So you ride?"

"Yes. After that bullshit in England, my parents banished me to the States—"

She held up her hand. "Wait? They *banished* you? People still do that?"

"Unfortunately, yes. They didn't call it that, but my father purchased this home and gave me the deed, while my mother gave me money to start up a business. They even managed to get my green card approved in record time." The faint lines around his eyes deepened. "The sooner I was gone, the quicker they could pretend I didn't exist. My scandal had put a real damper on their ability to get invited to parties."

Pain rolled off him in almost visible waves, and she once again flung her arms around him. She couldn't imagine anyone ever disowning their child because of a sex tape. The very idea just struck her as ludicrous, and she marveled at how different the world she grew up in was from Bryan's upbringing. Wanting to turn his mind to good memories, she cleared her throat. "So you bought a bike while you were over here?"

"Yep, the beast behind you is the first bike I bought in the US. I spent the next seven months driving across the States, going to both cities and small towns. Your country is an amazing place with its variety of people and habitats. It's like traveling to different worlds. And the freedom you have here just blows my mind. When I rode through Europe, Africa, and the Middle East, I always had to keep in mind that some of the areas I'd be driving through weren't exactly stable."

She grinned up at him. "That sounds like so much fun."

He gave her a bemused smile. "Did you ever go on long rides?"

"Yeah." She leaned away, and he supported her with his hands around her lower back. They fit together so well, her body curving into his as if they'd been made for each other. "I used to love riding up and down the California Coastal Highway. All that beautiful ocean and sunset views that would shatter your heart with their beauty. Nothing quite like being exposed to the elements, surrounded by nature rather than a car frame. Thought I'll admit I always stopped at a high-end hotel for the night and would usually get a massage. Man, that was fun."

He hugged her closer. "Maybe someday we'll ride together. I'd love to show you this bed-and-breakfast I found outside of Yellowstone Park. They have these hot-tub suites that are situated so you get the best sunset view you've ever seen."

An ache developed in her heart, a yearning for what she used to have, the freedom that was now missing from her life thanks to her stupid need for speed. "I'd like that."

He took a deep breath, then rubbed his lips against her temple. "Do you miss it? Riding on your motorcycle?"

Did she miss it? Of course she did. Memories of being young, beautiful, and carefree while racing through LA and Hollywood on her pink custom street bike played through her mind like a movie. She'd felt so invincible back then.

So happy.

Fuck yeah, she missed it, but she'd chickened out of every attempt to ride again.

"I do."

"That's what I thought. You know, I watched one of your movies today."

Happiness and the ever-present actor's inability to believe their own worth mixed within her. "Which one?"

"*Red Devil*, the one where you were in Hong Kong playing the role of a woman trying to stop a drug-smuggling ring."

"What did you think?"

"That I can't believe such an amazing, brave, talented woman is mine."

She leaned up and gave him a hard kiss on the lips. "Thank you."

"Don't thank me yet. You might not like what I have to say next."

She tried to keep from looking over her shoulder at the motorcycle, knowing where he was going with this. "Please, my lord, I don't want to drive it. Not now, not here. Please let us have a nice day together that doesn't end with me throwing up all over your beautiful bike."

"Do you trust me?" He stroked his knuckles over her cheek. "By the way, you called me 'my lord.'"

She tried to give him a seductive smile, but by the way the fine lines around his eyes crinkled, she didn't think it was working. "How about we go to the dungeon instead? You can shove hot pokers up my ass or something."

He laughed, a rich sound that soothed her frazzled nerves. "Tempting, but no. I have something I'd like to try. Hang on."

"Bryan, my lord, please. I don't want to do this. Don't make me do this."

"I'm not going to make you do anything you don't like. I have a backup vehicle we can use." His smile faltered for a moment, and he shook his head. "I can't believe I'm doing this. You must swear to secrecy that you will not reveal to anyone, ever, what I'm about to do."

Giggling at his sudden playful turn, relieved he wasn't going to push her into something she really didn't want to do, she nodded and pantomimed zipping her lips.

He gave her that devastating grin of his, then turned and began to walk away from her. She stared after him, admiring his ass in those jeans as he moved quickly toward an enormous ten-bay garage. Trying to keep from getting freaked out by the motorcycle, she looked around, and a flash of pink caught her eye. When she looked closer, some of her nerves fled on a tide of giggles. There, sitting next to an enormous pile of pads and other safety gear, sat a beautiful baby-doll-pink helmet.

Almost exactly like the one she used to have.

Nostalgia moved through her in a warm, bittersweet wave. Without being aware of even deciding to move, she found herself in front of the helmet and picked it up, turning it this way and that in the sunlight. On the back, done in small purple script, was her name. Well, that settled any thoughts she'd had that he might keep a pink helmet around for other female guests to use. Running her fingers over the smooth surface of the helmet, she felt bad that she wouldn't get to use it. Out of the corner of her eye, she glanced at the motorcycle, and her stomach gave a nauseous lurch.

Yeah, that wasn't going to happen anytime soon.

An engine started up in the garage, and she clutched her helmet, afraid of what Bryan was going to try and get her to ride. When she caught sight of Bryan behind the wheel of a golf cart painted like the Union Jack flag, she burst out laughing. He scowled at her and drove up, then stepped out of the golf cart.

His jaw firmed, and he crossed his arms. "It's not mine. It's Lawrence's."

"Sweet baby Jesus. That looks like something Austin Powers would drive."

He glared at her. "Piss off. I'm doing this for you. Even though you are a spoiled brat."

She laughed harder at the sight of his big, bad, sadistic ass standing in front of such an almost whimsical vehicle. Her giggles subsided as she thought about the implications of his words. He must really like her.

A lot.

Once he was sure he had her attention, he lifted his chin and gave her that growly Dom voice of his that melted her panties. "Unbutton your shirt."

The thought of being naked in public was very naughty and very arousing. Still, she had to play a little hard to get. It was so much fun. "What? People can see me!"

"No. I'm the only one who can see you. Trust me, Kira, and take off your shirt before I rip it off."

Fumbling with her buttons, she managed to get two undone before he did as he'd threatened, much to her delight. His tanned hands gripped the front of her pale green shirt and tore, sending buttons flying. A second later, he eased the cups of her bra down, revealing her swollen nipples. The heat of the sun on her pale skin was nothing compared to the blast of desire in his gaze. Her clit throbbed, and she pressed her thighs together in a vain effort to relieve the ache.

"Oh, that is pretty." He stood back, and she reached up to pull the cups back in place. "Hands down."

She did as he asked, praying to every god and goddess she could think of that no one saw her like this. Now if they were in Wicked, that might be different. She rather liked holding the attention of that many handsome Masters and beautiful Mistresses. It reminded her of the high she got from acting. And frankly, doing anything with Bryan aroused her into almost a frenzy of need.

Licking his thumb, he then brought it down to her exposed breast and ever so lightly traced the areola. Shit, it stung, but the more he touched, the more the sting became something else, something hot and dirty. She bit her lower lip and let the sensations he evoked take over. Abandoning herself to his touch, his care, was a decadent pleasure she'd begun to crave.

Feeling wanton, she arched her back, offering him whatever he wanted to take. A moment later the edge of his beard brushed her left nipple. She winced at the abrasive sensation. Then his tongue laved the tip of her breast, and she cried out. His rumble of satisfaction aroused her almost as much as his touch.

When he pulled back, she was panting. "Now, my sweet girl, into the golf cart."

She crossed her arms over her chest, plumping up her breasts for his hungry gaze, and teasing him with a little roll to her hips as she walked. "As my lord wishes."

He swatted her ass as she went by him; then he grabbed her arm. "Hold on one moment."

To her surprise, he stripped off his shirt and gave it to her. "I don't want you to catch a chill."

Grinning, she slipped his shirt on, the warmth of his skin and his scent still trapped in the fabric. She took a deep breath, then sat down in the golf cart, holding on to the side as he climbed in and started it up. She looked down and noticed the wheels on the golf cart were slightly oversize, more like those on an ATV.

They went down a gravel road that split off to a dirt road and another gravel road. He turned onto the packed-dirt road, and she took a deep breath, loving the smell of the forest they were driving into.

She leaned her head against his shoulder. "Where is this road taking us?"

"Your surprise."

She smiled against him and turned so she could spread gentle kisses over his bicep. Smooth and sun-warmed flesh passed beneath her lips, and she marveled at how different men's skin was from women's. The way his muscles tensed beneath her mouth made her giggle, and she realized she wasn't scared anymore.

He looked down at her. "You know, I think I can actually feel my testosterone level drop driving this thing."

She licked her lips. "I can help you out with that."

He gave her a feral grin. "Oh, I'm sure you can. But not here. It would scar me for life to think of Lawrence sitting where we had sex."

Laughing, she snuggled closer to him, casually touching him and just enjoying being with him. She was happy, really happy for the first time in what seemed like forever. That thought struck her as both sad and wonderful. Sad because she'd been so unhappy for so long; wonderful because she felt like she now valued her happiness more. She wanted to hug Bryan, to squeeze him tight and thank him for making her feel this way, but she didn't want to sound like a goober.

After maybe ten minutes, they pulled up to what looked to be a small cottage that belonged in a book of fairy tales. With stone walls and an English garden out front, it was one of the most charming things she'd ever seen. The little building sat among a stand of weeping willows, and it had a clay chimney pipe with a slight lean that extended off the roof. Behind the cottage and down a slight hill, she heard the rumbling of water, and she could smell a river.

Bemused by Bryan owning such a whimsical building, she arched a brow at him. "I never would have pegged you as the kind of guy who had a secret enchanted cottage."

He shrugged. "It came with the house. I've remodeled the inside to suit my purposes."

"You know, if you ever have children, they're going to want this for their own."

"Not bloody likely. I have no desire to have children." He snorted. "Can you picture me as a father? Because I certainly can't."

Surprised and slightly hurt for some odd reason, she got out of the golf cart and ran her fingers through her hair. "Never?"

"Never. Why would I? I like my life as it is. No worrying about Junior falling down the stairs and breaking his head or having some kid wake up at three a.m. to throw up on me. No way, and no thanks. I like my freedom, and I like my sanity."

"Wow, when you say it like that, kids don't sound very fun."

He shrugged and said in a low, almost sad voice, "Not everyone wants to be a parent or is meant to be. I'm just honest enough to admit it."

His words made her heart ache, and she kissed between his shoulders, wanting to lighten the mood. "For what it's worth, I think you'd make a good dad. But, on to happier thoughts: what's inside the cottage?"

"A surprise."

She scowled at him. "I can't believe my ass is sore from that little ride."

He snorted. "That's what she said."

Rolling her eyes, she moved closer to the cottage. "Really? We've dropped to that level of humor?"

She'd no sooner reached the small stone step at the front door than his energy poured over her a moment before he grabbed her wrists in both hands and spun her around. Removing his shirt from her body with more care than he'd shown her clothing, he soon had her bare-chested. "Take off your pants, everything. I want you naked and available to me."

She kicked off her shoes and pulled off her socks. After tugging down her jeans and stepping out of them, she pulled her panties down as well and added her bra to the pile. He growled, and her body gave an answering gush of moisture. A warm, deep throb started low in her belly. The delicious rush of adrenaline that accompanied him dominating her burst through her body like an intoxicating drug.

"Turn around."

She did as he asked, all too aware of how closely he watched her and slightly embarrassed by her body's imperfections. He'd seen her up close and personal before, just never in this bright a light. Firming her spine, she tried to let her anxiety go. This was Bryan. He adored her body.

His touch ghosted over the healing bruises and fading welts. "You have beautiful markings, love. Each one of them a testament to my ownership, a brand anyone can see marking you as mine. Raise your hair off your neck and don't move."

She complied, and a moment later, something cold and smooth snaked around her neck. It didn't take her long to realize he was putting his collar back on her. Emotion filled her until her breath caught in her throat. He trusted her, he wanted her, and she loved him.

Tears spilled from her cheeks as the realization came crashing over her.

Oh fucking hell, she'd fallen in love with him.

It had happened so quick, been so unplanned that she wasn't sure how to deal with it. But the marvelous feeling of the first blush of love spread through her, warmer than the sun. The collar tightened around her throat, not enough to be uncomfortable but enough so she was aware of it, aware of willingly wearing his collar, his mark of ownership.

She was his submissive, and she couldn't be happier.

After securing the collar, he carefully turned her and wiped the tears off her cheeks.

"Are you all right, love? Feeling a bit overwhelmed?" She nodded and sniffed. "We'll take care of you in a minute. Give me your wrists."

He picked up a pair of brown leather cuffs lined with sheepskin on the inside. They had two big brass rings, and when he bound each wrist in turn, she noticed how heavy and substantial they felt. These weren't pretty, decorative cuffs. These cuffs were meant for bondage. She couldn't wait to see what Bryan had in store for her.

"Spread your legs."

She quickly did, remembering how not so long ago his command would have shocked her instead of arousing her. Through some kind of magic he'd tapped into desires she didn't even know she had, but now that she'd found this kind of connection, she couldn't imagine how she'd ever live without it again.

Another pair of cuffs went around her ankles, and he paused to kiss her mound, his tongue snaking out and licking her slit. "Fucking delicious. I plan on eating a great deal of this pussy today."

She could only moan in response and quiver as he blew warm air onto her bare mound.

After standing, he took off his boots on the porch. Clad in only his worn jeans, he opened the door and led her into what looked like one big bedroom. Well, there might have been something other than the bed in here, but all she could do was focus on the huge, amazing, and terrifying stainless-steel four-poster bed dominating the room.

A canopy of steel grids topped the bed, and chains of various lengths hung from several points of the frame, dangling down to the bed below. There were big hoops attached at intervals to the posts of the bed, and after trying to figure out why they were there, it dawned on her the bed would be used for pretty much any kind of restraint her Master could want.

"Oh my. Is that from the Martha Stewart prison collection?"

He pinched one of the red marks on her bottom. "On the bed, Kira. I want you on your back."

She clambered onto the high bed, the white silk sheets slippery beneath her as she moved to the center of the heavenly mattress. Maybe after they were done, she could talk Bryan into napping out here. Birdsong and the rush of the river came through the open windows; the sheets smelled faintly of vanilla. When she rolled over onto her back, she couldn't help but sigh. Everything felt so good, and she was so incredibly alive. Outside the air took on the golden quality she loved. Lots of movies were shot in this perfect lighting for a reason.

It sure as shit made Bryan look good.

He stalked up to the bed with bundles of black rope in either hand. Tossing them onto the bed, he pulled out a pocket knife. The sunlight created delicious valleys and shadows over his lean, muscular frame, and she appreciated the hard work and dedication it took to keep himself in shape. It also made him feel oh so masculine when he pressed into her, and his obvious appreciation of her plump curves made her more confident than she'd felt in years.

After cutting two lengths of rope, he reached up and grabbed one of the chains. As he pulled it down, additional chain spooled out from somewhere hidden in the canopy.

"Right arm."

She lifted her hand, and he grabbed her wrist, snapping the chain to the cuffs with a solid snick.

"Other arm."

This continued for a good ten minutes, him requesting only movement from her and expecting complete compliance. He focused on his work as he checked the tautness of the chains, the circulation around her wrist and ankles, then made sure nothing was going to get pulled or strained. So even though she was literally chained up and at his mercy, she felt safe.

He paused next to her head. After staring at her for a long moment, he began to open his jeans. Her instinctive reaction was to reach for him, but the jangle of the chains brought her up short. Why the hell did he hardly ever allow her to touch him? She barely suppressed a frown as she looked back at Bryan.

Obviously he read her intent, because his lips curved into his devilish smile that meant she was in trouble.

"What's your safe word?"

"Pookie."

"What word do you use when you need to slow down?"

"Yellow."

"Good girl. I expect you to use them and will be very, very unhappy if you push yourself too far."

He tugged his jeans down so they rode below his hips, the tendon leading from his hip to his groin standing out from the curve of his body. Beneath he wore a pair of tight blue cotton briefs, and her whole body clenched at the sight of precum darkening the fabric over the tip of his cock. She used to think she'd never like a man's strong cum, that she'd always prefer the sweet taste of a woman, but once again Bryan had proved her wrong. Sucking him off, feeling him empty himself down her burning throat, had been an incredible turn-on.

"Open."

Grateful for the chance to please him, she eagerly sucked on him as he pushed his way into her mouth, his harsh groans sending an answering wetness between her legs. Her widespread legs that revealed every fold of her pussy to him. God, she couldn't even manage to feel embarrassed about being tied up and laid out before him like a human sacrifice. His ravenous reaction to her body shoved all doubts aside, leaving her feeling wanton. The collar pressed against her neck, and she thought about how pretty she must look to him, adorned in his jewels while taking his cock.

The chains clanked as she shifted her hips and kept pushing her mouth down over his cock. Because of her angle, she couldn't get him as deep as she had yesterday, but at least this time she didn't gag. The ring through the head of his cock was fun to play with, and she loved the way he'd thrust his hips when she tugged on it. She worshipped him with her mouth, her tongue, trying to tell him with her touch how much he meant to her.

"Shit, you're too bloody good at that." With a regretful mutter, Bryan pulled himself from her lips. He fisted his cock and massaged out a fat drop of precum. It clung to the curve of his piercing, and she groaned.

"Open."

She did, and he moved onto the bed next to her head. Slowly jerking his cock, he milked himself until more precum came out, enough to send one luscious drop into her mouth. She moaned and sucked on the salty liquid, loving the taste of his arousal. He tasted like sex.

He moved off the bed again and removed his pants. She bit her lower lip as he bent to pick something up, his ass flexing in a delicious way and his heavy sac hanging between his thighs, tempting her. When he stood, he had a small basket with a dark cloth over it.

"Close your eyes."

Trying to keep from pouting, she did and tensed when the bed dipped. Before she could prepare herself, she felt something gently pushing at the entrance to her sheath, something big, something warm, and something with a piercing.

His dick.

Her womb clenched down, and she wanted to cry with frustration. "Yellow. I'm so sorry, my lord. Yellow."

Instead of sounding pissed, his voice was incredibly kind when he said, "Kira, open your eyes."

She did, and a tear spilled down her cheek. "Yes, my lord."

"Good girl. This is how it's going to work. I'm going to have my cock inside of you. That is not something you have a choice over unless you decide to use your safe word. Don't fret, love. We're going to make sure you are very, very ready for me. Every time you say yellow, we stop, I make you come, and then we continue."

She stared up at him. "That doesn't sound very sadistic."

He grinned, but his gaze was soft as he stroked her spread thighs. "I'll take care of your needs. All of them."

Before she could respond, he'd laid down on his stomach and began to rub his goatee against the top of her slit. Pinching her labia together, he forced her clit to pop out of its little hood. Licking at the exposed nub while rolling her pussy lips, he quickly sent her into an intense orgasm. The angry throb in her womb subsided, and she once again yearned to be filled by him.

Holding her gaze, he fisted himself and slowly rubbed the head of his cock over her entrance, making her writhe against him. He fed just the tip of his dick into her, and her vagina clamped down like it was trying to suck him in. The relaxation of her orgasm faded, replaced now by an urge to take him more, deeper, now.

He eased a little bit more into her, working probably about two inches of his fat cock into her tight sheath. The uncomfortable tensing of her womb started again.

"Yellow."

He immediately pulled out and pinched her nipple, making her groan. "Good girl."

After mercilessly stimulating her clit to orgasm with a vibrator, he once again pushed himself in, deeper this time. Holding still, not forcing the issue, he took in a deep breath. Sweat stood out on his body, a silent testament to how hard he was fighting to be gentle with her. Moving her hips the littlest bit, she began to rise up to meet him, and he was almost all the way in when she began to tense up.

"Yellow."

His savage snarl as he pulled out both scared and thrilled her, almost as much as the dangerous look in his eye when he grabbed more rope. Moving quickly, the bobbing tip of his enormous erection slick with her fluids, he unhooked both of her legs. She stretched, but her relief was short-lived. He took her left leg and, pressing her ankle toward her butt, wrapped the black rope around it five times and left a small length of rope hanging down her inner thigh.

"If you feel any numbness, let me know."

"Yes, my lord."

He repeated the action with her other leg and sat back to survey his work. "Very pretty. But you need more."

He reached into the basket again and pulled out what looked like black clothespins. He tied the rope to each, shifting it around until it was the length he desired. She had no clue what he was going to do with it, but when he was finally satisfied with one side and moved to put the clamp on the other piece of rope, she realized what he intended to clamp with those pins.

"Oh, oh no, my lord. Please no."

"Silence."

He slapped her inner thigh, and part of his hit went over a healing welt. Her yowl of pain made him smile, and she raised her head up, watching in dismay as he grasped her right labia and clamped it with the clothespin. As if that wasn't bad enough, because of the short rope holding the clothespin to her leg, it pulled her labia open, exposing her to Bryan's gaze more fully.

It was so kinky, so dirty.

She loved it.

He did the other side, then leaned back on his haunches, his cock bobbing against his belly. "There we go. Nice and open for me."

He moved forward and braced his hands on either side of her head, the solid mass of his arms begging for her touch. Above her the chains clinked as she fought their hold, wanting to touch him so badly. He pressed his pelvis down and rocked the head of his cock over her fully exposed clit.

The sensation was intense, almost maddening in its delicious, sensual torture. Her mind began to shut down to focus only on the slow rub of his dick and the movement of his balls against her pussy. She was probably soaking him with her arousal right now, and she wanted to lick it off, to clean him and make him groan.

Reaching between them, Bryan took his cock in his hand and began to slap the tip on her clit. She arched and tried to buck him off, the direct contact hurting. He didn't relent, just tapping at her exposed bud until she began to anticipate the sting followed by the rush of pleasure. The erotic noise of his cock hitting against her wetness merged into the other stimulation, creating a dark hole of pleasure that she began to fall down. No, not fall, more like slide.

As always Bryan was a master at playing her body, and soon her cries of pain became moans of pleasure, his touch teasing and tormenting. She begged him to make her come, that she'd do anything for him. He reached back and pushed her knees up, the clothespins tugging at her labia in a new direction and awakening more nerves to this painful pleasure. Grasping her thighs together, he rammed his cock over her pussy, sliding between her slick, pinned lips, rubbing her clit. The collar around her throat pressed down as she raised her head to watch.

"Come for me, my little slave."

His rough words pitched her into the abyss, and she came hard. Her whole body shook and jerked, the spasms of her release making her blind with pleasure. He patted her pussy, sending a shiver through her body, before pulling off the clothespins. This sent two lightning bolts of pain through her poor sex. He made hushing noises while she whimpered. A moment later, the pressure on her legs eased, and she opened her eyes to find he'd cut her legs free.

Watching her carefully, he massaged her tight thigh muscles, all the tension melting away. Four good, mind-blowing orgasms combined with the endorphin rush of the pain had set her adrift, floating in the sky and only tethered to the earth by his will. She smiled at him, almost euphoric with happiness, and he grinned back.

"Good girl."

He repositioned himself between her thighs and pressed forward. This time she welcomed the kiss of his prick against her entrance, the gradual push and filling. There was pain—how could there not be after four years of no sex?—but it wasn't the horrible contraction-type pain. This was the pain of her body being forced to accommodate a man, her lord. She continued to drift, her limbs slack and her breathing deep.

She felt so full, so good, so connected to him. He shifted against her, and she sighed.

"Kira, look at me."

Opening her eyes was a struggle, but she managed and was rewarded by him smiling down at her. "I'm in all the way, love."

She contracted her vaginal muscles, and he sucked in a harsh breath. Oh, fuck yeah. He was in all the way, filling her and making her complete. Reaching up, he then unhooked her hands and drew them over his neck.

"Hold on."

The slow drag of his cock out of her gripping channel was delicious torture, but nothing compared to the pleasure of his erection pushing back in again. He kept the rhythm easy, pinning her hips when she tried to respond, not letting her do anything but grasp onto his shoulders. The movement of his body beneath her hands, the scent of their combined musk in the air, and the fierce lust in his gaze started a quickening within her that demanded more.

"Harder, my lord, please."

He didn't move any faster, but he seemed to push farther until the head of his cock pressed against a dense area deep within her. She desperately took a deep breath of air and let it out when he withdrew, tingles racing through her. The rough scraping of his chest hair against her nipples, the ache from her labia where it had been clamped, and the fading welts from his whipping all marched into a painfully beautiful whirlwind that stole her breath.

He captured her mouth in a kiss, sucking her tongue, murmuring wicked things against her lips, things he wanted to do to her, things he wanted her to do to him. Some of them shocked her, but others made her cunt clench in anticipation.

"You feel so good. Hot and tight. Your little pussy is trying to milk my cock. My perfect girl."

Joy mixed with her pleasure, and she reveled in the ability to finally give this part of herself to him, to finally be able to enjoy sex again. Oh, how she'd missed the intimacy of looking into her lover's eyes as her orgasm approached, something she did now.

Fighting to get the words out as her body wound tighter and tighter, she groaned out, "My lord, may I come?"

"Yes."

He sat up and began to drive harder into her, adding more pain to the mix. As doped up on adrenaline and endorphins as she was, he could have fucked her bowlegged, and she'd be begging for more. He began to massage her clit with his thumb, and she panted, straining against him, almost there.

"Come. Give it to me. Your Master demands it."

He pinched her clit and rolled it between his fingers, setting off her release again. This time it was hard, long, and earthshaking. He continued to thrust into her, his own breathing growing ragged. After a dozen hard poundings that made her feel stuffed full of his cock up to her throat, he stilled, then groaned and emptied himself deep within her. The jerk of his cock inside her body, the knowledge that she was giving him the most pleasure a woman could give a man, moved Kira in a profound way.

They lay pressed together, their bodies cooling and their breaths returning to normal. He slowly withdrew, tensing as she clamped down on him. "Mother of God."

"Oh, thank you, my lord."

She rained kisses down on every inch of his skin that she could. When she reached his pelvis, she recalled his harsh demands about licking her honey off his balls. Eager to please, feeling sensational and wanting this sense of ecstasy to never end, she moved onto the bed until her face was level with his balls and began to lick.

His cock twitched, filling more and more with each stroke of her tongue. Soon he was jerking his dick as she took his balls into her mouth one at a time, rolling them with her tongue. Her own body responded as if she was the one receiving oral sex, her pussy once again craving to be filled. Now that she knew she could have sex, finally, she was ravenous for it.

She wanted more.

Turning away from him, she went to all fours, her face down on the sheets and her ass up in the air, and gave a little wiggle. "Please, my lord. Take me as you wish."

He didn't question her, just moved into position behind her and guided himself into her eager pussy. "Bloody hell, woman. You're still as tight as a virgin."

She couldn't respond, too caught up in the long, slow slide of his cock into her waiting sheath. He reached her end sooner in this position and slowly pulsed his hips back and forth, rocking inside of her. "Touch your clit."

While she did, he traced and pressed on the healing whip marks covering her ass and hips, sending a harsh burn through her pleasure, a toe-curling sensation her mind quickly converted to pleasure. He pulled out and in, driving her higher, making her mad for him. Working her poor overstimulated clit, she whimpered with each thrust, tilting her hips to take more of him, to give him everything.

He increased the pace, shifting until he found an angle that made her writhe beneath him. His thrusts became harder, rougher, and she cried with the need to come.

"Having a hard time, love?"

"Yes, my lord. I've come so much I don't know if I can do it again."

"You can, and you will."

He spread her ass cheeks and spit down the crack, spreading the lubrication over her anus. Everything inside her tightened, her breath stilling as he continued to fuck her but also began to push his thumb into her ass. What must it look like from his position, to watch his thumb slide into her tight pink hole, all shiny from his spit?

It must have looked pretty fucking good because his erection swelled within her, and his breathing became ragged. He removed his thumb and thrust in two fingers, stretching her with a burn that lit a fuse inside her. A few more hard thrusts of his fingers and she pushed up onto her hands, slamming herself back into him.

The orgasm started deep in the pit of her belly, a terrific tension that threatened to break both her body and mind if not released.

"I'm going to come, my little slave. Going to fill you up again with my seed."

The thought of him feeling as good as she did, of being on the same precipice with her, gave her the edge she needed to finally come. She screamed as her release blasted out of her body and into her mind, blinding her with pleasure. He gripped her hips and ground himself against her buttocks, kneading her flesh while his cock jerked inside of her, spilling more semen into her, marking her as his in the most primal way possible.

She collapsed, her arms giving out, and Bryan grunted as he rolled off her. Reaching out, she then laced her fingers with his and held his hand. He stroked the back of her hand with his thumb, and she let herself be carried away by the tide of fading endorphins and complete relaxation.

CHAPTER TWELVE

The tiny seed pearls dangling from the edge of Kira's mask tickled her skin with their cool kiss. Tonight her outfit for her first trip back to Wicked as Bryan's submissive consisted of a sheer black robe and some chain-and-harness contraption Bryan had picked out. It made her feel like she was constantly being touched as the chains rolled with her movements. A section of chains draped over her bare breasts, and she rather liked the way her lord's gaze would grow darker as he examined her chest with a proprietary look. More silver chains hung between the pearls on her black silk mask, and they reminded her of what it felt like to be chained to her lord's magnificent play bed.

They'd spent the last two and a half months at either her place or his, making kinky, hot love every night and usually spending the days together as well. Kira's sister had initially been none too happy with the arrangement. Mary Kate made it a point to stop by often and poison the atmosphere with her presence. Bryan put up with it to a certain point, then very politely asked to speak to her sister in private. They hadn't had any problems after that, and Mary Kate had actually had them over for dinner at her home so Bryan could meet Kira's nieces and nephews.

Kira had already told her parents about the sex-tape scandal, though Bryan didn't know that. They'd been shocked, but when she'd shown all the charities he supported, all the work he'd done with setting up his own company and how he worked together with Jesse to help bring technology to third-world countries, they'd been impressed. Unlike Bryan's parents, her mom and dad were very liberal, and it took a great deal to shock them. After all, they had her as a daughter, so they couldn't exactly cast stones about people being caught doing things society didn't approve of. Not to say they loved the pictures of twenty-one-year-old Kira smoking a joint while sunbathing topless with her boyfriend, but they hadn't disowned her over it.

It also helped that her mother went faint at the notion of her daughter dating a lord. Kira was pretty sure her mother would have forgiven Bryan for pretty much anything, including murder, as long as she could say her daughter was dating *royalty*. Because everyone knows royal blood can't be bought.

Shaking her head to clear it of her mother's voice, she returned her gaze to her lord. They were in the main private dance section of the club, and boy howdy, was it rocking. The dance floor was what had once been the ballroom of the mansion. Now, the four levels above it had been cleared to the roof, and wrought-iron railings let people look down below. As if that wasn't crazy enough, there were four clear plastic cubes suspended over the dance floor, each attached to a different level of the club by a wrought-iron walkway, creating a lattice-like effect as she looked up. People were able to enter the rooms and have sex where everyone could see them, illuminated by the lights of the dance floor below.

Tearing her gaze away from a lesbian threesome, a Domme and two subs by the look of it, Kira stared out over the writhing bodies of the crowd. There were blue pillars in the middle of the floor that had velvet ropes the submissives could hold on to as their Master or Mistress did as they wished.

And wow, they wished a lot.

The scent of sex permeated the air, mixing with the smell of warm leather coming from Bryan's thigh next to her face. Around her neck lay what she liked to call her "in a committed relationship" collar from Bryan. The collar was actually a torque made of rose gold. Where the two heavy pieces of metal came together in the center, a large emerald dangled against the hollow of her throat. It amused her that the collar they used at home, the one she was comfortable with, was so much rougher than this one.

A leather strap with spikes and diamonds instead of delicate spun gold.

Mistress Jennifer strolled up with Shy in tow. "About time you two surfaced for air."

The women wore somewhat matching ensembles. Purple latex dresses in a pretty shade that reminded Kira of deep purple petunia petals. Where Mistress Jennifer's dress covered her from throat to almost her knees, portions of Shy's dress had been roughly cut out to reveal her pussy and nipples to the crowd. There was something extremely erotic about seeing Shy's pussy on display while her Mistress's body remained covered. It made the submissive look even more vulnerable than before.

Kira had been to Jennifer and Shy's home a couple of times with Bryan for dinner. The two women had been delighted that Bryan had finally found "his woman" and treated Kira like family. In an odd way, Jennifer and Shy were Bryan's family. They were his best friends, and he'd spent many a holiday with them.

While they hadn't played anything more kinky than poker together yet, the offer had been made to arrange a playdate for her and Shy together. Hell, Kira had wanted Shy since the time she'd helped Kira through her first whipping. What a mind-blowing night that had been. She glanced at Shy's face, memories of the other woman saying naughty things sizzling through her thoughts and body. Shy winked, and Kira looked away, embarrassed she'd been caught staring. Kira glanced up at Bryan, hoping he hadn't noticed, but that notion soon got blown out of the water.

"Kira, you've been rude and ignored Mistress Jennifer while staring at her submissive. Go greet Mistress Jennifer. Beg for her mercy."

She started to stand, but Bryan put his hand on her shoulder. "No. Crawl over, and after you have apologized, ask the good Mistress if you can have permission to kiss Shy's cunt. If you want to stare at her pussy, let me give you a better view."

Shock and desire lit Kira's body in flames. She and Bryan had done a lot in their time together, and he never failed to amaze her with his ability to make her feel wonderful. She'd done kinky things with him that would have shocked her in the past, but now she couldn't imagine living without. Before she knew it, she found herself crawling across the floor, too well trained to her lord's will these last ten weeks to disobey him.

Someone nearby laughed, and she heard a woman ask Bryan if his girl was available to play with. His answer got lost in the growing crowd, and Kira's cheeks burned hot with humiliation as she knelt before a bemused Mistress Jennifer. Parting her legs, she placed her hands on her thighs and lowered her gaze to the Mistress's boots.

"Please forgive me for my rudeness, Mistress."

With a soft laugh, Mistress Jennifer shifted her stance, widening her legs and projecting a power that floated over Kira's skin like snowflakes. Very different from her lord's burning presence, but pleasant.

"I believe your Master had further instructions as well, girl."

Pressing her hands against her legs, Kira tried to hide their nervous trembling. Adrenaline coursed through her veins, making her antsy. The crowd seemed to press in around them, drawn to her distress. Only the knowledge that Bryan was behind her, watching her, protecting her, gave Kira the courage to say the words. "Mistress, may I please have the pleasure of kissing your submissive's cunt?"

The toe of Mistress Jennifer's boot gleamed as she raised her foot and used it to lift Kira's chin in a limber move Kira envied. This angle also revealed Mistress Jennifer wasn't wearing panties, and her lovely pussy was covered with a fluffy down of blonde hair.

"You may." Shy shifted forward, but Mistress Jennifer stopped her with a slap to her exposed right breast. "Still."

Returning her formidable attention to Kira, Mistress Jennifer smiled. "As I was saying, you may, but Shy must keep her thighs pressed together as hard as she can. If you can make her orgasm despite the tight fit, I will let you pick out the size of the anal plug she'll have to wear for the rest of the night. If she can keep from coming for four minutes, then she gets to pick out the size of anal plug you will wear. And let me assure you, Kira, Shy will find the biggest hunk of metal she can to shove up your ass."

"Yes, Mistress." Kira's butthole clenched at the very idea, already sore from being pounded by Bryan last night as she shook with a series of full-body orgasms that left her speaking in tongues.

"Does that work for you?"

"Of course, Mistress."

The Dominatrix gave her a dry smile. "I was talking to your Master, girl."

Swallowing hard, she tried to ignore the laughter of those around her, whispers at how precious the innocent ones were. Most of the voices sounded friendly, but there were a few catty tones here and there that set her on edge. Bryan must have given his agreement because Mistress Jennifer gathered a handful of Kira's hair and forced her to scoot over and kneel before Shy. Kira had to brace her hands on the other woman's hips for support as Mistress Jennifer tightened her grip on Kira's hair.

"Stick your tongue out, girl. Oh, and Shy, after Kira picks out the plug she wants you to wear, I'm going to fist your ass, so you better hope she picks a big one."

Up this close, Kira could actually see Shy's pussy swell and quiver at Mistress Jennifer's words. While the idea of being fisted was intriguing when it was happening to Shy, Kira would run screaming her safe word if Bryan so much as mentioned it.

"Shy, pull your dress up and hold it at your waist."

Kira stuck out her tongue and shifted as Mistress Jennifer proceeded to use her face like a sex toy on Shy. There was something so impersonal about it. Kira wasn't sure how to feel. Usually she liked to take her time with a women, to work them up slowly, but the spicy musk of Shy's sex coated Kira's tongue, and she pressed her face closer, coaxing a groan out of Shy. The lack of control rankled her, and she struggled not to jerk away, not to fight the other woman's hold. If Bryan had been the one holding Kira's face to Shy's body, it would have been different, but Kira didn't have the same bond with Mistress Jennifer.

The Dominatrix laughed, then lowered her voice to a silken whisper. "Do you hear that? They're betting on who is going to come first, whose ass they'll get to see breeched. And Kira, your lord looks about ready to bust out of his leathers. You better be prepared for a hard fuck when this is over and he reasserts his claim on you."

With those words Mistress Jennifer managed to turn Kira's anxiety to arousal. Now it was Kira's turn to make needy sounds. Mistress Jennifer took her hand from Kira's hair and moved to stand behind Shy, pulling and pinching her nipples while Kira tried to work Shy's small clit from between her pussy lips. The other woman kept her thighs locked tight, but every time Mistress Jennifer pulled on her nipples, Shy would arch a bit and give Kira a chance to suckle on her clit.

The murmur of the crowd faded, and the focus of her world slowly narrowed into that inner peace she now craved. Submitting was like taking a vacation from life. Kira could just exist in a world of pleasure and delicious pain, safe and protected by her lord. While it was Mistress Jennifer and Shy touching her right now, the fact that they only did so at Bryan's sufferance made it hot. Her pussy was so wet she was afraid she would leave a wet spot on the floor before she was done.

"Two minutes," Bryan called out. "Come on, Kira. Make that pretty bitch scream. You know she's been dying for you to lick her."

Remembering how he liked to make her scream, Kira sucked the top of Shy's right labia into her mouth and bit down hard enough to sting. Shy responded with a full-body shudder and a moan of despair. Of course, Shy was a submissive. Kira knew from their conversations together that Shy was a masochist and loved pain. No wonder being gentle with the other woman wasn't working as well as it should.

Kira was used to vanilla sex between women, not this kinky shit.

Emboldened and rather liking how easily she was now working Shy up, Kira bit and sucked over every inch of soft flesh she could get to between the other woman's thighs. Shy trembled harder, her incoherent cries and begging for Kira to stop echoing in the room despite the loud music. With a harsh cry, Shy grabbed Kira's head and parted her thighs, shoving Kira's face against her sopping pussy.

Kira ate Shy like a ripe, juicy peach.

Within a matter of seconds, Shy began to cry out, and her little clit grew hard between Kira's teeth. She bit down, and Shy screamed, her body shaking with her orgasm. Kira began to pull back, but Mistress Jennifer stopped her.

"Keep nibbling her clit. She'll come over and over until you stop. Give her three orgasms."

Licking her way from the entrance to Shy's pussy all the way up to her hard nub, Kira did as Mistress Jennifer commanded and was rewarded by more of Shy's screams as she orgasmed. After the third, Kira wanted to come so badly she was tempted to touch herself.

Bryan's voice washed over her like a soothing balm, giving her something to hold on to before her desire swept her away. "Kira, come here."

She immediately removed her face from Shy's yummy sex and placed a soft kiss on the other woman's thigh before turning back to her lord.

Crawling toward him, she let him see her desire, her need for him. Ever since the first time they'd had vaginal intercourse, she'd been like a nymphomaniac, wanting him constantly.

He sat on the black leather couch like a king, relaxed among his peers but still radiating a strength and charisma that made him shine to her like a flame in the darkness. Compliments from the crowd about how well behaved she was, how beautiful, and how obedient all stroked her psyche in a warm caress. It reminded her of the adoration of her fans at a movie opening, a heady mix of disbelief that they were talking about her coupled with pride.

When she got close enough, he pulled her onto his lap, her thighs straddling his. Then he kissed her. She gave herself over to him, delighting in his hungry sounds as he licked the taste of Shy from her lips, and he kneaded her ass possessively. She belonged to him, and he took very, very good care of her.

The trust that came with that notion allowed her to relax and spread her legs wider when he reached between them to play with her pussy.

"Bloody hell, Kira. You're sopping wet."

She panted, straining to keep from rocking on his fingers. He slowly worked her pussy, massaging her labia and bringing more blood to the area until it felt like her sex was going to explode from the need. The entire time she held his gaze, knowing he liked to see her every reaction. Right now there were no secrets between them. Every wall she kept around herself to protect her heart from the rest of the world vanished before him, giving him an open path to her soul.

Mistress Jennifer leaned against the arm of the couch close enough to touch and watched Bryan work Kira into a frenzy. “I hate to interrupt before you give your girl her well-deserved orgasm, but Kira still needs to pick which anal plug Shy is going to wear.”

Bryan’s thumb halted right on top of Kira’s clit, and she shivered. “You are quite right. Kira, choose.” He turned her on his lap and tucked her up against his side.

There were seven club submissives standing before her in various states of dress, both men and women. Each held a closed gleaming wooden box. Almost in unison they opened the boxes, and the crowd that still gathered around them murmured. Inside each box on a bed of red velvet were gleaming silver butt plugs. The boxes were arranged so the submissive on her left held the smallest one, while the submissive on the right the largest.

Aware that the crowd was watching them and feeling the need to give them a good show, Kira turned her head to look at Bryan. “My lord, may I take a closer look?”

He nodded, and she stood, smoothing the diaphanous material of her robe over her curves and earning a little growl from her lord. Shy knelt off to the side, next to her Mistress, a content look on her face as Mistress Jennifer stroked Shy’s hair.

Biting her lower lip, Kira walked first to the smallest plug. The submissives kept their gazes lowered, allowing her to look her fill without being stared back at. When she reached the middle-sized plug, she paused as if considering but continued on. There were two plugs left. One almost as big as her closed fist and the other one the size of a fire hydrant. Okay, so maybe it wasn’t that big, but to Kira, it would be like trying to have a car park in her asshole. She couldn’t imagine Shy taking it without needing surgery afterward.

Kira turned back to Bryan and Mistress Jennifer, who were both watching her with small, almost identical devilish smiles.

She decided to play the moment up a bit. "Mistress Jennifer, you do plan on fisting your submissive tonight, don't you?"

Without hesitation, Kira took the second to largest plug with a sparkling blue crystal base. On impulse, she opened her mouth wide and slid the plug in, wrapping her lips around the slim part of the plug to hold it in place, sucking on it. Bryan almost jumped up from the couch but managed to restrain himself. God, she loved that, being able to drive him crazy with desire like he drove her insane with need. Her submission, her efforts to please him never failed to bring a positive reaction and she reveled in it.

Lowering herself as gracefully as she could to her knees, she crawled over the thick carpet to Mistress Jennifer. Behind her, one of the men made a soft, pained noise, and Kira shook her ass, earning another groan. According to society, she should feel ashamed and degraded. Good girls never, ever had sex with anyone but their husband behind closed doors with the lights off. Only sluts would do the kind of kinky play she was a part of now, or a damaged and weak-willed woman who craved abuse. But that wasn't the case. She felt alive and powerful in a way she'd never felt before. Here among Dominants strong enough to run entire countries using their charisma alone, she was the one who was making them feel good. Making their arousal spike and their collective attention hone in on her like a diamond lash.

Reaching Mistress Jennifer's feet, she sat back on her heels and let the other woman pull the anal plug from Kira's mouth.

Before Mistress Jennifer could say anything, Bryan reached over and pulled Kira to him until she knelt between his thighs. With lust blazing through him like a bonfire, he jerked his leathers open and brought out his cock. The veins on his erection stood out as he stroked himself once, gathering precum for her on the tip just how he liked it. To think, three months ago she would have been repulsed at the idea of eating his seed, but now she couldn't wait to make her lord come undone.

He put his arms back on the couch, an imperious figure looking down at her with complete control. "Suck me. You may use your hands and mouth."

She smiled at him, glad he was giving her the chance to prove her worth to him. Oh, she was more than aware of the jealous stares some of the submissives and Dominants were giving her. Lord Bryan was well-known within the club for his skills as a Dom, but Kira was the first woman to completely capture his attention like this.

Feeling territorial, Kira took as much of her lord down her throat as she could, enjoying his grunt of surprise at her aggression. She sucked him hard and fast, staking her own claim for all that were watching that he was her Dom, her Master, her lord, and she could please him better than anyone else.

All too soon Bryan jerked her up by the hair. "Enough."

His cock bobbed against her lips, and she sighed, making his thighs clench. "Yes, my lord."

With a slight grimace, he attempted to tuck himself back into his leathers. She waited patiently for him, knowing he would tell her what to do next, that she didn't have to guess his desires. From her right came a high feminine scream, and she looked over. Mistress Jennifer had Shy up on one of the tables and was shoving the fattest part of the anal plug into the submissive's stretched asshole.

It did not look fun at all.

Bryan leaned forward and whispered into Kira's ear, "Don't look so horrified, love. Shy and Jennifer have been together for three years, and Shy's body has been trained to take large objects."

"God have mercy. She's going to split in two, my lord."

He laughed. "She may be walking bowlegged, but do you really think Mistress Jennifer would hurt her? Think of how much care Jennifer took with you when you were injured because you didn't safeword out. Mistress Jennifer loves Shy and is giving her what she needs."

Kira considered this and nodded, feeling a bit less guilty about being the one who'd picked out the enormous plug. "I sincerely hope my lord never decides I need something like that in my ass."

He laughed and nipped her neck before leaning back. "Stand up and follow me."

She did as he commanded, and as they passed Shy, Bryan slapped the other woman's ass, earning a laugh from the crowd and a wail from poor Shy. They crossed the room quickly, with a dozen or so people trailing after them. Bryan didn't seem put off by their audience, but then again, he was probably used to that having been raised in the public eye.

They reached a white Lucite table in a corner of the room near the bar. It had metal rings going all the way around the edges and it didn't take her long to realize it was a bondage table. A shiver of apprehension went through her. When Bryan put her on the bondage table at home, it usually resulted in her becoming a sweaty, crying, blissed-out mess by the end of the scene. She wasn't sure if she liked the idea of being that undone in front of so many people. During the whipping scene, she'd had a sense of privacy from being unable to see those that were watching her. Now she could make eye contact with her observers, and she felt very exposed. In fact, the idea upset her, killing her desire and leaving her cold.

He tapped the surface, and she came to his side. Leaning close, she whispered, "Yellow, my lord."

Immediately he pulled her into a hug and kissed her forehead. "What is it that has you so scared, my beautiful girl?"

Now that he was asking her to vocalize her fears, she had a hard time putting those vague feelings to words. "I-I don't like the thought of people seeing me cry."

"Why?"

"It's...it's too personal." She swallowed and looked up at him, pleading with him not to make her do this even though her hedonistic side wondered how many orgasms he would give her. "My tears are only for you, my lord."

His mouth softened, and he stroked her cheek with his knuckles. "You are so sweet, but I'm afraid that won't get you out of this unless you wish to safeword out. What if I wanted to share your tears with the people watching? Of anyone on earth the members of Wicked would value your honest emotions for the treasure of submission that it is. There are some who have not had that experience in a very long time. I want share how beautiful you are when you submit, and I want you to show the other subs what wonderful things can happen if they trust their Dom. The people here watching us now are here because they value your submission. Look at all the other people and scenes they could be observing instead. Realize what a great compliment they are paying you with their attention."

She took a deep breath and tried to calm her racing pulse. From here, she could see that at various spots around them there were other scenes going on, including people openly fucking. Hell, poor Shy was somewhere in the area they'd left behind getting ready to be fisted in front of everyone. Kira thought about that and took a quick glance at the crowd watching her. All the chairs and couches surrounding them were now filled. While most of the Dominants had submissives at their feet, there were a few single Doms who watched her with a hunger that burned her from head to toe. Near the stage, two female submissives knelt together, apart from the crowd and totally focused on Kira and her lord. The yearning in the women's gazes made Kira's heart ache, and she realized anew how very lucky she was to have found Bryan.

It made Kira's worry of a few tears seem insignificant.

Besides, right now she'd given Bryan complete control of her to do with as he wished, and so far he hadn't disappointed her. And most importantly he'd never once pushed her beyond what she could endure. While he did work to expand her boundaries, if she said stop, everything stopped.

But she didn't want it to stop; she wanted more even if she was slightly embarrassed by her own very kinky needs.

"I trust you, my lord."

He smiled at her and gave her a soft kiss before murmuring against her lips, "The greatest gift any Master could ask for."

The deep bass of the music moved through her bones as he stepped back. He reached out and slid the robe from her shoulders, revealing her outfit of draping chains to the appreciative sounds of the people watching her. The top was shaped like a bikini, and the bottom links of dangling chains covered her like a skirt but hid absolutely nothing. In fact, she felt more naked with the chains than she would have in just her skin.

A breeze of cool air from one of the vents overhead kissed her, and her almost constantly sore nipples stiffened. She would have thought that with all of their rough play her nipples would have become used to the coarse treatment, but they seemed to be growing more sensitive to his touch. Right now she'd do anything he wanted for the chance to have his clever mouth on them, coaxing exquisitely painful sensations from her.

With a light, gentle touch, he began to remove her chain outfit until she was as naked as the day she was born. The pleased murmurs and compliments about her body from the nearby watchers warmed Kira from within. If she was being honest with herself and her desires, something Bryan greatly encouraged, she'd have to admit that she loved all the positive attention she was getting. In a weird way, it was a mixture of one of her worst nightmares and most erotic dreams.

When she'd been famous and had walked the red carpet quite frequently, she'd almost always have a dream before a big awards show about appearing nude on the red carpet, or having some kind of major wardrobe malfunction that would leave her naked before the massive crowd of photographers. Now she was naked before a crowd, but they liked her, and it was hard to be self-conscious about her nudity when all around her sat submissives in various states of undress. Deciding to play up to her audience, Kira turned and gave them a flirtatious smile.

Bryan softly laughed and stroked his hand down her back. "Careful, love. I don't want to have to stop to perform CPR if you give the Doms heart attacks."

He helped her onto the table, which immediately lit up with a rainbow of subdued colors beneath her.

Bryan must have caught her shocked looked, because he laughed. "The table responds to your movements, no matter how subtle. A nice tool for a Dominant to use while trying to teach a squirmy sub to stay still."

Trying to keep from squirming, she smiled up at him. "It's a good thing I'm so well behaved then, my lord."

The crowd laughed, and Bryan shook his head. "Brat. Let's see what we can do to test how well behaved you are."

He reached down around the side of the table and brought out a thick black leather strap. She tensed and he shook his head, giving her a small wink that showed that beneath his cold,

Dominant facade lay the man she'd grown to love. "Don't worry. I don't plan on beating you with this."

She gave him the best smile she could manage, and he took a moment to smooth her hair back from her face. Leaning down, he whispered in her ear, "Easy, love. If at any time you can't handle it, we stop. No big deal. This is, as always, about your pleasure."

"Thank you, my lord." She took a deep breath and let it out, missing Bryan's touch as he moved about.

He reached beneath the table and pulled out a bottle of oil and began to coat her skin with it. The scent of orange blossoms enveloped her, helping to relax her. With long, slow strokes, Bryan made sure every inch of her body was covered, and she sighed as he gave her a quick foot rub. Her Master knew just how to relax her, yet keep her aroused at the same time.

Using the hooks on each side of the strap, he fastened it to the table over her hips while leaving her pussy exposed. Another strap went over her rib cage below her breasts. He cinched it tight enough to hold her but not so tight she couldn't breathe. Next came a pair of cuffs on her wrists, secured to the rings next to her. When he put the ankle cuffs on her, he then spread her legs wide open and attached the cuffs to the table.

Completely tied down and at his mercy, she tried to fight the trembles shaking through her but couldn't manage to do anything more than pant. Blue, pink, and then purple light shifted beneath her, reminding her of being strapped to the Aurora Borealis. She felt vulnerable and wanted to be here less by the second. Bryan's soothing touch as he moved her helped center her and push away her panic. She'd been in much more precarious positions than this with her lord, and he'd kept her safe every time.

He came back so she could see him, and in his hand, he held a candelabra of different-colored candles. A big male submissive in a chain-mail loincloth moved into her line of sight, and Bryan handed the candelabra to him. Turning, Bryan nodded to someone behind her head. "Thank you, Master Finn, for lending me your submissive."

An older man's voice tickled over her like sharp electricity, the command in his tone undeniable. "Most welcome. Watching someone of your caliber break in a submissive is always a treat."

Bryan smiled, and when he looked back at Kira, the darkness in his gaze made her gasp. Oh, she knew that look. Part concentration, part excitement, and a whole bunch of lust. But underneath all those volatile emotions was a tenderness that had her whole body tingle with pleasure. She wanted to please him, to share the best experience possible for him as well. All she had to do was endure a little pain and do what he asked.

"Kira, I'm going to adorn your body with wax drippings. If you move and disrupt my work, I will be most displeased. If you manage to hold still, we'll be able to remove the drippings in one solid piece." He leaned over and gave her a soft kiss. "I would then take that mass of wax and have it framed and hung in my green room where I can look at it and remember this perfect moment with you."

She kissed him back, tickled pink about the idea of a part of her hanging among all that priceless and beautiful artwork. "Thank you, my lord."

"What's your safe word?"

"Pookie, but you know that, my lord."

"Yes, I know what it is, but I want you to know that everything that is about to happen is only occurring because you allow it. By using your safe word, you are giving both of us freedom. You the freedom to stop the scene at any time, and me the freedom to take you as deep into subspace as I can, to give you the most pleasure possible, without worry of injuring you or causing you harm. If at any moment you want this to stop, if it's too much, safeword out for me, love. I can't stand the thought of abusing your trust." The sincerity in his dark gaze made her melt.

She smiled up at him, his almost constant worry about her safety tugging at her heart. "Yes, my lord. I trust you."

Selecting a red candle, he moved out of her line of sight, and she tensed, her stomach a sour ball. She probably should have eaten more at dinner, but she'd been so keyed up she'd scarcely been able to do more than eat a few mouthfuls of her food. Now she regretted it because her stomach's churning increased to the point where a light sweat coated her skin.

A few moments later, a hot drop of wax dripped onto her leg. Hopefully it wouldn't leave a mark because they had a dinner party her parents were hosting tomorrow night. She was taking Bryan, and it would be their first public event out together. She would like to be able to wear something that didn't cover her from her ears to her toes.

She whispered, "My lord, no marks that can't be covered by my dress, please."

He looked up at her and gave her a small smile. "Don't worry, love. You may have a bit of redness tonight, but I won't leave any lasting marks that might raise questions. Now, hold still."

The burning trail moved up one leg and down the other, then across her belly and between her breasts. He hadn't gotten near any of her major erogenous zones yet, but that didn't stop the heavy arousal from setting in. She relaxed, giving him free rein to take her where he wanted her to go, because she knew that once the pain was over, the devastating pleasure would begin.

Bryan placed the red candle back and selected a white one. This time he started at her chest, and she could briefly watch the pooling of the wax at the top of the candle, then the careful drip. He didn't look at her face at all, concentrating intently on the way the wax dripped over her skin. He let a drop fall on her right nipple, and she couldn't help but scream. The table beneath her reacted to her movements, and bright yellow and red light splashed over Bryan, painting him in the color of flames. He leaned down and kissed her lips, seducing her with his mouth and turning the burn into a delicious, painful pleasure that started to shut down her thoughts and turn her attention solely to her body.

"Okay, love?"

Her clit throbbed to the beat of her heart, and she couldn't wait to have his mouth down there, his fingers, his cock. "God, yes. Don't stop."

After smiling at her, he resumed his task, dripping the wax down her other side in slow, controlled drops.

Next he grabbed a green candle, but this time, he let the wax fall on her left nipple, earning another scream.

Okay, that really fucking hurt, but she'd endured worse pain only to have Bryan make it into mind-dissolving pleasure. She just had to hang on until that happened.

She panted, trying to get past the pain, to get her body to switch it over.

He must have seen her struggle, because a moment later, his clever fingers were stroking through her exposed folds. He gathered some of her honey on his finger and spread it over her clit, dragging a groan from her. Pleasure finally began to overtake the pain, and she let out a shaky breath.

Still massaging her clit, he began to paint her belly with the green candle, sending little sizzles through her nerves that arched down to where he continued to toy with her.

All around them, the music pounded, and an odd taste filled her mouth. Before she could dwell too much on it, he began to drop the wax closer to her mound. Her breathing sped up. The anticipation was fair killing her, and she tried to breathe through the discomfort, but oh God, she knew it was going to hurt so badly. She held her breath and closed her eyes, willing herself to relax. She could do this; she just had to hold on a little bit longer, and that wonderful transformation would happen where he made her pain into pleasure.

Saliva filled her mouth, and her stomach lurched. Her legs and hands began to go numb, and all of her senses began to dull. Forcing her eyes open, she attempted to lift her head. Black dots swarmed the edges of her vision, like a thousand shadows converging on her. She tried to tell Bryan something was wrong, but by that point, it was too late.

Warmth surrounded her, and she snuggled closer, the smell of unfamiliar laundry detergent mixing with a men's cologne.

"Kira, please wake up."

The fear and the strain in Bryan's voice pulled her fully from the comfortable darkness. She opened her eyes and looked around. They were in what looked like a small, brightly lit medical room. An examination table sat to her right, and to her left a row of cabinets and a long counter. There was even an older African American man who looked like a doctor in a white lab coat.

Returning her gaze to Bryan, she found she was on his lap. A thick navy-blue blanket covered her, and Bryan's warmth cocooned her. She tried to remember how they got here, what had happened, but the last thing she could recall was getting up onto the bondage table.

"What happened?"

"Are you okay?" Bryan stared down at her, vacillating between worried and seriously pissed. "Why didn't you safeword out?"

"What?"

The doctor moved over next to them and put a hand on Bryan's shoulder. "Easy. Ms. Harmony, you're in the medical center at Wicked."

"Wicked has a medical center?"

"Yes, just to handle the small medical emergencies that tend to crop up during BDSM play." He gave Bryan's shoulder a squeeze and removed his hand. "Now, tell me, how do you feel?"

The command in his voice helped to clear her mind. "Nauseous and weak."

"You fainted, so that's to be expected. What's the last thing you remember?"

"Umm...Bryan, I mean my lord was strapping my hips down to the table, then...the last thing I clearly remember is him using the green candle on my chest. After that, it's all muzzy. Why did I faint?"

"Because you didn't safeword out," Bryan snapped. "Kira, why didn't you say something?"

She stared up at him, her anger kindling. "Look, I don't know what happened, but I swear I would have used my safe word if I knew I was going to pass out. I tried to say 'yellow,' but I couldn't get the words out."

Before Bryan could respond, the doctor interrupted. "Let's get you up on the examination table."

He did a routine series of tests, asked her a bunch of questions, then took a vial of blood with Bryan glaring at them the whole time. "Ms. Harmony, I'm going to have the lab run this to see if you're anemic. I'm pretty sure the reason you passed out is because of the excitement combined with your not eating a proper dinner."

When he said that last part, she felt like she'd been scolded by her dad. Pulling the blanket around her, she nodded. "I'm sorry."

The doctor smiled and patted her cheek. "I know you are, girl. You scared the shit out of your Master. I thought I was going to have to give him CPR when he noticed you'd checked out."

She glanced at Bryan, and guilt overwhelmed her. Tears burned in her eyes and then rolled down her cheeks when she blinked. "I'm so sorry, Bryan."

With a muttered oath, he stood and moved over to the table before gathering her in his arms. "You scared the fuck out of me, Kira. I thought I'd hurt you."

It had been such a wonderful, perfect evening, and she'd ruined it. She tried to tell him how sorry she was, but all that came out were muffled half words as she cried. Finally she gave up and just sobbed.

Bryan held and rocked her, stroking her hair until her cries petered off into sniffles. Wrung out, exhausted, and still feeling slightly ill, she slumped against him. Her voice came out rough as she said, "I got your shirt all wet."

The doctor handed her a wad of tissues before looking at Bryan. "Take her home, make her eat something, then make sure she gets plenty of rest. Nothing too strenuous for the next day or so, and she should be fine."

Kira wiped her eyes and took a hitching breath. "I'm sorry. I should have eaten. This is all my fault. I ruined your evening."

The doctor gave Bryan a sympathetic look. "She comes out of subspace hard, doesn't she?"

Bryan nodded. "Yes."

"Well, give her lots of love tonight, and she should be just fine." The doctor gave her a dark, intimidating look. "And you, young lady, eat before you do a scene next time, or once you're well enough, I'll personally paddle your ass, and you won't like it one bit."

"Yes, Sir."

CHAPTER THIRTEEN

Kira tugged at the strap to the purple silk halter top that was currently struggling to hold up her breasts. When she'd bought this dress last month for her parents' dinner party, it had fit great, but evidently marathon sex sessions in a dungeon didn't burn off as many calories as she'd hoped because it was extremely tight and uncomfortable now. A dull ache had started in her neck, and she rolled her shoulders, trying to ease the tension. She wished she could kick off her gold heels and sit, but she had to endure for at least another two hours until the charity auction was over.

Her salvation hailed her from across the room in the form of Bryan returning with two glasses of wine. He moved through the crowd, pausing now and again to speak to mutual friends. They knew so many of the same people she'd been surprised they hadn't met before Wicked. Maybe she'd seen him briefly before at some social function, then again at Wicked, and her brain had decided he was safe.

Sliding up next to her, looking like walking sex, Bryan smiled and handed her the glass of wine. "Did I mention how much I like that dress yet?"

She flushed and gave him a narrow-eyed look. Leaning in, she whispered, "If you tell me you want to fuck my tits tonight one more time, I'm going to have to kill you."

His deep rumble let her know she was in trouble before he even said a word. "*When* I'm fucking your tits tonight, I'll remind you of that threat."

"Hey!" People looked at them, and Kira cleared her throat and smiled. "You are a dead man."

"Prove it." He glanced down at his watch. "We've been here for three hours. Let's go."

"We need to stay a bit longer."

"Why? We've had dinner with your parents, talked with your sister and her husband, and you even managed to get me out on the dance floor. I'd say I've more than fulfilled my duties as your escort this evening."

She smiled, remembering how nice it had been to waltz with him. "Bryan, there is a lovely set of gold and green Depression-era champagne flutes going up for sale. I'd like to win them, which means we have to stay for the auction."

The lines around his mouth deepened as he gave her his grin that meant nothing but trouble. "Stay here."

As soon as he was gone, a few of her casual girlfriends descended on her, asking her who he was and where she found him. She enjoyed gossiping with them, getting caught up with what was happening among her friends. While she looked forward to spending time with Bryan, she felt like they needed to have at least two days a week where they could do their own thing. As it was, they were practically living together, and neither had said the big l-o-v-e word yet. She wanted him to say it first before she told him, as silly and juvenile as it sounded. Deep down, she knew he loved her—it was in his every action and every touch—but she was pretty sure he was afraid to say it. Though he tried to hide it beneath his cool facade, his parent's disowning him had hurt him deeply. She had a feeling he was afraid to say that he loved her. That was okay; she'd wait as long as it took for him to gather the courage to tell her.

Kira was laughing over something a friend had said when Bryan's energy brushed her back a moment before he touched her. His smooth, accented voice was like auditory sex as he said, "Ladies, if you'll excuse us."

Her friends tittered, and she rolled her eyes at how easily they'd fallen under his spell. She really needed to make him wear sunglasses so he couldn't enchant random women. He didn't do it on purpose. He was just a sensual man by nature, and women seemed to pick up on it.

Which made his open, affectionate gestures toward her in public all the more sweet.

Waving to her friends, she let him drag her through the crowd. “Bryan, what about the glasses?”

“I bought them.”

She gaped at his back. “That’s cheating! It was up for auction.”

“Yeah, well, they had a buy-it-now price, and I got it. They’ll deliver it to your house next week.”

“You are a bad man.”

He looked over his shoulder and winked.

They quickly made their good-byes to her family and headed out the main door of the restaurant. As soon as their feet hit the carpeted steps, they got blinded by flashbulbs. Ah fuck, the paparazzi. She’d forgotten a bunch of movie stars were affiliated with the charity now, and with them came the photographers. Bryan squeezed her hand so hard it ached, and her heart hurt for him.

She took the ticket stub from Bryan’s clenched hand and gave it to the valet before returning to Bryan’s side.

Leaning up, she placed her hand on his cheek and gently turned his head from the flashing bulbs. His anger seared her, and she watched him visibly struggle to let it go. She pressed her lips ever so gently against his, sighing when he responded. While he didn’t ravage her like he would when they were alone, he did kiss her well enough that she was almost unsteady when her car arrived.

“Hey, isn’t that the de Sade guy with Kira Harmony? Fuck, that picture just went way the fuck up in value. Jason, follow them!”

The crowd of photographers surged toward them, barely held back by event security. They swarmed like sharks with the scent of blood in the water, and Kira worried that she and Bryan might be trampled. These photographers would do anything to get a picture that they might be able to sell for six figures. A security guard yelled for someone to call the police, but that didn't stop the frenzy.

Bryan's face lost all of its color, and for a second, she thought he might pass out.

She needed to get him out of here ASAP.

The valet had to beep the horn to clear a space from the paparazzi, and the security staff was being quickly overwhelmed. The valet hopped out of Bryan's Aston Martin, and before he could give the keys to Bryan, she snatched them.

"Bryan, get in the car."

His eyes cleared for a moment. "Give me the keys."

"No. Get in the car."

He protested again, but she shoved past an overeager photographer and got in the car without responding. A few seconds later, Bryan followed suit and got into the passenger seat, his expression furious.

"Kira, what the fuck are you doing? Your license is still suspended for another two weeks. You can't drive."

A male photographer fell against Bryan's side of the car with a *thump*, and she watched as a few of the photographers started to push and shove one another. This was bad, really bad. She needed to get Bryan safe. There was no way in hell she was going to let anyone hurt him.

Anger seared through her, and she began to pull forward, the paparazzi blinding her with their camera flashes and only moving at the last second.

If that guy falling on the door had dented the car, she was going to kick their asses and give them something to really report about.

"Are you listening to me? Pull the fuck over! I'm not kidding!"

Finally at a point where she was able to pull out into the street, she eased Bryan's car forward into traffic. Two cars followed them, almost hitting in their haste to keep up with Kira. One of them, a blue sedan, cut off an incoming taxi and tailgated the car right behind Kira. From her other side, a white SUV rode up on the shoulder, earning more blaring horns.

"I've got this. Don't worry, I'll keep you safe."

"Pull over! You are breaking the law and could go to jail. Please listen to me! "

"No. I can do this. Now please be quiet so I can get us out of here."

Traffic began to clear ahead, and she checked her positioning. Gunning Bryan's car into gear, she shot through the gap before them, quickly gaining distance between them and the paparazzi. She almost hit a minivan that abruptly hit its breaks but managed to drive up slightly onto the curb to pass them.

There was no fucking way she was letting those bastards follow them and hurt her man.

"Kira! What the fuck is wrong with you? Slow down! You almost hit that car. Pull over."

She ignored him and continued to dart around slower-moving traffic while keeping an eye open for any cops. The last thing she wanted to do was get a ticket where she'd be photographed getting yelled at for endangering people's lives. Plus Bryan just might have a point about her getting into legal trouble for driving when she wasn't supposed to. But it wasn't like she was putting them in any real danger.

She knew what she was doing out here.

Car chases had been one of her specialties in the movies, and she knew how to get the most out of any vehicle, especially a fantastic car like the Aston Martin.

"Are they keeping up?"

Bryan didn't even look out the window. "Stop the car right now."

"No. I need to get us safe first. Now stop distracting me."

"Kira, I mean it. Stop the car. I'm asking you to stop, please."

She ignored him, taking a hard right onto the freeway. They merged into traffic, and she let out an exhilarated breath. "Fuck. That was fun."

"Stop the goddamned car, or I swear I will open my door right now and jump out!" He yelled so loud her ears rang.

Startled by his shout, she did as he asked, pulling onto the side of the freeway, her headlights illuminating the grass in front of them. "Are you okay, Bryan?"

"Am I okay? You broke the law, endangered both me and yourself, and didn't fucking listen to me at all! If I had a safe word, I'd have been screaming it four blocks back. What the hell is wrong with you? Are you determined to get yourself killed?"

Adrenaline still raged through her body and made her emotions sharper than usual. "What the fuck? You should be thanking me for rescuing you from the paparazzi."

"You didn't rescue me from anything. I can handle my picture being taken. I can't handle you totally ignoring me and putting yourself in danger. Don't you understand? Can't you see how reckless and dangerous your actions were?"

"Look, we're fine. I don't know what the big deal is. So I have a suspended license. Big deal. It doesn't mean I can't drive."

"That's exactly what it means. Did you even notice all the cars you almost hit? What about that minivan full of kids? You had to drive on the fucking sidewalk to get around them! What if there had been people walking there? What if someone had been in your blind spot and you got in an accident? How many more fucking times are you going to keep taking unnecessary risks before you get killed?"

His words stung, and she hated that he might have a point. "Every second of every day we could die. I could fucking choke to death on a potato chip going down my throat the wrong way."

"You choking on a potato chip isn't going to kill other people. Use some fucking common sense."

"No one got hurt!" she screamed, incredibly pissed that he kept making it seem like she was some psycho running around and trying to kill people.

He hit the dash hard enough to make her jump. "That's only because you got lucky."

"That wasn't luck. That was skill." Oh, she was mad, red-hot with anger. "You just want me stuck at home being a good little submissive that you can control. Fuck, look at how fucking overbearing you are already! I mean, I can't even fucking eat nonorganic food now because you worry that I'm going to get some type of rare toxic poisoning from the fucking spray they use on strawberries to kill bugs. Well, that isn't me, Bryan. I'm going to do what I want, and you're just going to have to deal with it."

"You're right. You are going to do whatever you want, and nothing I say is going to stop you." He closed his eyes and leaned his head back onto his seat. "I'm sorry, Kira. I can't see you anymore."

Stunned, she slumped back into her seat and pressed her hands against the center of her chest. All of her rage drained away so suddenly she felt weak. "What?"

Unbuckling his seat belt, he didn't look at her. "I can't trust you. You don't care what I have to say, you don't care about your own safety, and you don't respect me or my wishes."

"What are you talking about?" Her body broke out in a stinging sweat as a terrible hurt crushed her from within.

He turned on her, the pain in his gaze slicing through her soul. "I can't trust you to stop, Kira. I can't trust you to listen to me when you don't want to. And I can't trust you with my safety, let alone yours. I'm done. I can't do this anymore. Either it ends now, or it will end up with one of us in the hospital. I care about you too much to be the one who puts you there."

"I'm sorry!" She reached for him, and he jerked away. "Please don't go. I'm sorry. I really am."

He opened the door and stepped out, slamming it behind him. Walking the opposite direction of his car, illuminated by the brake lights, he pulled his cell phone from his pocket. She sat there, frozen like that, until his figure was no more than a speck on the horizon, waiting for him to come back.

But he didn't.

CHAPTER FOURTEEN

Bryan's life was now measured by a different concept of time. He no longer lived by the calendar and clock, but rather by how long it had been since he'd last seen Kira. Five weeks since he'd left her. Three weeks since she'd stopped calling. One week since she'd stopped e-mailing him. One day since he'd received her collar back in the mail.

Sweat dripped down his face as he ran hard on his treadmill, trying to outpace his demons.

He missed her immensely.

With Kira gone, he found himself drifting, not really having a sense of purpose anymore. When he'd left her, he'd left a part of himself behind too. He'd never experienced emotional pain like this, not even during the sex tape scandal and his subsequent banishment.

The hour mark rang out from the treadmill, and he considered pushing it, then caught a glimpse of himself in the mirror and slowed down. His muscles stood out in sharp relief from his body, all the fat gone from his constant exercising and not having the will or desire to eat.

He looked like shit and felt like shit from the inside out.

Breathing heavily, he snagged his towel off the treadmill and wiped his face and head. Before he left the room, he picked up Kira's collar from where he'd placed it next to the treadmill, a physical reminder of why he couldn't take her back. This hunk of metal had symbolized their mutual trust, their respect for one another. Their possible love and future together.

Striding into the showers off his personal gym, he stripped out of his sweaty clothes and, despite his dark thoughts, gently placed her collar on the counter where he could see it from the shower. The emerald at the center sparkled beneath the bright lights, and he remembered how beautiful it had looked on Kira.

Images of their time together flew through his mind. Her laughter, her cute scowl, and finally her intense concentration as she wove through traffic, totally ignoring him and putting them both in danger. If she hadn't passed out the night before because she didn't safeword, he wouldn't have been nearly so pissed, and sure that they weren't right for each other.

The hollow ache in his chest that had never really gone away flared to life as he thought about the picture of their kiss together. True to his prediction, the paparazzi had dredged up the old stories about him, but it didn't change anything. The public had moved on to new scandals, and his grainy video from the past didn't warrant a second look. Thank God no one had realized Kira was driving on a suspended license.

He couldn't help but wonder if part of the reason he hadn't been on the cover of every tabloid was because Kira had taken a risk to lose the paparazzi on their tail. Had she saved him from another round of being torn apart in the public eye? Did he make a mistake in ending this with her?

No, he did the right thing. With her reckless disregard for her own personal safety, it was inevitable that she wouldn't safeword with him when their play got too extreme, and she would be grievously injured. But bloody hell, he didn't understand it. She'd gotten so good at telling him "yellow" when she needed to slow down. He thought he could trust her, but it had never occurred to him that he would be the one who needed a safe word, that it would be his life that was put in danger. He still had nightmares about looking into the window of the minivan as they drove past it on the curb, and the stunned and terrified faces of the people inside.

He had to stay away. If he talked to her, just once, he had no doubt he'd forgive her for everything she'd done and beg her to come back. But if he did that, he'd only be inviting trouble and chaos into his tightly controlled world.

Toweling off, he donned a thick black robe and belted it around his waist. Grabbing the collar, he then shoved it into the big pocket. The last thing he wanted Lawrence to see was him carrying it around like a teddy bear. Fuck, he'd even slept with the stupid thing last night because it held the faintest trace of her perfume.

He hoped to avoid Lawrence all together. He hadn't been able to tell Lawrence exactly why they'd broken up, only that it was for Kira's own good. As close as he was to Lawrence, the idea of telling him that he'd broken up with Kira so he didn't kill her during sex just wasn't going to happen. The old man, while not overly vocal about it, let his disapproval of the situation be known. Since his butler was the one who answered Kira's phone calls, Bryan guessed Lawrence had a right to believe Bryan was acting like a stupid bastard.

Bryan certainly felt like a stupid bastard.

Moving through the first level, a maid intercepted him. "Begging your pardon, Lord Sutherfield, but Mr. Lawrence could use a hand in the basement."

Since Bryan didn't allow anyone but Lawrence into his dungeon, he nodded. "Thank you."

He hesitated a moment before opening the door. On the other side and down the stairs lay the room where he'd made Kira bloom for him. The place where they'd shared each other in just about every way a man and woman could. He didn't know if he could handle the emotional pain of seeing his dungeon again, this time without Kira's presence filling it with her bright light.

Mad that he was letting a memory keep him from his dungeon, he jerked the door open and stepped through before slamming it behind him. He took the stairs two at a time, eager to get out of this room after he helped Lawrence with whatever he needed. When he reached the main floor, his empty stomach clenched, and his heart lurched.

Everywhere he looked he could see Kira. Fuck, he could actually *feel* her. The illusive electric tingle that ran through his body when she was around now sizzled along his nerves. Almost against his will, he took a deep breath of air and despaired when he smelled nothing more than leather and the faint hint of a lemon-based cleaning solution.

"Lawrence? Where are you?"

"Over here, sir."

He followed the sound of his butler's voice to where the manacles hung from the wall. Lawrence held one of the shackles with a dismayed expression. "My lord, I'm afraid I broke one of your shackles while polishing the brass."

Normally Bryan wouldn't have cared, but those shackles were antiques made during the Victorian era. "Here let me see it."

Lawrence held it up. "It's easier if I show you, my lord. It isn't latching properly."

Before Bryan knew what was going on, Lawrence had snapped the shackle onto Bryan's wrist. "Can you get out, sir?"

Bryan jerked at it once and tried to pull it off. "Seems to be working now. Hand me the key."

"I'm sorry, sir, but I don't have the key." Lawrence took a step back. "I'm afraid you'll have to ask Ms. Harmony to let you out."

"What?" The strength left his legs, and he leaned back against the wall, the chains clanking next to him.

From the other side of the stairs came her low, husky, beautiful voice. "Hello, Bryan."

Despairing, he stared at his butler. "Why?"

"Because, sir, Ms. Harmony needs to speak with you, and you refuse to give her the common courtesy of letting her say her piece. It is not only poor manners. It is stupid, and you are too good of a man to do this."

He kept his head turned away from Kira, but she danced on the edges of his vision like a mirage. "You're fired."

"Very good, sir." Lawrence gave him a small bow and walked away.

"I mean it!" Bryan yelled.

"Just like your father meant it, sir. And your grandfather. And your great-great-great grandfather to my great-great-great grandfather."

The steps creaked lightly as Lawrence went up the stairs, and all too soon Bryan found himself alone with Kira. He should look at her, yell at her, demand she let him out, then call the police on her and Lawrence for scheming this up. But oh God, he could smell her perfume as she came closer, and his soul reached out to her even as he struggled against acknowledging her presence.

"I'm sorry it has to be like this, Bryan, but I have to talk to you."

She sounded so very tired and almost defeated. Movement came from the corner of his eye, and he tried to stare at the wall, the floor, anything but her. The edge of her long, amazing auburn hair came into view, and he could no longer resist. He stared at her, drinking in her beauty, starved for a glimpse of her beautiful amber eyes.

Today she wore a long, flowing empire-waist dress in a deep chocolate-brown velvet that flattered her coloring. The neck was low enough to show a hint of cleavage, and her breasts—full, ripe, and creamy—begged for his touch. He looked away from her chest and back to her face, catching her staring at his body like he was staring at hers. When their eyes met, that familiar electricity jumped between them, and he stopped fighting the inevitable.

He was a complete tosser.

He loved her.

They belonged together, like the sun and the moon, and he would have to find some kind of balance to make this work.

"Bryan, I need—"

"Kira, I'm sorry I was such a rotten bastard. I shouldn't have ended it like I did. Please, let's give it another go." The words tumbled out in an uncharacteristic babble before he could stop. Even as he cleared his throat in embarrassment, a great sense of relief filled the emptiness those words left behind.

She gaped at him, the color draining from her cheeks. "I can't."

"Why not?" He jerked at the chains. "Let me out of here, love. We can go upstairs and talk like civilized adults. Maybe have a glass of wine, and I can have the chef make us an early dinner."

"I can't."

"Why not?"

She opened and closed her mouth a few times before taking in a deep breath. "Bryan, I'm pregnant."

"You're what?" A white, rushing noise filled his head, and a sudden clammy sweat broke out all over his body. "My baby? How?"

"Of course your baby!" She took a step back, every physical defense she had going up. With her arms crossed, she glared at him. "I made a mistake, okay? I got my weeks messed up with my pills, and I accidentally skipped a week. It's my fault. I take all the blame."

His heart hurt for her. He felt like he knew Kira better than she knew herself, and right now she was almost screaming with the need to be held. But he couldn't grab her if he was shackled to the fucking wall. Taking a deep breath, he found his focus. The only thing that mattered now was Kira and their baby.

Bright, startling clarity lit his mind from within, and the implications of that finally set in. Staring at her, he swallowed hard and said, "I'm going to be a father?"

She nodded and a tear rolled down her cheek but she gave him a defiant look. "I'm going to keep the baby. If you choose to be in the child's life as his or her father, I won't stop you. If you want to bow out of the child's life, I will accept that as well, but you will sign over all rights of the baby to me before you do."

He stared at her, unbelievably insulted that she would even think he wouldn't want to have a baby with her. Didn't she know anything about his feelings for her? She drove him absolutely fucking bat shit. "Kira, bloody hell. Unshackle me, woman!"

To his dismay, a bad situation only got worse as Kira began to cry. Poor girl. She was so sure he was going to leave her again. Her trust in him was gone. She sniffed and dashed a tear away. "No, because if I do, I won't be able to stop myself from kissing you, and that would be wrong. I gave you a thousand chances to get back together with me. You didn't want me, and you made it very clear. I won't be with you just because we are going to have a baby."

He wanted to scream and shout that he loved her, but he managed to keep his voice calm. "I didn't want to be with you because I was afraid someday I'd kill or maim you."

"No, Bryan. You didn't want to be with me because you can't trust me or control me. I understand that, and I know it is a fatal flaw in our relationship."

He shook his head, trying to clear it of his racing thoughts. Now was not the time to argue with her. Especially since he was chained to the wall and she held the key. He needed to be calm right now even if his world had suddenly changed in a life-altering way.

Taking a deep breath, he let it out and tried to catch her gaze. "How far along are you?"

"Thirteen weeks-ish. Either I'm measuring big, or they're a week or so off." She pressed the material of her dress over her belly, and there was a small but distinct bump. Then she stroked her belly, and it seemed to soothe her. The tense line of her shoulders eased, and she took a deep, watery breath.

"Is the baby healthy? Are you healthy?" He smacked himself in the forehead. Her broken pelvis. Panic tried to seize hold of him, to make him think about all the horrible ways Kira would suffer through the pregnancy, but he managed to keep his cool. The last thing he wanted to do was freak her out even more. "Kira, are you able to carry a baby?"

"Yes, we are both fine, and yes, I can carry a pregnancy to term. I'll have to have a C-section when it comes time for delivery. And maybe bed rest if the doctors think it's necessary at the end of the third trimester."

He tried to move toward her, but the shackle brought him up short. "Please unlock me."

She gave him a weak smile. "I can't, not down here. Don't make me turn you away. I need you to be a friend right now, okay? If you want this to work, you need to give me some space. I don't want to do this alone, but I will if you push it."

He choked on his pride, on his own needs, and nodded. "Fine. Fine." Taking a deep breath again, he began to shift the focus of his world around, to make this beautiful woman carrying his baby the center of it all...like she already was. "Kira, if you will, please go upstairs and give the key to Lawrence. May I please call you tonight?"

She looked nervous and terribly vulnerable. Damn, she needed him, and he was totally failing her. He had to rebuild her trust. "I don't know."

"Just a phone call. Nothing more. We need to talk. Friends talk to each other, don't they?"

She gave him a suspicious look. "You won't try for more?"

"I swear it."

A little over a month later, Kira stretched out on her cream suede couch with a tired yawn that Bryan found adorable. They were at her apartment tonight having just come from visiting their friends Jesse and Anya. The Dom and his former nanny had gotten engaged while vacationing in France together, and they'd had an engagement party for their friends and family. They'd all had fun tonight, and Bryan had noticed how Kira kept giving him odd looks. He tried not to read anything into it, because with her mercurial moods, he never really knew what she was thinking.

He couldn't help but smile at the memory of standing with his friends Isaac, Jesse, and Hawk at the party. He'd kept an eye on Kira where she sat gossiping with a group of submissive women from Wicked in Jesse's garden. They'd laugh and sneak little peeks in the Doms' direction, then lean forward and whisper to each other. This usually led to more laughter. It had eased his heart to see Kira so happy. She had such a wonderful spirit, and she made people happy just to be around her. She certainly made him happier. His life was almost perfect, well as perfect as it would ever get with a brat for a sub.

There were a couple of times where he really wished he was still her Dom so he could spank her ass. Her round, beautiful, fucking perfect ass. No, no thinking about that. He desperately tried to think about something not sexual and keep from remembering what it felt like to bugger her.

Tight, hot, and perfect.

Kira stretched out next to him, drawing his attention to her body as she let out a soft sigh. At nineteen weeks, the bump on her belly was now a pronounced curve, something visible even in the empire-waisted gowns she now favored. Well, gowns combined with running shoes. She'd said a tearful good-bye to her high heels last week, saying her feet were too swollen to fit in them.

Now, full of eggplant parmesan and chocolate raspberry cake from the party, she was as content as a well-fed kitten. Kira smiled at him. "Feet, please."

Rolling his eyes, he pulled her feet onto his lap. "You are utterly spoiled."

She merely smiled and closed her eyes, the movie she'd put on a background hum of noise. They'd been spending more time together at night, and he rather liked the quiet intimacy of it. So many steps had been skipped when they first got together, and he tried to use this time to let her know that no matter what, he'd be there for her.

Clearing her throat, she wiggled her toes at him. He shifted her feet forward a little bit, not wanting her to feel his erection. Things had finally smoothed out between them after many long talks about what went wrong. He admitted he may have been a bit overbearing, and she admitted that she might have a problem with impulse control, at the top of their lungs. Those hadn't been easy conversations, and more than once, it had ended with one of them leaving in a huff, but it had cleared the air between them. He didn't want to freak her out and push her right now. Her hormones were a mess, and it wasn't unusual for her to go from weeping, to laughing, to weeping in less than a five-minute time span.

Made a man want to drink.

He pressed into the arch of her foot, earning a groan that made his dick jerk. It reminded him of the noises she made when she came for him. Not touching her in a sexual manner was getting harder and harder, no pun intended. Her body had begun to fill out, and her already nice breasts were now the things of his hottest wet dreams. His friends had been full of advice on how to woo her back, and their number one rule was to let her make the first move. He assumed the men might have a point because both

Isaac and Jesse were engaged to women that adored them. Wouldn't hurt to heed their advice.

But fuck, he thought he might die of blue balls first.

She moaned again and rubbed her heel into his thigh, perilously close to his cock. This evening her dress was a pretty light blue color that reminded him of a spring sky. Her hair was on top of her head in a messy bun, and she'd placed a small white rose from Jesse's garden behind her right ear. She wore a pair of dangling blue topaz earrings that brushed against her neck, marking places on her that he'd love to kiss. The feeling of her smooth skin beneath his fingertips was enough to have him ready to rut on her like a beast.

She was absolutely stunning.

He was so wrapped up in his thoughts he almost didn't hear her say his name. "Yes, love?"

"I asked if you were excited about finding out the sex of the baby next week."

He laughed. "Excited and terrified."

"Why terrified?"

"Because I'm afraid that if we have a little girl like you, I won't stand a chance against her. And if we have a little boy like me, you'll run for the hills."

She smiled at him and toyed with a stray strand of her hair. "Thank you for taking such good care of me."

"It's what a Dom, I mean, a friend does."

She opened her eyes the slightest bit, leaving them heavy and with an unexpectedly sensual look. He noticed for the first time that she'd put on some kind of silvery eye shadow. It made her already beautiful eyes glow. "Did I tell you about one of the fun parts of being pregnant?"

He snorted and pulled on her big toe. "I must have missed it somewhere in between your constant caterwauling about all the not fun things about being pregnant."

She laughed. "Poor Bryan. You really have been so kind to me."

He met her gaze for a moment, then looked away, scared she would see his true feelings for her. How desperately in love with her he was. Trying to keep things light, he picked up her other foot and began to press on her heel with his thumb. "You better make sure I get lots of those 'World's Best Dad' coffee mugs."

She stayed silent, watching him touch her. He had the distinct feeling she was checking him out, in a sexual way she hadn't used since they'd broken up. The old electricity started to fill the air between them, and he debated on going with it or pulling back. The last thing he needed right now was her pissed at him for overstepping his bounds.

"Bryan?"

The husky tone to her voice almost made him groan. "Yes, love?"

"Aren't you going to ask me what one of the nice parts of being pregnant is?"

He smiled, but the delicious tension didn't ease between them. "Sorry. I missed my lines. What is one of the fun parts of being pregnant?"

She traced the tip of her finger down the side of her neck, drawing his gaze to the delicate curve of her collarbone. "It makes my orgasms insanely good."

He froze, unsure of what she was doing, hoping and praying it would somehow involve letting him bring her pleasure in a much more carnal manner. Clearing his throat, he resumed rubbing her feet. "How so?"

"Well, the doctor said it's because there is so much blood in that area now, that in some women their vaginas become extrasensitive." She ran her finger over the edge of the top of her dress, her hard nipples tenting the thin fabric. "I'm one of those lucky women."

"Well, that... Fuck, Kira. What do you want me to say? You've spent the last six weeks laying down all these rules about only being friends, and then you pull a mind fuck on me like this. It's not fair to either of us, and I won't put up with it." He moved her foot off his lap. "I need to go."

She sat up quickly. "Wait, please don't go. I... Shit, I'm doing this all wrong. Please sit back down."

He took a weary seat and ran his hands through his hair. "I'm trying as hard as I can to respect your boundaries, but even I have my limits. So you need to think very hard about what you're doing here, because I won't be some fuck toy you can pull out whenever you want and then stick back on the friend shelf when you're done."

To his shock she reached over and cupped his cock, giving it a squeeze through his pants that had him arching into her touch. "I know that."

"Bloody fuck." He shuddered as she continued to squeeze him. "Woman, don't think that just because you're pregnant you won't have to face the consequences of your actions. I'll still punish you."

She removed her hand, but before he could mourn the loss of her touch, she straddled his lap. "I want those consequences. I miss you, my lord."

His stared at her, not quite sure he'd heard her correctly. "What did you call me?"

Her flush spread from her chest to her hairline, but she managed to hold his gaze. "My lord." She leaned forward and gently brushed her lips over his. "This doesn't mean I'm going to put up with you trying to run my life outside of the bedroom, but I'm willing to give it a try again if we go slow."

He gave a tortured laugh as her hot core pressed against his erection. "This is going slow?"

"No, but right now I need you to be my Master. I miss it. I miss you. Just please go slow."

He shook his head. "How slow are you talking about?"

"Slow and deep. I want as much of you inside of me as I can take."

His dick tried to punch a hole through his pants, but his mind hesitated. Maybe she was having one of those hormonal surges that crept up on her every now and then. Except those usually left her throwing something at his head in anger, then crying that he made her throw something. He wasn't sure who the insane one was here: her for having a split personality or him for sticking around to deal with it.

"Are you sure?"

She jerked down her top and bra so her breasts spilled out. With a quiver in her voice, she placed her hands on his shoulders. Those soft, lovely hands he'd missed so much. "I trust you, my lord." A shift in her posture brought his gaze down to her breasts, and his mouth watered.

For a long moment, he stared at them, marveling at how her nipples were now a deep rose color instead of their usual pink and how they'd gotten a bit bigger. Delicate blue veins were visible beneath her pale skin. He traced one with the tip of his finger, fascinated by the lush changes of her body, overwhelmed by her faith in him. Though he'd never considered it before, there was something extremely sensual and arousing on a primitive level about knowing that this woman carried his child.

Cupping her breasts, he then brought the tip to his lips and gently brushed his beard over the nub. Her instant gasp and the jerk of her hips made him smile. "How sensitive are these now?"

"Very, very, very sensitive."

He gave her nipple an experimental lick, delighting in how she groaned out his name. Her tits had an additional weight to them now, and he wondered how heavy they would get when her milk came in. Keeping his touch light, he toyed with her breasts, going from one tip to another, worshipping her with his mouth and tongue. She began to rock on his lap, driving his arousal to the point where he feared he would come in his pants.

He continued to torment her, to let her body know he could be trusted to give her what she needed even if her mind still didn't fully trust him. They had shit to hash out; he knew there would be some tough fights on the horizon, but this physical bonding between them would go a long way toward repairing the gulf.

She ground her pelvis against his, her hips jerking and her breath coming out in harsh pants. The lovely scent of her arousal surrounded them, and he rubbed his chin back and forth over her breasts, making her hiss and writhe.

Reality intruded for a moment, and he forced himself to pull back from her bounty. "The doctor said intercourse is okay, correct?"

"Yes. As long as you don't hog-tie me and hang me from the ceiling, it will be fine."

Gently squeezing her breast, he gave her a smile that let her see how much that mental image aroused him. "We'll save that until after the baby arrives."

Her eyes grew big and round, fear and desire mixing into a heady blend that called to him. "Yes, my lord."

If he didn't get inside of her soon, he was going to die.

"Get up and take off your panties. Then I want you to open my pants, straddle me, and ride me until you come."

"Yes, my lord."

He had to help steady her while she pulled her underwear down, but her long skirt hid her sex from his view. Not that it mattered. Right now he wanted to be inside her with a desperation that bordered on insanity. Together they opened his pants, and when she pulled his stiff dick out, she made a happy little purring sound. Her full breasts wobbled with her movements, and he wondered if her pussy had changed as well.

"Gather up your skirt. I want to watch my cock slide into your cunt."

She shivered but did as he asked. At the first sight of her very swollen sex covered with a tempting layer of russet curls, he bit back a groan. He'd only seen her cunt this deep of a red color after they'd done a particularly hard caning session. Cupping her with his hand, he found her soaking wet.

"Is this sweet cunt more sensitive as well?" He slid his finger between her labia, and she almost fell against him. Laughing, he cuddled her close. "I'll take that as a yes."

Her warm breath heated his skin as she whispered, "Please. Let me suck you off."

"Later. Right now I need to be inside of you."

Reaching between them, she fisted his cock and guided it to her entrance. Just as the tip pressed against her, he grabbed her hips in a firm hold. "Promise me you'll stop if it hurts. Please, Kira."

"I promise." She pressed her face against his neck and groaned as the first inch sank in.

Holy shit.

Her pussy was hotter, tighter, and more amazing than ever. If this was what sex with a pregnant woman was like, he might keep Kira pregnant all the time, even if it meant dealing with her split personality. Sliding into her was almost too good, and he had to pull back his lust and try to regain his focus on her.

She clung to him, gently rocking, until he was seated all the way inside. They stayed like that for a long minute, the occasional reflexive clenching of her pussy making him twitch. She slowly moved back up, the air shockingly cool on his dick after the heat of her body.

She rubbed her lips against his neck, then whispered, "I missed you so much."

His throat closed up in a most unmanly fashion as he held her tight. "Me too, love. Me too."

They fell into an easy rhythm, long and stroking glides that had them both panting and straining. Her first orgasm almost caught him by surprise. One minute she was moaning and sighing; the next she snapped her hips, and she screamed out her release. The strong contractions of her vagina against his cock felt like a hand squeezing his dick, and his toes curled at the overwhelming sensation.

He managed to bite his inner cheek hard enough to hold back his own orgasm as she writhed and moaned on his lap, her plump bottom resting on his thighs as aftershocks radiated through her. Eager to see how easy it was for her to orgasm now, he gripped her hips hard.

"Again."

"What?"

Reaching between them, he gave her nipple a gentle pinch that had her yelping. "Come again. Ride me, Kira."

She drew in a quivering breath and did as he asked. Bracing her hands on his shoulders, she raised herself up until only the tip of his cock remained inside, then came down hard enough that the sensation of being fully sheathed snapped through him like a whip. He removed his hands from her hips and grabbed the cushions of the couch, afraid he'd bruise her if he touched her right now.

Up and down she went, her eyes closed, her face slack with pleasure. The bounce of her breasts captivated him, and when her next orgasm rolled over her, he grabbed her and held her close, suckling her nipple while she screamed and contracted around him, her little fists grabbing his hair and trying to pull him off her breast even as she thrust her chest to his mouth. God, how he loved a submissive's internal battle to do as her Master wished even as her body screamed about the sensation being too much.

Releasing her nipple with a *pop*, he reached down to where they were joined and stroked his fingers over her stretched labia, to her now postorgasmic, soft clit.

"Kiss me."

Their lips met, and she practically devoured him. He could feel her desperation, her loneliness, her need for him in her frantic kiss. Keeping his hand busy stroking her little bud back to stiffness, he fisted his other hand in her hair hard enough to sting and slowed their kiss down, took possession of it. She struggled against his grip, then softened and allowed him access to her mouth with a sigh. Lovely, warm, and pliant, she filled his arms and his heart like a dream.

Once her clit was hard again beneath his fingertips, he gripped her hips and began to raise and lower her on his lap. Their gazes met and held. All the feelings he'd been bottling up, trying to keep contained, spilled out.

"I love you."

She gasped and stilled, his cock deep within her. "I love you too. So very much."

Not wanting any distance between them, he pulled her closer, and as they kissed, Bryan thought his heart might beat right out of his chest. Each stroke brought him closer to the edge until he shook with the effort of holding back.

He loved her.

"Come for me, my beautiful girl. Please your lord."

Two hard thrusts later, she finally broke for him, moaning and crying out her release against his neck, her little teeth nipping his skin in a way that made cum boil in his balls. The first blast of pleasure wiped his mind clean of everything but the sensation of pouring his seed into her body, of filling her up with him, of reaffirming his bond with his submissive, his woman, and hopefully someday soon, his wife.

Hand in hand, Bryan and Kira strolled through the rose garden of his estate, excited beyond belief at the news they'd received at the doctor's office.

Pausing by a fading pink rose, Kira leaned down to smell it. Her long hair fell forward over her shoulder, a bright sheaf of red in the late afternoon sunlight. The pretty pale green sundress she wore made the freckles on her chest and shoulders stand out, and he wondered if she'd put on sunblock today and if he should get her a hat. Wisely, he decided not to mention it as she got rather snippy if she felt he was being overprotective with her…at least outside of the bedroom.

She glanced over at him and caught him staring. "What? Do I have a booger hanging out of my nose?"

Rolling his eyes, he brushed a strand of her hair back as she straightened. "Here I was, composing a poem about your beauty, and you, being the typical crude American that you are, think I'm checking out your snot."

She giggled and rubbed her belly. "True. If I had so much as sniffled, you would have shoved a tissue up my nose by now and been on the phone with the hospital."

Choosing to ignore that, he held her hand again, and they walked toward the surprise he had waiting for her on the other side of the garden. "Have you thought of any names?"

"Well, now that we know the bump is indeed a girl, I would like to do something that combines the names from our families. My mother sure hinted hard that she'd be delighted if we chose to follow the 'grand family tradition' of giving our daughter my mother's name as a middle name."

"Thank God her name is Diana. I'd hate to stick a baby girl with a name like Gertrude or Matilda."

"Hey, I kinda like Matilda."

Snorting, he gave her butt a pinch. "I'm sure you do."

They slowed, and Kira stepped closer, then pulled his arms around her. There was more space between them now with her ever-expanding belly in the way, but he loved that solid proof of their union. He needed to get her to agree to an even more visible and permanent representation of their love.

"Kira?"

She looked away from a butterfly she'd been watching and smiled up at him. "Yes?"

"Marry me."

He winced. Fuck, he'd had this huge speech planned about how wonderful their lives would be together, how much it made sense, and how much he loved her. But what came out sounded more like a command than a request.

She pulled back, confusion and yearning filling her expressive face, but also pain and sorrow. "Bryan, you know I love you, but I don't know if I can marry you."

"Why ever not?"

She swallowed hard. "Because I like how things are now."

He took a step toward her, hurt not only by her rejection but by how she took an automatic step backward. "What are you talking about? I swear to you. You will never need or want for anything. I will keep you safe and provide you with the best life possible."

"I know that, and that is part of the problem."

"You don't want to be happy?"

"No, no. Give me a second to try and say this right."

She began to pace, and he backed off. The last thing he wanted to do right now was rouse her unpredictable temper, then deal with the tearful aftermath. Shit, if he survived her pregnancy without her killing him, he should go into hostage negotiations.

"Bryan, I love you, I really do, but I can't live being kept in a gilded cage. I feel like you'd prevent me from taking any risks, from having any dangerous excitement in my life outside of the dungeon. Whenever I drive with you now, you always insist I ride in the passenger seat. I don't want to ride. I want to drive."

He pinched the bridge of his nose, trying to remain calm. "I'm so protective of you because I care about you. If anything happened to you, or our daughter, I would die."

"I know, and that's why I don't think we can get married. If you're this protective of me, what will you be like with our daughter? Will you try to keep her in a bubble as well? What if she has my taste for adventure? What if she wants to climb trees that she may fall out of, run through fields that may have holes she could twist an ankle in, or go off on her own adventures? I worry that you'll force her to be a proper English lady. That she'll have to live her life constantly being told what she can't do and have to walk around on eggshells."

His anger slipped his tight control a bit. "Are we talking about our daughter or you, Kira?"

"Both." Her lower lip trembled.

"Is anything I say going to make a difference? Or are you already set in your opinion of who and what I am?" He gritted his teeth and took a deep breath. "If I loosened my hold a bit, would you marry me?"

Now she began to cry, and he pulled out the tissues he now carried with him everywhere and handed one to her. She took it and blew her nose. "I don't know. I want to be with you, I really do. I want the fairy tale of marrying my handsome lord and living happily ever after, but this is the real world with real problems. How do I know if you'll ever be able to really trust me again? How do I know you won't go all overprotective crazy with our daughter?"

Suddenly, he realized he did have a way to show her how wrong she was. He smiled down at her, and she stared at him like he'd lost his mind.

"Bryan?"

"Follow me."

He grabbed her hand and ignored her sputtering protests as he pulled her along. They passed through the edge of the garden and came to the grassy meadow that separated the house from the woods. There, gleaming in the sunlight, with the door freshly painted in tones of blue, purple, and yellow, sat the cottage. He'd wanted to save this surprise until the garden out front had been planted, but he hoped she liked it.

Kira stopped in her tracks. "What is that doing here?"

"Come on."

Together they walked through the soft grass, accompanied by the sound of birds chattering around them. He could easily imagine spending more summers here, watching their children play, growing old and sharing that same joy with their grandchildren.

Fuck, he was becoming as soft as a girl himself.

They reached the cottage, and Kira paused to examine a potted pink geranium at the foot of the steps. It held a small balloon that said It's a Girl on it in sparkly writing.

"When did you do this?"

"That must be from Lawrence. I had the cottage moved stone by stone while we went on that three-week tour of visiting your family all over the United States. I was just waiting until we knew if our baby was a boy or a girl. I wanted this to be my gift to you."

"That is one of the sweetest things anyone has done for me, ever."

He cleared his throat and pretended to examine the cottage, while in truth hoping she didn't notice the way her words made his face flush. "Let me tell you. Keeping you away from this side of the house has been a right pain in the arse."

She grinned at him. "I was wondering why you suddenly wanted to molest me every time I went near the laundry room. I thought maybe you had a laundry fetish in addition to all the other freaky shit you like."

He laughed and rubbed her bottom. "I seem to recall you are rather fond of my 'freaky shit' as well."

"Hmm, that is true." She looked up at the door. "Is the bed still in there?"

"No. It's in storage right now. I'm having it upgraded and then put down into our dungeon."

Her golden-brown eyes went wide. "Upgraded? Oh God, now I'm scared."

"Sure, the thought of jumping the Grand Canyon on a mule doesn't scare you, but a sex toy built for your pleasure does."

She giggled, a happy sound that helped to ease the hurt of her rejection of his proposal. "So what's inside?"

He gestured to the door. "Open it up and see."

She took the steps as quickly as she could, and he stayed behind her, ready to catch her if she slipped. Fairly bouncing with excitement, she opened the door and gasped.

"Oh, my sweet lord."

Swallowing hard, he tried to still the knot of worry twisting his gut. "You don't like it?"

Looking over her shoulder at him, with more tears filling her eyes, she shook her head and stepped into the room.

The walls had been painted a fresh, butter yellow with green, blue, purple, and still-wet pink butterflies gracing the border at the top. Lawrence must have run out here when Bryan called him after the ultrasound to tell him the sex of the baby. Where the bed had been now stood a massive, state-of-the-art baby jungle gym. There were slides, brightly colored and safety-plastic-coated rails, swings, and one wall had been transformed into a giant chalkboard with a bucket of pastel chalk nearby. The floor was covered with a soft, brightly colored foam mat that the salesman had assured him would keep his children safe. He'd even had a small ball pit installed despite his misgivings that it would be a place where germs could breed and potentially give his children the plague. The plastic used in the construction of the jungle gym was also supposedly germ proof and guaranteed not to give off toxic fumes or contain any chemicals that were known to cause cancer.

She slowly walked over to the slide, and her shoulders shook as she made a low keening noise. Alarmed, he moved quickly to her side.

"I'm sorry, love. If you don't like it, I'll—"

"No, no." She turned in his arms, her face lit from within. "You don't understand."

Unsure if he should pretend he knew what the hell she was talking about, he shrugged.

Giggling, she covered his face with light kisses before pulling back. “I do.”

“Do what?”

She held up her hand and wiggled her ring finger. “I do.”

He took a step back, leaning against the side of the jungle gym. “Really? All I had to do was buy you a slide?”

“No, idiot. If you’re willing to let our daughter play on something like this, there may be hope for you yet.”

Before she could change her mind, he pulled the ring out, sucked her finger to get it wet, and slid it on.

Holding her hand out into a beam of sunlight streaming in through the cottage window, she gasped. Rainbows bounced off the walls as the four-carat, rose-cut diamond blazed like a falling star. The ring had been given to him by his paternal grandmother after she passed, and it had been in his family for four generations. It made him almost burst with pride to see it on Kira’s finger. She turned her hand this way and that, smiling the whole time. His heart seemed to double in size when she gave him her brilliant, amazing smile.

“It’s so pretty.”

“If you don’t like anything, we can change it.”

“No, it’s so sparkly.” She threw her arms around him and hugged him as tight as she could with the bump between them. “I love you so much.”

“You are everything I ever wanted, even when I didn’t know what that was.”

She took a deep breath and let it out slowly. “I’m sorry I make you worry so much. Mary Kate and I had a talk a few weeks ago, and I think I’m beginning to understand how much it sucks to worry about someone you love. I think about some of the dangerous things I’ve done, then try to imagine what it would be like if it was our baby doing those things, and I feel almost sick with dread. I know this sounds terribly selfish and immature, but I never really realized how horrible it feels to be worried about someone. I know I made you feel that way, and I’m so very sorry. I promise that in the future I’ll think before I act.”

Part of him wanted to lecture her on just how much her reckless actions had hurt him, but that was the past, and he didn't want to spoil the moment. "That's all I ask, love."

SHE NIBBLED THE side of his neck, knowing how that was an instant turn-on for him. "So…is it naughty of me to wonder if you might tie me up to the jungle gym and have your wicked way with me?"

Laughing, he ran his hands up her bare arms to the straps holding her dress in place on her shoulders. "Yes. Very naughty. You know what we do to naughty girls around here."

"What's that?"

"We punish them and love them and then punish them some more until they have to be carried back to their house by their fiancé in a sweaty, exhausted, sexually satisfied heap."

Giving him a seductive grin, she traced her fingertips over her nipples. "You'll have to catch me first."

He did indeed chase her, having fun stripping her bit by bit. Eventually he caught her and fulfilled his promise of leaving her exhausted, sweaty, and very, very well loved.

ANN MAYBURN

Ann is Queen of the Castle to her wonderful husband and three sons in the mountains of West Virginia. In her past lives she's been an import broker, a communications specialist, a US Navy civilian contractor, a bartender/ waitress, and an actor at the Michigan Renaissance Festival. She also spent a summer touring with the Grateful Dead-though she will deny to her children that it ever happened.

From a young age she's been fascinated by myths and fairytales, and the romance that often was the center of the story. As Ann grew older and her hormones kicked in, she discovered trashy romance novels. Great at first, but she soon grew tired of the endless stories with a big, wonderful, emotional buildup to really short and crappy sex. Never a big fan of purple prose (throbbing spears of fleshy pleasure and wet honey pots make her giggle), she sought out books that gave the sex scenes in the story just as much detail and plot as everything else without using cringe worthy euphemisms. This led her to the wonderful world of erotic romance, and she's never looked back.

Now Ann spends her days trying to tune out cartoons playing in the background to get into her 'sexy space' and has learned to type one handed while soothing a cranky baby.

Loose Id® Titles by Ann Mayburn

Available in digital format at http://www.loose-id.com or your favorite online retailer

The Breaker's Concubine

The CLUB WICKED Series
My Wicked Valentine
My Wicked Nanny
My Wicked Trainers
My Wicked Devil
My Wicked Masters

The VIRTUAL SEDUCTION Series
Sodom and the Phoenix

In addition to digital format, the following titles are also available in print at your favorite bookseller:

The Breaker's Concubine

The CLUB WICKED Series
My Wicked Valentine
My Wicked Nanny
My Wicked Devil

The VIRTUAL SEDUCTION Series
Sodom and the Phoenix

CPSIA information can be obtained at www.ICGtesting.com
Printed in the USA
LVOW07s1655071015

457264LV00048B/87/P

9 781623 007409